Murder in Season

A *Murder, She Wrote* Mystery

A Novel by Jessica Fletcher & Jon Land

Based on the Universal television series created by
Peter S. Fischer, Richard Levinson & William Link

BERKLEY PRIME CRIME
New York

BERKLEY PRIME CRIME
Published by Berkley
An imprint of Penguin Random House LLC
penguinrandomhouse.com

ISBN: 9781984804372

Berkley Prime Crime hardcover edition / November 2020
Berkley Prime Crime mass-market edition / May 2021

Printed in the United States of America
1 3 5 7 9 10 8 6 4 2

"If I could work my will . . . every idiot who goes about with 'Merry Christmas' on his lips should be boiled with his own pudding, and buried with a stake of holly through his heart."
—EBENEZER SCROOGE IN CHARLES DICKENS'S
A CHRISTMAS CAROL

Chapter One

The holidays are murder, I tell you."

I smiled through the steam rising off my tea and lowered the cup back to its saucer. "Can I take that to mean you won't be out caroling this year?" I said to Dr. Seth Hazlitt across the table at Mara's Luncheonette.

"Have you ever heard me sing, Jess?"

"As a matter of fact—"

"Question answered, then, *ayuh*. But there is the matter of the annual Christmas parade."

"Please tell me I don't have to play Mrs. Claus again."

"If I have to play Santa, you have to play Mrs. Claus. That's the deal."

"When exactly did I agree to that?"

"The first time you said yes."

"That was five years ago."

"Just one more year, Jess. I promise."

"That's what you said last year . . . and the year before."

"Did I?" Seth mused, fingering his chin. "Must've slipped my mind. No surprise, given that I'm a year older. That's the best thing about aging: It gives you an excuse to ask people to do what you know they don't want to. Tell you what—you find someone to replace me as Santa this year and you're off the hook. At least, according to the forecast, we won't be dealing with any snow. Seasonal temperatures and clear skies— that's what the weatherman says, *ayuh*."

"It's weather*person* these days, Seth."

"Is it, now? And who exactly made that rule? Is it written down anywhere? Because I'd love to see it. In my mind, there are weather*men* and weather *ladies* and they're both weather *people*."

Just then Sheriff Mort Metzger ambled through the door and joined us at the table, taking his usual seat. "I miss anything?"

"We were just exchanging Christmas wishes," Seth told him.

"In that case, here's mine," he said, tilting his gaze toward me. "A holiday season free of murder. How's that sound, Mrs. F.?"

"Works for me, Mort."

"Are you still going to visit your nephew Grady in New York?"

"Now that I'm back home, we decided to move the festivities here."

I'd long ago stopped counting the days since the fire that had nearly cost me my life forced me from my beloved Victorian at 698 Candlewood Lane. I'd been staying in a suite at Cabot Cove's swanky Hill House hotel, weathering any number of setbacks encountered by the construction crew. The fire had spared the old home's structure and I'd done my utmost to preserve as much of the original period detail as possible. With a healthy insurance payout aiding the restoration, my instructions had been to *spare no expense.*

Three words I shall never speak again. I had witnessed any number of fitful stops and starts, do-overs, and alterations to the original reconstruction plans. I had remained steadfast in my desire to preserve as much of the house as possible and create a precise replica of what I'd lost, instructions that had proven impossible to comply with for several random, and often conflicting, reasons. I was forced to compromise and then compromise some more, leading to all those dreaded delays and cost overruns. The end result was an exterior beautifully true to its original form, but a newly minted interior with fresh character it would take some time for me to get used to.

The final and most recent setback, which had followed my being granted a provisional certificate of occupancy so I could move back in, was the need to replace the property's septic system after the current one failed final inspection.

"Why?" I'd asked the inspector, Carl Cragg, my fisherman friend Ethan's cousin.

"Because it's old."

"So am I. Should I be replaced, too?"

"Inspecting you isn't in my job description, Mrs. Fletcher. And the system's no longer up to code."

"It was up to code before the fire," I told him.

"Grandfathered," Carl Cragg explained. "The reconstruction of your home changed that status."

For the first time, I found myself wishing our quaint town had a more modern sewer system. In any case, the crew had begun digging this morning, with an additional few days' work in the offing. Today being Monday, with any luck they'd be done before Christmas Day on Sunday.

Across the table at Mara's, Seth Hazlitt shook his head, grinning warmly. "Grady Fletcher . . . It's been forever and a day since I've seen that boy."

"That *boy* is in his mid-thirties now with an eight-year-old boy of his own."

"About the age Grady was when he came to live with you, right, Mrs. F.?" Mort asked me. "When you were still living in Appleton."

I nodded. My late husband, Frank, and I had taken on the responsibility of raising Grady following a tragic accident that claimed the lives of his parents. Frank and I had stepped up, not hesitating to volunteer our efforts, which became the best decision we ever made. I often tell people that the happiest day of our lives was when we brought him home and the saddest was when he left for college. The proudest day of my life was when I played the role of parent at Grady and his beloved Donna's wedding. And they'd even named their son Frank after my beloved husband.

"The timing couldn't be better," I noted. "Celebrate my first Christmas back home with family."

"Does that mean I'm not invited?" Seth asked lightly.

"That depends."

"On what?"

"Are you bringing the pie?"

Seth nodded. "So long as you promise not to tell it was baked right here by Mara."

"Why?" Mort asked him. "As I recall, Doc, your own baking efforts didn't exactly win any ribbons."

"How do you know?"

"Because I was one of the judges at the Founders Celebration the year you entered. Enough said?"

Seth frowned. "I suppose. Baking is women's work anyway."

Which drew a broad grin from Mort. "Did you hear that, Mrs. F.? We've got us a genuine dinosaur here. Wake up and smell the new century, Doc. It sure beats the scent of your strawberry rhubarb, from what I recall."

Mort cast me a wink as Seth's features crinkled in a fashion typical of our very own town curmudgeon, who happened to still serve as primary care physician for a large chunk of Cabot Cove. Seth seemed to enjoy nothing more than pointing out, when we were out for a walk, all the folks he'd delivered as babies. It left me wondering if there was anyone native to our town he hadn't delivered.

"Anyway," I said to Mort, "I'd like to invite you and Adele over for Christmas dinner, too."

"That's mighty kind of you, Mrs. F., but . . ."

"But what?"

The sheriff of Cabot Cove seemed to be struggling for words. "It's just that, well, Adele isn't exactly the most sociable sort, you know."

"I know that's what you always say when I suggest

inviting her to anything. Maybe I should give the woman a call, issue a personal invitation."

Mort looked less than enamored of the prospect of that. "Just don't let her bring any food, please. For your own good."

"That bad?" Seth asked him.

"Bad doesn't begin to describe it. Let me put it this way, Doc. Adele's first job was in the kitchen of a Howard Johnson's."

"That chain pretty much went out of business years ago."

"My point exactly."

My phone rang, an incoming call from the all-too-familiar number of my contractor, Ben McMasters.

"Don't spoil my breakfast," I greeted him.

"We've got a problem, Mrs. Fletcher."

"Oh no. What is it this time, Ben? Don't tell me you found a sinkhole when you dug out the old septic system."

"Actually, ma'am, we found a body."

It had been a body. Judging by the condition of the bones, though, that had been a long time ago.

"I feel like I'm dressed up for Halloween," Seth Hazlitt told Mort and me.

Seth's worn woolen suit and loafers were hardly conducive to an examination of those bones and an accompanying wooden chest, six feet down in a trench Ben McMasters's crew had dug to lay the fresh piping that would be connected to my new septic system. Ben had provided Seth a pair of coveralls, which he pulled over his clothes before donning the extra pair of work boots Ben always kept in his truck.

"They don't fit," Seth groused.

"Too big or too small, Doc?" Ben asked him.

Seth showcased the freedom his feet had to roam inside the worn lace-up boots. "What does it look like?"

"Hey, too big is better than too small."

"Not by too much."

As Cabot Cove's de facto coroner, Seth would perform a preliminary examination of the skeletal remains. We'd have to wait for a Maine State Police crime scene team to remove both the bones and the old wooden box the construction team's efforts had revealed. I watched Seth move awkwardly toward the ladder, appraising it the way one might a trip to a root canal specialist, as a pair of Cabot Cove deputies who'd arrived ahead of us to secure the scene looked on.

"Is this the first time you've dug this deep into my lawn?" I asked McMasters.

"You mean what used to be your lawn, don't you, Mrs. Fletcher?"

"Well, now that you mention it . . ."

"And the answer's yes, ma'am. Truth be told, nobody would have found those bones if the order to replace your septic system hadn't come down."

"Yup," said Mort, whose face crinkled the way it did when he'd swallowed something sour, "Mrs. Fletcher here seems to be so lucky when it comes to death. You might even say she attracts it."

I was too busy watching Seth descend the ladder to

pay much attention to what Mort was saying. I had something else on my mind I wasn't ready to share with him yet, figuring it was better to listen to what Seth had to say once he climbed back out of the hole, or from down inside it.

"You've got that look, Mrs. F.," Mort said, moving in front of me just as I started to draw closer to the resting place of my septic system.

"What look is that?"

"Your 'I've got a secret' one. Care to share?"

"This isn't the first time I've replaced the septic system, Mort. The one they're ripping out was installed fifteen years ago, I think, give or take."

"So?"

"So the workmen dug up this part of the lawn back then, too, and there were no bones to be found."

Mort took off his hat and rolled his eyes. "So you're saying the remains could have been here no more than fifteen years."

"Actually, I think somebody buried them here much more recently," I told him. "At some point while all the construction here was underway, sometime in the past few months."

"In which case, they must not have figured on the septic system replacement mandating the yard being dug up," Mort concluded, not bothering to argue my point.

"Neither did I."

"But it wasn't you who moved the bones here, right, Mrs. F.?"

"Not that I remember, anyway," I quipped. "And you said it perfectly, Mort, when you used the word *moved*. Those bones, and whatever's in that chest, must have been hidden somewhere else for a time, maybe a long time, before somebody found their opportunity to stash them where he or she figured they'd never be found."

"In your backyard. Which proves my point."

"What point was that?"

Mort fitted his hat back over his still-thick hair, sprinkled with more dabs of gray now. "That you attract death, at least murder."

"You're assuming the person those bones belonged to was murdered."

"Aren't you?"

"I prefer to wait and see where the evidence takes me."

He rolled his eyes again, then cast his gaze toward the hole into which Seth Hazlitt had disappeared. "With you, Mrs. F., it always leads to the same place."

Seth looked almost comical trudging about the bottom of the six-foot trench in the bulky work overalls and oversized work boots. He looked bloated, puffy with air, his feet sloshing around the mud that lined the trench thanks to Cabot Cove's high water table. He almost fell a few times and banged up against the trench's earthen walls on several occasions.

He'd finally gotten himself steadied enough to crouch amid the mud to examine the mix-matched clutter of bones, which looked as if they'd been dumped into the hole like the contents of a trash bag.

"I can tell you they're human, *ayuh*," he called up to us without changing the direction of his gaze.

I watched him sifting gently through the next layer of mud, coming out with several bones. Each time he plunged a hand into the muck, he seemed to come out with another one, at least a chipped fragment.

"These are the remains of a man—I can tell you that much," Seth said, finally looking our way.

"How can you be sure, given the bones' degraded condition?" Mort said down to him.

"Narrow pelvic cavity. Women have much wider ones, so babies can pass through."

Mort sneaked a peek down toward his belt buckle. "Right. I knew that. Must've forgot. That all?"

"Not quite," Seth said, examining what looked to be a section of skull large enough to be recognizable. "This man's been dead a real long time. I can tell by the degraded remains of his teeth. He lived in a time before dentists and oral care became the norm, that's for sure."

"Care to be more specific?"

"I'd be guessing."

"Then by all means," Mort urged, "guess."

"Late eighteenth or early nineteenth century. I'll be able to narrow it down much further with an accelerator mass spectrometer to do a proper radiocarbon test."

"You don't have an accelerator mass spectrometer, Seth," I reminded him.

"Because our good sheriff keeps taking it out of my budget requests. If I had one of the darn things, I'd be able to do a more proper job as medical examiner."

"De facto medical examiner," Mort corrected.

Seth was inspecting the skull in his gloved hands.

"De facto or not, this medical examiner can tell you there's a symmetrical depression in this skull here."

"A result of blunt-force trauma, you think?" Mort queried, squinting to see the skull better.

"A fall would be just as likely," Seth said, looking up at us and then at the rungs he had grasped on his way down. "Maybe got pushed off a ladder."

"Don't give me any ideas, Doc."

Seth stopped suddenly when his furrowing about the muddy floor of the trench revealed another bone that looked to have suffered far less degradation, with remnants of decaying flesh that still hadn't totally decomposed. Several more followed that must've been similarly dumped, but a bit off to the right of the original find. I thought I saw Seth's eyes bulge before he rose from a crouch and clambered up the ladder, his too-big work boots slipping off the rungs. He actually lost one altogether as he neared the top rung and accepted Mort's help to boost him from the hole so as not to have to put pressure on his stockinged foot.

"You look like you just saw a ghost, Doc," Mort noted.

"Couple of them, it turns out," Seth told us both. "Because there's not one set of bones buried in that hole; there's two. The second set looks to have belonged to a woman, and she didn't die a couple hundred years ago either." His eyes moved from Mort to me, then the two of us at once. "More like one year back, two at the most, based on the state of the remains."

Chapter Two

Near as I can tell, anyway," Seth continued.

Mort twisted toward me. "You hear that, Mrs. F.? *Two* bodies buried in your backyard instead of one. And I'm betting it turns out they were both murdered. Tell me—before I got to Cabot Cove, did anybody die in this town who *wasn't* murdered?"

"I agree with you in this case," I told him. "Someone took the opportunity to move both sets of remains here at a time no one would notice my yard being dug up, someone who clearly has something to hide. And whatever that something is, it must be somehow connected to both bodies, not just one."

"Well," Seth said, slipping back into his loafers, "at least we can safely assume the same killer didn't kill them both."

My eyes fell on the mysterious box, still partially submerged in mud. "And maybe whatever's inside that can tell us why someone would go to such great lengths to hide their remains."

I'd grown familiar with colonial furniture for a book I was researching at one point. From this distance, the box appeared to be actually more of a chest. An oblong curved lid fastened atop its rectangular shape, maybe two and a half feet high by four and a half feet wide and two feet deep. That was standard size, more or less, for colonial and early American times, I assumed because it fit neatly in the back of horse-drawn wagons and could fit comfortably in pretty much any corner, nook, or cranny in homes of the time, known for their smaller rooms. The golden-shaded exterior I could make out from ground level was speckled with mud that still left the iron latches, handles, and wrappings evident, along with a matching key lock. I recognized the wood from its shade and grain as oak, common for those times. And this chest had the look of an elegant piece fashioned by a master craftsman, a theory supported by how well it had weathered the years in spite of likely being hidden away for most of them.

That suggested the chest had been owned by someone of means, someone from the gentry class that had been left over from the days of British royalty. I ran the timeline in my head, noting to myself that Cabot Cove had been founded in 1791 as a seaport and northern hub for trading ships. Those ships swept north across the Atlantic toward Canada to take advantage of the steering winds and currents, before angling south. Cabot Cove's was the largest open ocean port this far north at the time. You had to sail all the way to Boston to find another, and I imagined that the two venues often battled to provide docking for the same traders sailing back to Europe from points south, or from Europe heading toward the West Indies and South America.

"Mrs. F.?" Mort prodded, jarring me from my thinking. "Earth to Mrs. Fletcher . . ."

"Yes, what?"

"You looked like you were someplace else altogether."

"I was—in my mind."

"She does make a fair living as a writer, after all, Sheriff," Seth reminded him.

"Does she, now? I've got no idea where she finds the time to write in between solving murders." Mort looked from Seth to me. "But she's got her work cut out for her with these two."

"We need to have a look inside that chest," I told him. "How long before the state police can get a crime scene unit here?"

"They're a bit short staffed, this being Christmas week and all, but the fact that bones were found got them moving, so I'd say any minute."

"Speaking of Christmas . . ." Seth started, the words aimed at Mort.

"No."

"You don't even know what I was going to say."

"Yes, I do, Doc. You were going to ask me to play Santa Claus at the Christmas parade, because you ask me to play Santa Claus every year."

"And every year you say no."

"And this year will be no exception. The town is used to you as Santa, anyway."

Seth looked down at his stomach. "Every year I seem to need less padding. Come spring, Jess, maybe I'll join you on your jaunts through town on a bicycle. I must say, Sheriff, you're missing the spirit of the season."

Mort took off his sheriff's hat and flapped it by his side. "Who died and left you in charge, Doc?"

"Agnes Weatherby, last May at the ripe old age of ninety-one, after organizing the parade for thirty-five consecutive years. That leaves the committee big shoes to fill."

"There's one thing I really liked about Agnes Weatherby."

"What's that, Mort?" I asked him.

"She wasn't murdered."

Just then, a gaggle of voices drew our attention to the far corner of my brochure-new house. A trio of figures appeared, a pair of young women wearing jeans flanking a well-built man with muscular arms showcased in a formfitting shirt and a shock of hair that looked dry-cleaned. The well-built man was holding a cordless microphone, and one of the women held what looked like a news camera on her shoulder. The trio moved purposefully our way, Mort tensing alongside me.

"What have we got here?" Seth wondered aloud.

"Whatever it is, Doc," Mort followed, "it can't be good."

They ground to a halt directly before us with the

trench in the background. The well-built man trained all of his focus on me, as if Mort and Seth weren't standing right there with me at all.

"Mrs. Fletcher, I'm Tad Hollenbeck from *Stalker*."

"*Stalker*?"

"The television show."

"There's a television show called *Stalker*?"

Seth Hazlitt leaned over and whispered into my ear, "Tawdry tabloid show nobody in their right mind watches, promoting wacko theories."

If Tad Hollenbeck overheard his words, he wasn't showing it. Despite his considerable musculature, I had the distinct impression he was holding his stomach in.

"And you made our radar, Mrs. Fletcher. Well, more accurately, Cabot Cove made our radar."

"What on earth for?"

"Try being the murder capital of the world, at least the country. Per capita, anyway. How many was it last year?"

"I don't keep count."

"Then let me tell you. It was—"

Mort cut the man off before he could continue. "There's gonna be another if you don't back off and state your business, son."

Hollenbeck's gaze darted to the crime scene tape erected around the ditch that had been dug in my backyard. "Judging by that crime scene tape, I'd say there's already been another. I'm here to do a story on why so many people seem to be murdered in Cabot Cove. There are several working theories."

"Can't wait to hear them."

"You've heard of the Bermuda Triangle, I assume, Sheriff Metzger," Hollenbeck said to him, even though his eyes remained on me.

"You seem to have done your homework," Mort said, hardly used to outsiders knowing his name.

"It's my job. I'm a reporter."

"Not if you work for *Stalker*," Seth mumbled, just loud enough to be heard.

"Anyway," Mort picked up, "I know enough to know that so-called triangle is down near Bermuda, not up here in Maine."

"We're working on the theory there may be something like that at work in your town. A kind of blip in the universe, an anomaly."

"A *what*?" From Seth.

"Call it a cosmic depression."

"Do I have to?" I asked Hollenbeck.

"Do you know what a sinkhole is, Mrs. Fletcher?"

"Is this a quiz?"

"Just an analogy."

"A sinkhole," I told him, "is a hole in the ground caused by some form of collapse of the surface layer, normally caused by collected water that has no place to drain."

"I think Cabot Cove lies in the center of a metaphysical sinkhole."

"In other words," tried Mort, "our murder rate can be tied to something in the air."

Hollenbeck nodded. "Not far from that, yes, Sheriff Metzger, and I intend to prove it."

"Better be able to pull that off before I run you out of town, son," Mort warned him. "Folks here like to be left alone, especially during the holidays. I'd listen to what I'm telling you, if you and your friends don't want to wake up Christmas morning in a jail cell."

"How do you explain it, then?"

"Explain what?"

"The murder rate."

"Son, I was a New York City homicide detective in the bad old days before I moved here, if you want to talk about murder rates."

Hollenbeck swung toward Seth. "You must be Dr. Hazlitt."

"Guilty as charged," he said, pleased at the fact that the TV reporter had recognized him.

"Residents here ever complain about the water?"

"Complain about *the water*?" Seth repeated, dumb-founded.

"The wells and regular supply all come from the same aquifer. You ever have it tested?"

"Why would I?"

"Just another theory we're pursuing, that maybe the water has high concentrations of toxins, either known or unknown. Toxins with psychotropic prop-erties that result in violent tendencies. There's prece-dent for that, you know."

"Really?" Mort challenged. "Where?"

Hollenbeck ignored his question and swung back toward me, gesturing for his cameraperson to set up a shot. "You mind if I get this on tape, Mrs. Fletcher?"

"As a matter of fact, I do."

"You seem to be at the center of a lot of these mur-ders."

"Just like you seem to be trespassing on my property."

The young woman angled the camera my way as Hollenbeck thrust his microphone in my face. I stretched my arm forward and covered the lens with my palm.

"You were saying, Mr. Hollenbeck . . ."

He lowered the microphone. "You wrote your first book here in Cabot Cove."

"Yes, I did."

"A *murder* mystery."

"That's right."

"People died."

"They normally do in murder mysteries."

"And you've written, what, fifty of them?"

"Something like that. Why?"

"Means you've killed an awful lot of people, Mrs. Fletcher."

I couldn't help but groan. "Because of something in the water, you think?"

"Or the air, or the ground, or the barometric pressure. An anomaly, like I said, or maybe several of them working in concert. An impossible convergence of elements that our investigation intends to prove to explain all the people getting murdered here." Hollenbeck aimed his next words at me. "For real, I mean."

Seth eased himself forward. "Is this going to be the subject of an episode of *Stalker*?"

"I'm considering a series of episodes, maybe a week's worth, actually. Would you be up for an interview, Dr. Hazlitt?"

Seth's eyes seemed to glisten. "Well, I . . ."

I looked at Mort, who shook his head at Seth's rumination over the possibility of appearing on national television.

"Because," Hollenbeck resumed when Seth's voice tailed off, "your perspective would lend a lot to the story, an incredible amount, really."

"You think?"

"How long have you been practicing medicine in Cabot Cove?"

"Oh, well . . . a long time," Seth stammered, before suddenly forcing a smile. "Long enough to know where all the bodies are buried, you might say."

"Literally, it would appear," Hollenbeck said, peering beyond us at the crime scene tape that had been staked in the ground all around the hole where Ben McMasters's crew had uncovered the remains of two bodies. "And have people always dropped dead from foul play at the rate they do now?"

Mort moved in between Hollenbeck and Seth, cutting off whatever answer the good doctor might have been about to give.

"Mrs. Fletcher," he said, while keeping his eyes on the reporter, "would you like to press trespassing charges against this gentleman?"

Hollenbeck's gaze again tracked over Mort's shoulder to the two Cabot Cove deputies standing vigil over the trench, the nearby backhoe silent and workers continuing to mill about while waiting for their boss to tell them what to do.

"Speaking of buried bodies . . ." He swept his gaze toward me. "In your very backyard, Mrs. Fletcher?

This is just too rich to believe." He gestured toward the young woman with the camera, stopping just short of snapping his fingers. "Get this on camera, Selina. An active crime scene would make for great B-roll."

Selina started to raise the camera, and Mort forced it back down.

"Hey!" protested the other young woman.

"Who are you?"

"I'm Angie, the producer, Sheriff."

"Well, Angie the producer, this is private property. No taping allowed without the owner's permission."

"Is that actually a law?"

"If it's not, it should be. Take me to court if you want. Nearest federal bench is Boston. See you there."

Hollenbeck eased his hands into the air, a show of subservience, relenting. "I think we've got enough for today anyway," he said to me, as if Mort wasn't standing there at all. "Just one more question, Mrs. Fletcher: How many bodies was it this time?"

"It was nice meeting you, Mr. Hollenbeck," I said with a smile as I sidestepped away from him.

"Fine," he shot back, holding his ground, "so long as you know I'm not leaving town until I get to the bottom of whatever's really going on in Cabot Cove."

"When you find out, Mr. Hollenbeck," I called out in his direction, "please tell me."

As soon as Hollenbeck and his crew had taken their leave, Mort glared at Seth, shaking his head. *"Long enough to know where all the bodies are buried,"* he repeated. "Really, Doc?"

"I got carried away, all right?"

"You actually watch that show, don't you?" I said to Seth.

"I like to keep up on things."

"Sure." Mort nodded. "I get it. Things like psychotropic toxins in groundwater and metaphysical sinkholes."

"*Stalker* covers other stuff, too."

"You mean like that theory that the Chinese have built a maze of tunnels beneath the entire country to spy on us?"

Seth's eyes bulged. "See, I knew it! You watch the show, too! That episode ran last week!"

"Not me," Mort responded sheepishly. "Adele."

"And you just happened to be listening at the time," I noted.

"Adele keeps the volume loud 'cause of the hearing damage she suffered blowing things up in the Marines."

Mort could tell by our expressions that neither Seth nor I was buying that.

"Okay, once in a while," he admitted. "When I'm flipping through the channels."

I couldn't stop shaking my head while holding back a smile. "And you just happen to stop on *Stalker*. Or does the TV do it on its own?"

"It's the top-rated show in its time slot, Jess," Seth said, looking toward Mort as if they were kindred spirits now.

"Interesting tidbit for a small-town doctor to know," I noted.

"Hey," Seth said defensively, "I'm a student of pop culture."

Mort scratched at his scalp again. "What the heck is that exactly, anyway?"

Seth fingered his chin. "You know, I'm not really sure what it is, but I know it when I see it."

Mort fitted his hat back on. "You really want to appear on trash television, Doc?"

"It's not all trash," Seth insisted.

"Didn't you just say no one in their right mind watches it?" I asked him.

"Well, the show is a great stress reliever."

"Stress reliever?" said an incredulous Mort. "You're eating pie at Mara's every afternoon at three o'clock." He cast his gaze in the direction in which Tad Hollenbeck and his two-woman crew had disappeared around my house. "I wish we could still just run people out of town for no good reason at all."

Mort's phone rang and he started walking off, stopping long enough to wave a reproaching finger in Seth's face.

"And don't go telling that reporter I said that either."

"You've been on television, Jess," Seth said to me after Mort moved away to answer his phone.

"Many times."

"Some big shows, too."

"A few."

He sighed. "Not many media types clamoring to interview small-town doctors."

"You always told me how much you valued your

privacy. You always say that's what you love most about living in Cabot Cove."

"Well, maybe I had things wrong," Seth huffed.

At which point Mort strode up to us, putting his phone in his pocket. "The state police crime scene unit went to the wrong address, Sandalwood Street instead of Candlewood Lane. They're on their way now."

Chapter Three

While waiting for the state police crime scene unit to arrive, I busied myself with more of the chores that would allow me to reclaim 698 Candlewood Lane as my home. That process started, appropriately enough, with placing my vast book collection in the rebuilt bookshelves that adorned both my living room and upstairs office. Actually, in the house's original form, spaces were reserved for books in every room, an accommodation I had insisted be meticulously re-created in this remade version, no matter the expense.

Somehow, the formality of that made it appear forced. Shelves now existed for books, instead of being appropriated for their placement. I missed the spontaneity of the way it had been before, the random clutter that had long made the house mine. I'm very orderly, except when it comes to books, as if they must be granted an exception to the rule. Clean what you must, but spare no book its place.

The question I've probably been asked more than any other is when I knew I wanted to be a writer. I've formed any number of answers over the years, often dwelling on my struggles to get published over more years than I care to admit. The most truthful one, though, is how I loved losing myself in the stacks of my local library as soon as I was old enough to read. I started in the children's section, filled with beanbag chairs and the scent of the jelly beans the children's librarian was fond of handing out as a way to cajole us kids to keep coming back.

I, of course, required no such cajoling. I graduated to the middle-grade and then young-adult sections of the library before finally moving on to the array of stacks reserved for adults. I was still a child at the time, and perusing the neatly shelved books made me feel I'd finally been granted access to a secret place previously denied me. I didn't give much consideration, if any, to becoming a writer at that point, but the desire to do so rested in my unconditional love of books. The feel of the pages as I flipped them, the smack a book made when closed after the last one was turned, the familiar, comforting smell.

Pondering that made me realize I missed the smells of my old house as much as anything, maybe most of all. Construction crews can replace, rebuild, or repair pretty much anything, but they can't re-create the smells that collect over the years like memories and are often just as personal. I'd been back in the house for just a week now, but it didn't feel like home yet. I thought the return of the books I'd either restored or replaced would do a lot to remedy that, making my home once again feel like the local library where I'd spent a great deal of my youth.

I owe so much to that library, all libraries, really, which is why it was such a pleasure for me to serve as president of the Cabot Cove Friends of the Library. No cause was more important to me, nor would one likely ever be. And with each book I shelved, I started to feel more at home. I lifted them from boxes marked to correspond with specific shelves, doing my utmost to re-create the order that had predated the fire. The process proved refreshing, therapeutic, and even cathartic.

I was home, starting to clatter away on my laptop on my kitchen table, where I did my edits, or the brand-new iMac in my upstairs office, where I was currently slaving over a first draft. As I did in my life, I let the stories take me where I needed to go. And, as I also did in my life, I found myself surprised when I got there.

"Mrs. F.?"

Mort's summons almost made me lose my balance atop the stepladder I needed to reach the topmost bookshelves. I recovered my balance, stepped down, and looked his way.

"The state police are here," he said.

I normally enjoy watching crime scene techs work, admiring their meticulousness and keen powers of observation. But it was too chilly, and too much work awaited me back inside the house, for me to linger outside through the whole of the process that began just short of noon.

The techs pulled dark overalls over their clothes, much as Seth had. Then they clubbed plastic booties over their shoes so as not to contaminate the crime scene once they lowered into the newly dug trench in my backyard. While I'd been inside, Seth had taken his leave to shower and change his clothes, telling Mort he couldn't stand the lingering stench that had accompanied him out of that same hole in the ground. There wasn't much more he could do here anyway, given that the crime scene techs were certain to take possession of both sets of human remains in order to run proper DNA and dating tests to learn everything they could about whomever they belonged to.

That process proved painstaking and laborious, as the crime scene technicians sifted through the six-foot-deep trench like gold miners of old, careful to disturb the sodden layers of earth as little as possible while uncovering more and more bones. Ultimately, they would add up to the remains of two human beings and would likely provide firm indication as to the manners of their deaths; or, in the case of the skull Seth had already examined, whether the depression was caused by a fall or something more malevolent.

I noticed the techs were working around that old oak chest, saving its inspection and removal for last. They wouldn't open it here amid the elements, not without an understanding of what its contents might be. Since the chest had been buried on my property together with the skeletal remains, presumably there was a connection between its contents and the two sets of bones.

Of course, it was difficult to estimate exactly when the skeletal remains and colonial-era chest had been buried here. It could have been anytime in the last year or so, really. My landscape needed to be redone entirely, so there were no flower beds or grass to hinder the perpetrator's efforts. Just a lot of bare ground heavily laden with impressions of thick tires belonging to any number of construction vehicles and equipment.

The one thing that was clear and undeniable was that my home's reconstruction had offered a splendid opportunity to move the bones and old chest here from wherever they had been hidden prior. And that raised the question of where exactly that was and why someone had deemed the effort worthwhile in the first place. That suggested two things in my mind: First, that whatever had led the culprit to relocate the bones and chest to my property was worth the risk. And, second, that that person must've been a resident of Cabot Cove, since how else would they have known about the opportunity presented by the ongoing reconstruction of my home?

I tried not to form the word *murder*, because no indication of that existed yet. Of course, people didn't routinely bury surreptitiously those who died of any other cause. When someone goes to such lengths to secure remains, not to mention the potential treasure trove of evidence inside that colonial chest, a nefarious reason is almost always to blame.

Mort had to attend to some other business for a

time, leaving the two Cabot Cove deputies to secure the scene with the Maine state policemen who'd joined the crime scene unit in my backyard. I spotted contractor Ben McMasters and his work crew hanging back on the unlikely chance they'd be given the okay to resume their work.

"Ben," I called as I approached him.

He cast me a frown. "Sorry this is going to put us behind, Mrs. Fletcher."

"Totally out of your control and nothing you need to apologize for," I told him. "But I do have a question. Any idea when that hole might have been dug?"

He took off the ball cap he was wearing, smoothed his hair, and then fit the cap back over his head. "We've been racing so hard to get things wrapped up before winter, we've had workmen literally bumping into each other. A few times I had to introduce myself to some of the very crews I'd hired."

"Meaning . . ."

"Meaning it could have happened right in front of me and I may not have noticed. Or whoever did the burying could have come out on a Sunday, when my crews were off. Since you can't see the backyard from the street, they might as well have been invisible."

I thanked Ben for telling me exactly what I expected to hear, even as I hoped to hear otherwise, and retreated back inside to relieve the wintry chill I could feel down deep in my bones. I flipped on the television to check the weather forecast for Christmas week, which remained dry and just a bit warmer than average, with no snow in the offing, which meant no white

Christmas this year. In the process, I happened to cross over a rerun of the *Stalker* tabloid TV program in which another of their correspondents was reporting from a town where aliens were being blamed for a series of unexplained disappearances. Typical fodder for the show under whose auspices Tad Hollenbeck had come to Cabot Cove to investigate our unusually high murder rate.

An anomaly, like I said, or maybe several of them working in concert. An impossible convergence of elements that our investigation intends to prove to explain all the people getting murdered here.

That was Hollenbeck's working theory, and more power to him if he was able to latch onto that so-called convergence. In my mind, a much more rational explanation for why the murder rate in Cabot Cove vastly exceeded the norm was because we paid attention. Blame me, in other words, for spotting murder in many cases where an accident or natural causes might have otherwise been the ultimate disposition.

I've been here one year. This is my fifth murder. What is this, the death capital of Maine? On a per capita basis this place makes the South Bronx look like Sunnybrook Farm!

That had been one of Mort's first reactions to our uncommonly high murder rate, and I could only hope that Tad Hollenbeck never managed to track that quote down. Meanwhile, I busied myself by shelving more books, the house becoming more and more home again with each successive one, as the light began to bleed from the afternoon sky. Outside, members of Mac's crew had set up portable construction lights around the trench so the work of the state police crime scene unit wouldn't be deterred by the fall of night.

As it turned out, though, they finished just short of that. Mort had returned some time ago and I overheard him haggling with the state policemen over chain of custody. It was determined, quite expectedly, that the state police would take possession of the skeletal remains but that the old chest and its contents would remain here in Cabot Cove in the possession of our Sheriff's Department. The two deputies who'd been on scene all day donned evidence gloves (even though the chest had already been dusted for fingerprints) and placed the chest in the back of Mort's department-issue SUV. That the SUV was four-wheel drive and showroom new had finally gotten him to retire the red Cadillac Eldorado he'd tooled about town in through his first years on the job. The change coincided with the explosion in summer residents and business, which required more traffic stops, better conducted with a real police vehicle, though Mort often mused that he wished there was a convertible model.

Once the crime scene was cleared, Ben McMasters's work crew would be free to resume removal of my old, and installation of my new, septic system. But that would likely have to wait until after Christmas at this point, and I figured Ben and his team wouldn't be back to work until the following Monday at the earliest.

I gave the chest an up-close-and-personal look after the deputies had loaded it into the back of Mort's SUV, Mort using his flashlight to guide my efforts.

"Anything come to mind, Mrs. F.?"

"I don't think it was down there long, Mort," I told him.

"And you think this why exactly?"

I took the flashlight from his grasp and ran it along the chest's uniform coloring and texture. "We had a wet fall, right?"

"One of the wettest ever."

"The ground was saturated throughout town, the creek beds and water table near their highest level ever. That level would have easily reached six feet down to the trench where Mac found the chest and human remains," I said, as I continued moving the flashlight beam about. "But there are no water marks or scoring anywhere. That means whoever did the burying did so after the water table leveled off and the ground firmed up again as fall's chill set in."

"So sometime in the last month or so?"

Again I indicated the chest's incredibly pristine condition. "I'd say even the past week or so."

He pondered that for a moment. "Suggests it was done by somebody familiar enough with Cabot Cove to know about the water table. By the way, Mrs. F., remind me to put in for more security cameras in my next budget."

"More as opposed to none, you mean, outside of those traffic cams on Main Street you talked the town elders into."

"All the same, I'm going to check around the neighborhood to see if anyone might have one of those doorbell cams. You never know, do you?"

"No," I told Mort, eyeing the chest again through the flood of the flashlight beam, "you don't."

* * *

Mort had cleared off one of the desks normally occupied by a deputy for us to place the chest on, which took virtually the entire space. The state police crime scene techs had confirmed the latch wasn't locked, meaning the missing key posed no issue and we didn't have to call a locksmith.

The shift dispatcher was at his station well off to the side, leaving Mort and me on our own for all intents and purposes, though I had the strangest feeling we were being watched through the sheriff's station's ample windows.

"You mind closing the blinds?" I said to Mort.

"Not at all, if they worked. Sorry."

I shrugged and repositioned myself to block sight of our efforts from anyone looking in. "You want to do the honors?"

"Care to hazard a guess as to what's inside, Mrs. F.?"

"It's not a body."

Mort frowned. "That's comforting enough, I suppose."

He eased hands encased in evidence gloves to the curved, oblong lid, just about to lift it when the entry door banged open.

"Sorry about that." Seth Hazlitt chortled, backing his way through the door with a take-out box from Mara's in hand. "But I figured you could use some—"

He stopped when he saw the object of our attention on display.

"Why do I get the feeling I interrupted something?"

"Because you did, Doc. That said, what'd you bring us?"

"Mara's signature club sandwiches, three of them. Three pieces of pie, too," Seth said, laying the take-out box down on the raised reception desk. "But all that can wait."

"Notice anyone about outside?" I asked when he drew even with us.

"Not a soul, Jess. You know how folks get when the temperature drops into the twenties."

"You're sure?"

"It's a full moon. If there was anyone out there, I would've noticed them."

"Given that you never miss a thing." Mort nodded.

"I'm glad somebody noticed."

"Yes, sir, a real master of observation. That's you, Doc."

With that, Mort pointed downward.

"What?" Seth asked him.

Mort pointed again, and this time Seth looked down at his shoes to find that he'd donned a mismatched pair, one black and one brown.

"Will you look at that? If that doesn't beat all . . . Maybe that *Stalker* reporter was right about there being some kind of toxin loose in this town. Maybe the whole epicenter is located in your backyard, Jess, and now I've been exposed and afflicted."

"Sure, Doc," said Mort, "that explains it. Now, step back."

Mort returned his gloved hands to the top of the lid, angling for a purchase that would allow him to lift it open. The lid rose with the slightest of creaks, light shed from the ceiling-mounted fixtures pouring in.

"Looks like this is more in your neck of the woods than mine, Mrs. F."

The chest was crammed with ragged journals bound in faded, tattered leather, arranged in a series of neat piles that all featured stray unbound pages peeking out among them. There were also frayed document carriers, tasseled closed with thick leather twine looped around the topmost one I could clearly see.

"That's quite a collection," Mort noted.

"And remarkably well preserved, *ayuh*," Seth added.

"The chest isn't airtight, but the seal was tight enough to keep moisture out and the ground can make for a great insulator, so long as something's buried deep enough to avoid seepage or contamination by groundwater."

"Sounds like whoever did the burying wanted to keep the contents of that chest as well preserved as possible," Seth offered, his eyes starting to widen. "In which case . . ."

"In which case *what*, Doc?" Mort prodded.

Seth looked toward me. "How old you figure this chest to be, Jess?"

"Late eighteenth or early nineteenth century," I told him, explaining what I'd already concluded for myself.

Seth was almost shaking with excitement. "Seventeen nineties maybe?"

I nodded. "Of course. That would fit."

"My stars, I should think so. After all these years . . ."

"What's got you in such a tizzy, Doc?" Mort asked him.

Seth's eyes were glistening as he regarded the contents of the old chest as if they were the Holy Grail. "I think I know what we're looking at here."

Chapter Four

I always figured they were lost forever," Seth continued. "Everybody did."

Mort edged a bit closer to him. "Figured what was lost forever, Doc?"

Seth thrust a trembling finger toward the chest. "I believe we are looking at the long-lost founding documents of Cabot Cove."

"Why would anyone bother to lose them?" I asked him.

"Long story; whole bunch of long stories, actually, Jess. But what you're looking at here just might be among the greatest troves of primary-source writing from the colonial era left anywhere."

"That sounds all well and good, Doc," Mort Metzger said, scratching at his scalp. "But how exactly did these founding documents end up buried in Mrs. F.'s backyard? And why?"

"How long before the state police get back to you with the test results on those bones?" I asked Mort.

"It's Christmas week, Mrs. F., which means it's difficult to say. Depends if the lab's running with a short staff. I already did my best to put a rush on things, but we don't even have firm evidence of any crime here, other than the fact that whoever buried those bones and this chest here trespassed on your property to do it."

"There is that depression in the older of the two skulls, Mort," Seth reminded him. "Spotted it myself, as you'll recall."

"And you said it was damage as likely done from a fall as with some kind of blunt instrument."

"What if it was murder?" I postulated.

"I knew that was coming," said Mort, rolling his eyes.

"Hear me out, the both of you. These founding documents resurfaced in my backyard after having gone missing for over two hundred and twenty years. Now let's assume, just for fun, that the older set of bones belonged to a murder victim from the same era. That he was killed with a blow to the head at the same time those documents were hidden away."

"My first thought," started Seth, "would be that it must involve the town's founding fathers in some respect. The first five families to settle in Cabot Cove, after coming north from Boston under the auspices of one John Henry Cabot."

"That's who the town is named for?"

"Not right away, Sheriff, but yes, and for good reason. John Henry Cabot was a hero of the Revolution, a master strategist who commanded a cavalry regiment under General Nathanael Greene. He distinguished himself at both the Battle of Guilford Court House and the Battle of Hobkirk's Hill. While Greene remained in the southern theater waging guerrilla war against the far superior numbers of General Charles Cornwallis, Cabot took over command of the Continental Army's troops from Rhode Island northward, including portions of New York."

"That's one founding father," I noted. "Why don't you tell Mort about the other four?"

"Wait a minute," Mort said. "Their descendants ride in Averell Cooperman's carriage at the head of the Christmas parade every year."

I nodded, making a *sh* sound with a finger pressed against my lips and then whispering, "Seth's afraid of the horses."

"I am not!"

I stared at him.

"Well, maybe a little." He looked back at Mort. "In no particular order, our other original founders were Earl Grove Hutchinson, John Van Webb, Franklin McMullen, and Wyatt Rackley. They'd all carved out a great degree of success around Boston before heading up this way."

"If they were so successful down there, Doc," said Mort, "why venture up here at all?"

"The way I've heard it told was that they didn't cotton well to the religious persecution that arose from the puritanism that was taking fresh hold at the time, this being the early 1790s. Believe it or not, that spawned what some called a 'religious tax,' of all things, on the goods they imported from Europe and Asia."

Being a history buff, I found all this fascinating,

especially since I'd never really heard this part of the story before. "So they were traders."

"The seagoing trade made up a primary source of their business, but they were also among the first to establish textile mills and factories. Hutchinson owned a farm and a sawmill, too, and his family would ultimately start the first grocery chain in the country. Van Webb pretty much stuck to the import-and-export side of things, his primary export business derived from the products made at Hutchinson's sawmill. Cabot, of course, was a champion of industry responsible for the largest textile mills in all of New England, including the old Cabot Manufacturing Company right here off the interstate. Wyatt Rackley, on the other hand, trafficked in saloons and brothels. He ultimately headed west to expand his business interests and never returned to Cabot Cove."

All this was vaguely familiar to me. "Which brings us to Franklin McMullen."

"Owner of the first cannery and fishery in Cabot Cove history. He was known for having quite a temper and was reputed to have won at least two pistol duels in his time. In the last one, he mortally wounded the nephew of the sitting governor of Massachusetts, one John Hancock. So you might say he had his own reasons for fleeing north."

Our eyes all fell back on the contents of the old chest unearthed just hours before in my backyard.

"I was wondering if those documents might tell us more still," I suggested.

"As in, why the owner of those older remains may have gotten his head bashed in, Mrs. F.?"

"That's what I was thinking."

"I'm not sure whether my jurisdiction includes deaths more than two hundred years old," Mort said.

"Leave it to me, then," I told him.

"Okay," Mort relented, flapping his hands in the air, "okay. And I'd love to hear your thoughts about how those more recent remains ended up in the same hole as the older ones. How old did you say they were, Doc?"

"I didn't for certain, but I think twelve to eighteen months would be a fair estimate from Cabot Cove's de facto medical examiner."

"I've met all the current descendants still living in Cabot Cove but don't know any of them all that well, with the exception of Clara Wizzenhunt," I noted.

"I was over to see her at Shady Willows just the other day," Seth offered.

"How's she faring?"

He shrugged. "Good days and bad, more of the latter every month."

"I worked with her for years on the Friends of the Library."

"She's had the same book on her nightstand for over a year now," Seth said, sighing through the sadness lacing his voice.

"I always thought Cabot Cove's founders came north to make their fortunes," I said, eager to change the subject.

"Makes for a nice story," Seth told me, "but the truth is they were of substantial means already. Even way back then, you had to have money to make money, and our founders turned Cabot Cove into the most successful port north of Boston. The raw materials they imported from Europe, silk from Asia, and cotton shipped up from southern plantations became the basis for the factories that, combined with a thriving fishing industry, turned Cabot Cove into the envy of New England—the whole of the Northeast, really. All thanks to the five original founders who settled here."

I looked toward Mort. "You know what I'm thinking?"

"Do I have to guess?"

"I'll spare you the trouble: We need to interview the descendants of the five founders living in town. Because if anybody knows anything about how those founding documents ended up in my backyard—"

"It would be them," Mort completed, looking as if he wished he hadn't. "How do I get myself into these things?"

"I think I can handle a few interviews on my own," I told him. "They're not suspects, after all."

Mort's gaze flitted back to the contents of the old chest. "Not yet, anyway. We better team up." He eased the lid closed, as if that would be enough to stop our ruminations about the mystery that had been unearthed earlier that day in my backyard. "Now, what exactly are we supposed to do with this?"

"We need to take it to Mara's," I suggested.

"Does the chest look hungry to you, Mrs. F.?"

"To store in one of her walk-in fridges, Mort, to keep the pages from degrading."

Seth nodded. "Because a refrigerator is also a dehumidifier."

"Exactly," I said.

"Kind of like murder on ice."

"We'll see."

Seth took his leave to go back to work on organizing the upcoming Christmas parade, leaving Mort and me to transport the old oak chest to Mara's. Mara herself had already gone home, but the hostess made space for us on a floor-level shelf in one of the walk-in refrigerators in the back. It was chilly inside with a steady hum.

"Mrs. F.?"

"I was just thinking. . . ."

"Please don't."

"Think?"

"Nothing good ever comes of it, at least for me."

"Then close your eyes."

"Why?"

I reached down to the chest's lid. "So you don't see me bringing home some reading material for the night."

I couldn't resist the opportunity to bear witness to history written by those who lived it, and I figured that something in what Seth Hazlitt was certain were the long-lost founding documents of Cabot Cove might explain why they'd been squirreled away for so long, only to end up buried in my backyard. Had it not been for the need to replace my septic system, the documents and the skeletal remains separated by two hundred years would have gone undiscovered for decades. And I knew the questions that had arisen earlier in the day would keep me up long into the night:

Where had the founding documents of Cabot Cove been kept prior to being relocated to my backyard? Who had buried them there? And who belonged to those two sets of bones divided by centuries, the older of which showed clear evidence of a possible murder?

Pondering questions like that in real life was surprisingly akin to working out how to fill plot holes in my books. Invariably, I box myself into a corner where a character's actions and motivations confuse even me. Also invariably, revelations appear that I hadn't been expecting, forcing me to reverse engineer their existence and find their purpose in the book.

I work out the details of my stories as I'm writing them, just as I was doing now. Only instead of a printed partial manuscript lying before me, there was a centuries-old tattered document carrier, what might be called an early American portfolio, to tuck conveniently under one's arm, wrapped in thick leather twine. I pulled on a pair of latex gloves to keep any skin oils from the contents and unspooled the leather twine wrapped vertically around the document carrier. I felt as if I was spinning the combination dial of some mysterious vault holding untold riches. The twine came free, dangling down off the edge of my brand-new kitchen table as I folded back the cover, pausing ever so briefly just to smile.

How long had it been since I engaged in this oft-repeated ritual, seeking comfort in my routine? I'd forged a new one in the months I'd spent at Hill House hotel, but it never took, not really. Everything felt forced, wrong. Now I was back among my plates and dishes and cookware, the house starting to smell of books again. The modifications were obvious and impossible to deny, but this was still home, however reconstructed. The kitchen light remained too dull to work by, which meant nothing to me because it was my kitchen and my light. I recalled the very same lamp from the first night my husband, Frank, had taken me to see 698 Candlewood Lane. I remembered a lot of things about the house in the aftermath of that showing as we struggled to put an offer together, though it was this very kitchen I remembered most of all.

Meanwhile, it amazed me that these documents had managed to weather the years miraculously intact. That attested to the probability that they had been tucked away in a safe and dry place before someone stored the chest in some kind of dehumidified chamber.

I cautiously peeled back the flap to reveal the documents contained inside. Even then, I almost didn't want to slide the worn, yellowed pages, which I could see were frayed along the edges, from the document carrier, as if doing so might be a betrayal of the town I so loved. Yet these pages, and all the others contained in that oak chest, represented a mystery that had to be solved.

As was my custom, I turned on the television set on the counter, my old thirteen-inch now replaced by a slightly larger flat-screen. I kept the sound low, just loud enough for me to know there was a world out there beyond this kitchen and to chase away whatever loneliness might have crept in while I sat alone in the dark of night. Sometimes it was tuned to the Weather Channel, but usually CNN, as it was tonight, although I was tempted to flip through the channels in search of a Christmas movie. Once I began my work I'd forget it was on or even there at all, but its presence and the sound of voices were comforting at the start.

Not wanting to risk damage to the contents of the document carrier, I eased the entire clump of mismatched documents out at once. I was mindful of the weathered pages being stuck together and resolved not to try to separate any that resisted my grasp even in the slightest.

The topmost pages, I quickly noted, came from the log of a ship called the *Sansabel*, chronicling in exquisite detail a voyage in the captain's scrawl. I pictured the man seated at the desk in his cabin dipping his quill pen into an inkwell under candlelight that made my kitchen day-bright by comparison. He would have dutifully recorded the day's events each night before retiring. The content consisted of distance covered on what course, along with anything that had waylaid the voyage, from weather to sightings of possible pirate or enemy ships. There were details about crew members being punished with sanctions or lashes, having committed offenses ranging from tardiness to theft of foodstuffs. The latter was apparently treated very seriously at sea, and according to the log one offender had been punished with six lashes dispensed by the ship's steward on the foredeck. The captain wrote of how this pained him because the young man was his nephew, but at sea even more than on land it was necessary to enforce equal justice under the law.

I recalled how the five founders of Cabot Cove had established our town to be a thriving port and imagined many of the documents contained in the oak chest would pertain to that fact. Ships' logs, manifests, maps, charts, business dealings, transactions carried out in various ports of call, and so on. The *Sansabel* was a freighter, ferrying textile goods in the form of clothing and uniforms, made to order in many instances, across the sea, then being loaded with many of the raw materials the mills required to continue churning out inventory. The sea and network of inland waterways spun the turbines that allowed textile mill workers to cut, sew, and plume the cotton and woolen materials, hemming them into wearable items to be shipped to Europe. When one coupled that with the open ocean port conveniently situated at the hub of the northern trade route across the Atlantic, it was easy to see what had made Cabot Cove so attractive to its original founders. They had struck gold without ever planting a shovel in the ground to mine.

I was perusing the logs in an increasingly cursory fashion, taking mostly to skimming, when a tattered fragment of a page separated itself from the back of a log entry and dropped to the table. It had been torn down the middle, as if someone had intended to discard it altogether and might well have succeeded with at least the other half of it. But this half remained, wedged amid a random ship's log these many years, dislodged tonight after centuries.

The document was yellowed and faded. It was clearly a table of some sort, with categories listed across the top, beneath which were columns of hand-scrawled listings that were too degraded for me to clearly identify. The first category, in bold letters courtesy of the era's printing presses, was labeled *NAMES*. So, too, a fragment at the top featured the word *MANIFEST*, beneath which under a magnifying glass I was able to discern in cursive letters *On Board the*, followed by the handwritten *Sansabel*. Next came the cursive *of* accompanied by a blank line on which *Boston* had been written out.

Boston, not Cabot Cove, I thought, making a mental note there.

Unfortunately, the only other features I was able to discern were a series of names written in what looked like the same handwriting that filled in the blank lines above. They were centered, more or less, beneath *NAMES*, but the fragment's degraded condition prevented me from making out any of the specifics beyond that.

I had a sense this might be a vital clue in whatever mystery I'd latched onto.

". . . Cabot Cove . . ."

At first, I figured I must have heard the soft words emanating from my new kitchen television wrong. But a glance toward the screen revealed none other than Tad Hollenbeck, microphone in hand, doing a promo for a coming edition of *Stalker*. I quickly grabbed the remote and turned up the sound just as a jumpy video of Mort, Seth, and me inside the sheriff's station earlier that evening, shot through the window with the colonial chest in plain view, filled the screen.

"Is this the key to the latest murders to take place in Cabot Cove, Maine?" Hollenbeck said to the camera. "What secrets does it contain that might help us better understand why this small town has become the murder capital of the country?"

Just as the camera zoomed in on our now blurry faces, my phone rang, *MORT* lighting up on my caller ID.

"You saw it, too?"

"Yup, on Fox."

"I'm watching CNN."

"Nice to see Tad Hollenbeck is blowing through his ad budget at our expense, Mrs. F. I'm going to have a little talk with him tomorrow and I'd like you with me."

"I don't know, Mort. You might find yourself the subject of another segment."

"Not if Hollenbeck's in jail." He stopped, then started again. "Find anything interesting in that document carrier?"

"Maybe."

I heard him sigh. "I hate when you say that, Mrs. F."

"What on earth for?"

"Because with you, *maybe* always means *yes*, and *no* means *maybe*."

"What does *yes* mean?"

"*Watch out*. How about we have breakfast at Mara's and then go have a little talk with Tad Hollenbeck?

"Speaking of which, I've already thought of someone we need to see tomorrow morning before we pay a visit to Hollenbeck."

"Care to give me a hint, Mrs. F.?"

"A ship called the *Sansabel*."

"What kind of ship?"

"That's what we need to find out, Mort," I said, thinking of the one man in Cabot Cove who might be able tell me the meaning of that page fragment I'd been unable to decipher.

Chapter Five

The founding documents of Cabot Cove, you say?" said Fred Hardesty, tugging on the edges of his shiny black mustache as he tended to do whenever excited. "The two of you have brought me an early Christmas present."

Just minutes before, Mort and I had entered his antiques shop, located at a site once occupied by a mercantile shop owned by one of our town's original founders, John Henry Cabot. We'd made sure to leave Seth Hazlitt at Mara's shortly before nine Tuesday morning so we could get there for the store's opening, to avoid the Christmas crowds certain to demand Fred's attention through much of the day.

His eyes practically bulged out of his head when I slid over a plastic sleeve containing the fragment marked *MANIFEST*, which I had stored in the refrigerator overnight. Hardesty had been president of the

Cabot Cove Historical Society even longer than I'd served as president of the Friends of the Library. No one knew more about the history of our town, and I'd enjoyed hearing Fred speak about this or that any number of times at various civic functions and never tired of his stories. He maintained a virtually encyclopedic knowledge of all things Cabot Cove, and if anyone might have an inkling of what this ship's manifest contained, it would be him.

Meanwhile, his antiques shop remained one of the must-visits and true mainstays of Main Street. Fred had managed to weather the storm of chain stores moving in around him. If anything, their presence had made his shop even more fashionable for its downhome quality and superb selection, which formed a treasure trove of wonderful period pieces peeking out from behind others beneath a magnificent nonworking cut-crystal chandelier that had been a staple of the store ever since it had opened.

Hardesty could opine endlessly on the origins, lineage, and source of all the items he lovingly displayed, the chandelier in question being the one item he'd refused to part with under any circumstances. The story was, it had been presented to the original founders of Cabot Cove by a nobleman and trader who claimed it had once hung in the Palace of Versailles. I had no idea of its true value, and Fred might not have either, given his devotion to the piece as part of the history of our town. The master craftsman who'd fashioned the chandelier had cut the crystals in such a way that natural light was reflected out in a magnificent kaleidoscope of color.

Everything in his cluttered shop came with a story attached, and I stopped in occasionally as much to hear them as to view whatever new merchandise he'd been able to bring in. I must say I had a dual purpose for dropping by today, given that there was no better way to celebrate my return to 698 Candlewood Lane than to bring home a few fresh furnishings. Nothing spices up a house better than antiques, and I had my eyes set on both a beautiful Victorian settee and an early twentieth-century dresser that was perfect for my guest room.

"They were buried in my backyard," I told him, picking up on what had brought me to see him that morning. "Workmen found them yesterday while digging a trench for my new septic system."

"I heard it was bones they uncovered."

"That, too, and I guess human remains are more interesting to folks than the contents of an old chest."

Fred tugged again on the end of his jet-black mustache. He had long made a habit of dressing in woolen suits better fit for the ages most of his wares dated from, keeping the air-conditioning blasting on high during the summer to avoid roasting to death within the heavy material. Today that suit was a brownish herringbone I took to be an authentic Edwardian-era three-piece from 1901 to 1910, when King Edward VII sat on Great Britain's throne.

"Not to me," Fred said to both Mort and me, itching to get a look at the document I'd tucked into that plastic sleeve for safekeeping. "Now, let's see what you've got there, Mrs. Fletcher."

"How long have you known me, Fred?"

"Oh, round about twenty-five years or so. Pretty much ever since you moved here, I suppose."

"I think that's long enough to call me Jessica."

"I'm a creature of the past, and thus of formality. Look at it as a show of respect."

"In that case, thank you, *Mr. Hardesty*."

"How's the Cabot Cove Library's collection wing coming, by the way?" Fred asked me.

"Well, I wouldn't call it a wing—more like a closet."

"I'd still love for my first-edition Edgar Allan Poe story collection to be the first donation."

"Even if it means parting with 'The Purloined Letter'?" I asked him, knowing that story centered around hiding something in plain sight was his favorite.

"A sacrifice I'm willing to make toward the greater good, Mrs. Fletcher."

Mort rolled his eyes, and I smiled as I handed Fred the plastic sleeve, which he took gingerly in his grasp as if it were a Fabergé egg. Mort's phone rang and he moved aside to take the call.

"You okay on your own, Mrs. F.?" he said, holding the phone away from him.

I looked toward Fred Hardesty behind the counter. "I think I've got a handle on things."

"Good. I've got something I need to do at the station. Don't leave without me."

Mort was already moving for the door, and part of me wondered if he'd called himself so he'd have an excuse not to receive a history lesson.

"You can fill me in on everything when I get back," he said, the same bells that had jangled when we entered the shop jangling as he exited.

Instead of regarding the page fragment right away, Fred Hardesty moved to a raised counter that came up just short of his chest. He maneuvered one of those bendable desk lamps into position over a black blotter resting on the counter's surface. It looked hot enough to burn through the blotter. Fred then positioned it directly over the plastic sleeve and raised a pair of magnifying spectacles that had been dangling in front of his shirt.

"Oh my," he managed at first sight. "Oh my . . ."

"What is it you're seeing, Fred?"

"Something I've suspected for a very long time."

"Something to do with the *Sansabel* and her cargo?"

"Everything. You see, Mrs. Fletcher, the *Sansabel* was a slave ship."

Chapter Six

This all ties in with the five founders' move up here from Boston," Hardesty continued, while I tried to make sense of what he'd just said.

Cabot Cove as a port of call for the slave trade? This was the first I'd ever heard even an inkling of such a thing.

"Not a lot of people have a clear sense of the history involved here, Mrs. Fletcher. Slavery was outlawed in Massachusetts in 1788."

"So if the founding fathers of Cabot Cove were involved in the slave trade," I postulated, "they'd need to find another port of call to continue their efforts."

"Hence their move north and the establishing of a major port right here on the Maine coast."

"Why has nothing about this ever come out before?"

"You already know the primary explanation for

that: because the documents attesting to the truth have been hidden these many years." Fred pushed the magnifying spectacles up on his nose and pointed toward the document contained within the plastic sleeve. "There've been plenty of rumors and stories over the years, but that is the first evidence attesting to the fact that the founders of Cabot Cove weren't all they were cracked up to be."

It was hard to get my arms around the probability that my beloved Cabot Cove had been founded as a center for the slave trade, that much of the mythos of the establishment of our town had been a lie.

"If this were a more complete document," Hardesty resumed, while I was still trying to collect my thoughts, "you'd see more headings across the top after 'names.' There'd be categories for sex, age, and size, which was more commonly referred to as 'stature' at the time."

"But the names, the ones I could make out anyway, were Anglo."

Hardesty nodded. "Of course they were, because that's what the chief mate, whose duties included being in charge of the cargo, named them once they were brought aboard. It was easier and far more convenient than identifying them by their African names. Remember, they spoke no English and, I imagine, in many cases were too terrified to speak at all."

"Terrible to refer to human beings as cargo."

"All the same, that's how slaves were looked at in those times by traders like the men behind the *Sansabel*," Fred said, tugging at his mustache again.

I couldn't get past the notion that the much-celebrated Earl Grove Hutchinson, John Van Webb,

Franklin McMullen, Wyatt Rackley, and John Henry Cabot of lore had made their fortunes on the backs of innocent human beings. I know the times were different and such things should be viewed through the cultural lens of the time. In my mind, though, slavery was a reprehensible aberration no matter how it was couched. If nothing else, the motive for someone to have gone to such great lengths to hide the documents was starting to sharpen in focus. They might have thought they were doing what was best for the town, wanting to preserve Cabot Cove's roots as a fishing village and manufacturing center going all the way back to the initial years of its existence.

"Consider me available," Fred started, "to review all the documents in that chest from a historical perspective, Mrs. Fletcher."

"That will be up to the sheriff, but I'll definitely convey your offer to him."

Hardesty regarded the remaining portion of the *Sansabel*'s slave manifest again before moving his gaze back to me.

"Our founders did wonderful things in these parts as well. You should keep that in mind when judging them."

"It's just that I find the mere notion that Cabot Cove was built on slave labor revolting."

"Perhaps the remainder of those documents can provide a better idea as to the extent of that."

Mort timed his return to the antiques shop well, arriving just as Fred Hardesty was finishing up his analysis of the manifest from the *Sansabel*. He parted with the document reluctantly, to the point where I almost had to pry it out of his hand.

"Don't forget my offer to inspect the remainder of the documents, Mrs. Fletcher."

"We'll likely take you up on it, once we get things a bit more sorted out."

He nodded as the morning's first real customers entered the shop to the sound of jangling bells.

I stopped near that turn-of-the-century dresser I was so taken by. "Beautiful piece," I said.

"Want me to hold it for you?"

"If you wouldn't mind. I have just the place for it."

"Done!" Fred said, readying one of his SOLD placards to place upon the dresser.

Then I spotted something else near the dresser amid the shop's clutter, something that made me do a double take.

"Can you hold this for me as well, Fred?"

He readied a second placard and spotted the item I was referring to. "For your grandnephew?"

"What do you think?"

"That he'll love it, Mrs. Fletcher."

Mort was leaning against his SUV when I emerged from the shop. "Ready to get on with some real police work, Mrs. F.?"

"Tad Hollenbeck?"

"He's staying at one of the motels off the interstate that are always packed during the summer. I called over there before coming to get you. No answer in his room, so we'll have to track him down."

"Which should be very easy," I said, as Tad Hollenbeck walked through the entrance to Mara's, just down and across the street.

Tad was casting his gaze about the crowded restaurant, seeming to study the tables, when we entered behind him.

"Looking for something, Mr. Hollenbeck?" Mort asked him.

He swung with a start. "Good morning, Sheriff, Mrs. Fletcher. . . ."

Neither of us returned his salutation.

"You send your cameraperson and producer back to New York?" Mort asked him.

"Hardly," a surprisingly at ease Hollenbeck responded. "They're out shooting B-roll of the town for the story. You know."

"No, I don't. Why don't you explain it to me?"

"They're accumulating footage of the various places around town where murders have been committed."

"Just murders?" Mort asked him.

"That's the focus of the story, Sheriff."

"Because it occurs to me there are other crimes you could include. Like lying to a police officer or misrepresenting your identity, both of which you're guilty of."

The bravado washed off Hollenbeck's expression as quick as that. "I don't think I follow you."

"I think you do, Mr. Hollenbeck," Mort said as I looked on, wondering where he was going with this. "I called the *Stalker* offices this morning after seeing that promotional spot that aired last night. I think you know the one, since you put Mrs. Fletcher and me on tape without our permission. They told me you'd uploaded the ad without approval and had been suspended as a result, that you were no longer on the '*Stalker* beat,' as they called it."

"They said that?"

"Their exact words."

"It's not accurate. I already wasn't salaried anymore, but I've still been filing reports and stories on a freelance basis."

"Including the one you're planning on Cabot Cove?" I asked him.

"That was the plan," he said, nodding.

Mort didn't look like he was in the mood to back down. "What about those rumors of you fabricating or embellishing stories?"

Hollenbeck grew tenser. "That's a private matter between me and the producers. And let's not be naïve, Sheriff. *Stalker* is in the business of embellishment."

"Right. I spoke to them about that as it pertains to Cabot Cove. I even mentioned your, er, theories about toxins in the water and rips in the interdimensional time-space continuum."

"I never said anything about rips in the time-space continuum, interdimensional or otherwise."

"Really? My bad, then. You can take it up with your former bosses when you get back to New York. They're eager to have a chat with you. If you leave now, you can be there by midafternoon."

Hollenbeck tried to make his expression look harsh, severe, but couldn't quite pull it off. "I'm not going anywhere without my story."

"*Your* story, Mr. Hollenbeck?" I interjected.

"That's what it is."

"I would have thought *the* story would be a more accurate way of phrasing it," I said, realizing something. "This story seems awfully personal to you."

"All my stories are personal to me, Mrs. Fletcher, just like yours are to you, I'm sure."

"Your stories," Mort said, echoing Hollenbeck's words. "You mean like the one about the hybrid alligator people? Or maybe the one about the Boy Scouts of America's involvement in the Kennedy assassination. Now, that was a doozy."

"It was also legitimate."

"Right," Mort followed. "All you left out was that they were conspiring with the Girl Scouts and the whole thing was about those cookies they sell every spring. Yup, a real doozy. I can see why you were fired, Mr. Hollenbeck."

"Suspended," he corrected.

"Right," Mort said, cutting him off, the diners closest to us growing quiet in order to listen, "you're freelance now."

"What really brought you to Cabot Cove, Mr. Hollenbeck?" I asked him.

"How many times do I have to explain it?"

"Apparently at least one more, because what you've told us so far doesn't wash," Mort interjected.

"Maybe somebody gave me a tip," Hollenbeck said, his voice flailing a bit.

"Who?" Mort asked.

"You don't really expect me to give up my sources, Sheriff, do you?"

"I expect you to leave town and take your cockamamie theories with you."

"I can no more do that than you can stop arresting people."

I could tell Mort was fighting to restrain his temper. "Doing our jobs, in other words."

"That's right."

"Wrong," Mort snapped, sticking his chest out. "And I'd love to make you the next person I arrest."

"On what charge?"

"Let's start with disturbing the peace."

"Whose?"

"Mine for starters, son. Stick around another day, and I'll come up with some more."

A cocky sneer spread over Hollenbeck's face. "You know, you're not the first yokel who's tried to run me out of town."

Mort managed a smile as he turned to me. "Yokel. He called me a yokel, Mrs. F." The smile slid from his face when he looked back toward the reporter. "You impress me as the kind of man who's used to making enemies, Mr. Hollenbeck."

"Comes with the job, Sheriff."

"Then you should keep in mind the job you claim brought you here because of our excessively high murder rate."

"Should I take that as a threat?" Hollenbeck posed, clearly pleased by the prospect, welcoming the challenge Mort had thrown before him.

"No, just a reality, according to you."

Mort glared at Tad Hollenbeck all the way to the door.

"He's a piece of work, isn't he?" I said.

Mort was still looking the reporter's way. "I can

think of other ways to describe him, but that's as good as any."

"Mort—"

"Save it, Mrs. F. I know I gave him the confrontation he wanted."

"I'm worried he may have taped the conversation to edit selectively and air as part of his story."

"Then it's a good thing I recorded it, too," Mort said, extracting his phone from his pocket.

Which rang on cue.

"Seth," Mort said, putting the phone on speaker. "What's up, Doc?"

"How long you been rehearsing that, Sheriff?" Seth asked him.

"Would you believe it just came to me? I'm with Jessica at Mara's, so she's on, too."

"Two of you enjoying a second breakfast without me?"

"Just having a little conversation," Mort told him.

"Saves me the trouble of calling Jess, too. I just heard from the state police crime lab. The two of you need to get over to my office right away."

Chapter Seven

We headed over to Seth Hazlitt's office immediately, greeted by Bing Crosby singing "White Christmas" through a stand-alone speaker that looked like a football. His receptionist ushered us into the back, where a trio of exam rooms was located. Since they were all taken, and Seth was currently with a patient, she led us to a fourth room, which had been converted into a dedicated children's area/playroom, Nat King Cole's "The Christmas Song" playing now, with chestnuts roasting over an open fire. Seth often mused about taking on a younger physician to handle some of his overload, but the mere possibility that a younger doctor might have intentions of replacing him someday was enough to dissuade Cabot Cove's favorite primary physician from doing so. Seth might be a committed curmudgeon in his sixties now, but he had managed to stay up on all the features of modern medicine and had also found his way to negotiating the maze of the modern health care system to make himself more relevant than ever.

The empty kids' room featured only tiny cube-like chairs better occupied by the likes of first and second graders. Mort and I remained standing while we waited for Seth to join us. The door opened after five more minutes and he closed it behind him.

"Took your sweet time getting here," he said from within his white lab coat, the front pocket of which was stuffed with lollipops.

"We were waiting for you, Doc," Mort told him.

"Well, I've got a boatload of patients to see, so let me fill you in on the details."

Seth sat down on one of the kid-sized chairs, leaving Mort and me no choice but to take the two matching ones opposite his. Seth took a scrap of notepaper from the same pocket in which the lollipops were squeezed and put his reading glasses on.

"First off, the victim from sometime around the turn of the nineteenth century was murdered, all right. State police crime lab folks believe the weapon that left that depression I found in his skull was a hatchet."

"Interesting choice for a weapon," Mort noted.

"Pretty common back then, though."

"You said 'around the turn of the nineteenth century,'" I chimed in. "Could it have been earlier?"

"It was a general approximation, so, yes, of course. Figure a margin of error of a decade or so, either way."

"So that would make closer to around 1791 a possibility."

"Is that important?"

"Let's just say the founders of Cabot Cove weren't everything they were cracked up to be," I said, and proceeded to fill him in on what I'd learned from Fred Hardesty earlier that morning.

"Cabot Cove as a hub for the slave trade? Now, that's a big change in our history."

"Hardesty says there were rumors, tales told without any evidence to back them up."

Seth weighed my statement briefly before responding. "Because, you're thinking, the evidence was hidden in the old chest that only showed up on your property yesterday."

"It didn't just show up; it was hidden there by someone who can likely shed a lot more light on whatever's going on here."

"Which brings me to the second victim," Seth said.

Mort looked toward me. "Did he just say *victim*?"

"He said *victim*," I confirmed.

"Based on the state of the remains, the second victim was killed somewhere between ten and sixteen months ago. State police techs tell me they'll be able to narrow that down further in their next round of tests, but at this juncture they were able to confirm it was a woman, age around thirty-five to forty. Turns out they found a distinctive chip on a rib in her chest."

"She was shot, in other words," I interjected, before Mort had a chance to.

"Bullet penetrated the heart, by all indications. She would have died almost instantly."

Mort shifted in his kiddie chair and nearly fell off. "Which tells me," he began, recovering, "that whoever buried those bones in Mrs. F.'s backyard either killed this woman or knows who did."

"Fair assumption, I'd say," Seth agreed, turning toward me. "This must be a first even for you, Jess. Two murders separated by a couple hundred years."

"And almost certainly connected by the contents of that chest they were buried with, some secret in Cabot Cove's past," I added.

"Like the slave trade, you think?"

I shook my head. "As much of a historical game changer as that might be, it doesn't seem enough to be the cause of two murders two hundred–plus years apart. But something clearly connected the two victims."

"The contents of that chest, you figure, Mrs. F.?"

"That's what we need to find out."

But that would have to wait until the evening's rehearsal for the Christmas play was over. We were putting on *A Christmas Carol* this year, part of a rotation with stage versions of *It's a Wonderful Life* and *Miracle on 34th Street*. We were using a boilerplate theater group version of the play as always, but that version required tweaking to accommodate the limits of our actors and staging in the high school auditorium. The single annual performance would take place on Christmas Day immediately following the Christmas parade, in keeping with long-held Cabot Cove tradition.

I would be serving as narrator, reading portions of Dickens's original text to help the audience keep track of the action on stage, somewhat abbreviated by time constraints, since we wanted to keep the performance to ninety minutes or less. That had the added effect of giving the actors fewer lines to memorize, a blessing for the likes of Seth Hazlitt, who was playing the Ghost of Christmas Past.

The painted sets were all in place for our rehearsal, our volunteer carpenters and set designers having done a magnificent job. It brought back to mind my own humorous failings building sets at the famed Appleton Theater, where I first met my late husband, Frank, while we were volunteering on the same production. Fortunately, our relationship survived my becoming the first ever volunteer to be fired, my performance so poor I was politely told my services would no longer be needed after that particular play. Good thing my talents were much better suited to putting pen to paper or, these days, fingers to keyboard.

I'd color-coded the portions of the play's script I was to read out loud into a microphone off in the wings of the stage. At this rehearsal, I had trouble keeping my focus on the pages I was flipping through as the cast ran their lines. In between blocks of narration, I found my mind wandering to those two clearly connected murders and what role the long-missing founding documents of Cabot Cove might have played in either or both of them. So I was glad when the rehearsal neared its end, and I nailed the final lines of the performance on cue just past ten o'clock in the evening, exhausted after such a marathon session, which included a takeout dinner paid for out of what we called the "Christmas budget," which funded the parade as well.

"He had no further intercourse with spirits, but

lived upon the total abstinence principle, ever afterwards; and it was always said of him, that he knew how to keep Christmas well, if any man alive possessed the knowledge. May that be truly said of us, and all of us! And so, as Tiny Tim observed, 'God bless us, every one!'"

The cast gave me, and themselves, a rousing ovation for a job well done, everyone feeling we were ready for opening night. That's when I saw Mort enter the auditorium from the rear, his stride all business as he approached the stage, stopping just short of the stairs.

"Let's go, Mrs. F." His gaze found Seth next. "You, too, Doc."

"Where we going?" Seth asked him, garbed in his fanciful Ghost of Christmas Past costume.

"Surfsider Motel, where Tad Hollenbeck was just found dead."

Chapter Eight

Well, this is an easy one," Seth said, after examining the body of Tad Hollenbeck on the motel room's single bed and eyeing the empty prescription pill bottle on the cheap night table. "That's a prescription for the generic version of Ambien. We are very clearly looking at either an accidental overdose or a suicide here." He cocked his gaze my way. "Sorry to disappoint you, Jess."

His stiff woolen costume creaked every time he moved.

"Well," I started, "it would've been quite the irony if Mr. Hollenbeck had been murdered in the very town that has a propensity for it, according to this segment for *Stalker* he was working on."

"At least suicide gets me off the hook as a suspect," Mort noted, only half jokingly.

"Good thing you had an alibi, just in case, Sheriff,"

said Seth, as he continued a by-the-numbers examination of the body. "From what I can tell, he's been dead between one and two hours."

Hollenbeck's head was propped up on a pair of pillows, his arms and feet splayed to the sides. He was fully clothed and looked so much to be no more than sleeping that I thought he might come awake at any moment. The old box-style television set on a dresser before him was on, but the sound had been muted.

The Surfsider was the oldest of all the area motels, having resisted the tides of change and motel modernity thanks to an owner who lived on the premises and liked things just the way they were. He didn't make much money, but he didn't need much either.

"Nice Christmas present, anyway, Mrs. F.," Mort said to me. "A body in Cabot Cove that wasn't murdered."

"Errr," I started.

Both Mort and Seth swung toward me, flashing an identical look of something between wariness and despair.

"What?" they asked in unison.

"Have you known many suicide victims to swallow a bottle of sleeping pills while watching television, Mort?"

"I've only investigated a handful of them over the years, so I can't really say."

"Dealt with a couple in my time," Seth started, "but I can't really say either, *ayuh*."

"Please tell me that's all, Mrs. F."

"Almost, Mort."

"*Almost?*"

I turned back toward Tad Hollenbeck's body lying atop the bedcovers. "Cause of death was suicide by an overdose of zolpidem tartrate," I said. "That's our working theory."

"Because it happens to be what happened," Seth maintained.

"Then where's the water?"

"Water?" from Mort.

"If he took a bottleful of pills before lying down on the bed like we found him, where's the glass of water he used to swallow them?"

Seth and Mort looked at each other.

"She's got a point there, Doc," Mort conceded.

Seth scowled and shook his head. "Well, by gum, why didn't I notice that?"

Mort retreated into the bathroom, the light already burning, and spoke to us from there. "Two of those plastic cups, one used and the other still wrapped up. What looks like toothpaste residue on the open one."

"Okay, Jess," Seth started, as Mort reemerged from the bathroom, "assuming, and I stress the word *assuming*, you're right, that would mean the killer would have either force-fed the pills to the victim while he was still alive or post-mortem. Have I got that straight?"

"If it was done prior to death, there'd be trauma around the mouth and face from the pills being shoved into the victim's mouth, and his mouth and nose being held closed until he swallowed."

"No trauma here, at least none that's visibly evident," Seth noted.

"And that tells us it must've been done postmortem."

Seth nodded. "Meaning the pills would have collected in the back of the victim's mouth or down his throat, since a corpse can't swallow."

With that, he moved back to Tad Hollenbeck's bedside and, latex gloves still donned, used a penlight to examine the inside of the dead man's mouth.

"Nothing," he reported, thumbing the penlight's switch.

"Which leaves us where, exactly?" Mort posed to me.

"Looking for another cause of death, I imagine. And—"

"Why is there always an *and* with you, Mrs. F.?"

"Just lucky, I guess. And in this case I think you should bag that used plastic cup in the bathroom, Mort. Because maybe the killer ground up the sleeping pills and diluted as many as he or she could in water, in which case that residue on the used cup wouldn't be toothpaste at all."

I looked toward Seth.

"A corpse can't swallow pills, but could the killer have poured a glass of diluted sleeping pills down his throat?"

Seth weighed the prospect of that, moving his head back and forth to the side. "If you held his head back and pinched his nose closed, I suppose so, yes, it's possible."

My eyes went back to Mort.

"You may want to have Tad Hollenbeck's nose dusted for prints, Sheriff."

"I can see it now," Mort mused. "'Come to Cabot Cove for Christmas, where there's a body under every tree.' Happy holidays, Mrs. F."

* * *

A state police crime scene unit had already been dispatched, responding with much more haste than they had yesterday, given that tonight they'd be dealing with what now could be considered an active murder investigation. An autopsy would be the next course of action, vital in this case given the circumstances surrounding Hollenbeck's death.

"Okay, I'm confused," Mort said. "Did Tad Hollenbeck die from an overdose of sleeping pills or not?"

The question was aimed at both of us. I gave Seth a few moments to jump in, but he looked toward me, yielding.

"Seth, can you check the victim's arms for bruises?"

He nodded, grasping where I was going with this. "In case he was held down while somebody poured the diluted contents of the pills down his throat."

Seth checked the victim's arms carefully, then moved away from the bed and snapped off his latex gloves. "No bruises I can detect here, Jess. Nothing of note at all. Best we leave the rest of the examination to the state police folks."

Mort looked back toward me. "Any further thoughts before they get here, Mrs. F.?"

"Someone went to a lot of trouble to make this look like a suicide, Sheriff."

"Some*one* singular?"

I nodded. "Based on the fact that Seth found no bruising to indicate he was held down, that would be the working theory, yes."

Mort took off his hat and scratched at his scalp, mussing his hair. "Makes no sense I can see."

"What else don't you see?" I asked him.

"I don't follow you, Mrs. F."

"Looking at this as a normal crime scene."

"There's no such thing as a normal crime scene. You know that."

"Humor me."

"Well," Mort said, twirling his gaze about, "there are no signs of a struggle, which would suggest Hollenbeck knew his killer."

"Or killers," Seth elaborated.

"Either way, if somebody forced him to drink ground-up sleeping pills, a struggle would have almost certainly preceded that. But there are no indications of one whatsoever."

"I'm assuming this place doesn't have security cameras," I ventured.

Mort looked as if he found that funny. "I'm not even sure the Surfsider has a computer, Mrs. F."

I looked toward Seth. "What if Hollenbeck was unconscious when the killer poured the contents of that cup down his throat?"

"Same result as if he swallowed the contents willingly. He'd die."

"How long would it take, Doc?" Mort asked.

"Hard to tell without knowing how many sleeping pills actually dissolved. Best guess if the bottle was full or close to it: an hour at most."

We hadn't examined the body until nearly eleven o'clock, and I didn't know how that jibed with the overall timeline.

"Where are Hollenbeck's producer and camerawoman?" I asked Mort.

"The room three doors down."

"Strange they'd rent two not next to each other."

"Guess we'll have to ask them why, Mrs. F."

"One of them called the sheriff's station after Hollenbeck failed to respond to their calls and knocks," Mort said, closing the door to Tad Hollenbeck's room after him, with Seth Hazlitt left behind to keep it secured. "The deputy I left babysitting them got the manager to open the door with his passkey."

And it was indeed still an actual key, the Surfsider having not yet converted to the key-card system. No surprise there.

"If I didn't know better, Mrs. F., I'd say Hollenbeck staged the whole thing to better make his case for Cabot Cove being some kind of cosmic epicenter for murder."

I nodded. "His final story likely leading to his best ratings ever. Something was all wrong about him, Mort."

"Just one thing?"

"I'm talking about beyond his demeanor. If I didn't know better . . ."

"But you always know better, so what's on your mind?"

"I'm not sure. Not yet anyway."

Selina Sanchez was the woman who'd been manning the camera in my backyard the day before. Angie Lawrence, who was slightly older, was Hollenbeck's producer. Mort's deputy took a post immediately outside the door to ensure that Mort and I weren't interrupted. The murder of a tabloid TV reporter of some repute and fame was certain to draw media attention once word leaked out. And it could very well have been that the sheriff's station wasn't the only call these women had made. Maybe they'd called the network behind *Stalker* to report in. Maybe a second news crew was already well on their way to pick up the story from there. And once the news reached the wire, all bets were off on how many reporters would be converging on Cabot Cove in the coming days or even hours.

The two young women, both in their early to mid-thirties, sat on separate full-sized beds, leaving deep impressions in the ragged mattresses. One was bouncing slightly, clearly nervous and unsettled. Before the deputy moved outside to wait for the state police, he introduced the bouncy one as Angie and the other, who was still as a rock, as Selina. That figured, given that her profession involved handling a camera.

"I remember the two of you from yesterday," Mort started. "We kind of met in the backyard of Mrs. Fletcher here."

"Why did you bring her?" bouncy Angie asked him.

"Since you were up here to do a story on murders in Cabot Cove, I'm sure you're aware that Mrs. Fletcher consults with the Sheriff's Department from time to time."

"'Time to time' seems to be a lot," Selina offered from the other bed.

"Tonight, most recently."

"Wait," said Angie, stopping her bouncing so she could lean forward. "Are you saying that Tad was *murdered*?"

"I'm not saying anything right now, other than we're investigating his death. What led you to call for one of my deputies?"

"We were supposed to meet up at nine thirty," Selina said. "When he didn't answer his door or phone an hour past that time, we called."

"When the manager and deputy opened the door," Angie added, shivering as her gaze met Selina's, "at first, we thought he was sleeping. Then . . ."

Her voice tailed off. She didn't go on.

"It was suicide, wasn't it?" Selina picked up. "I mean, we saw that empty pill bottle on the night table."

"That's what we're investigating," Mort told her, leaving it there. "What was the purpose of your nine thirty meeting?"

The women looked at each other, both reluctant to speak.

"Ladies?" Mort coaxed.

"This afternoon Tad told us the network had suspended him," said Angie.

Mort nodded. "So this meeting . . ."

"Was to plan our next moves for the story," Angie completed.

"What moves would you have to make, now that he'd been suspended?" I couldn't help but inquire.

"Tad said he didn't care, that it was for the best," Angie resumed. "He said this story was too big for *Stalker* anyway."

"Something else," Selina added. "We were supposed to spend today shooting footage of past Cabot Cove murder scenes for B-roll—you know, like for background. But that's not what we shot."

Mort was making notes in his magical memo pad, which never seemed to run out of pages. "If you weren't shooting footage of these past murder sites, what were you shooting?"

Selina and Angie exchanged a glance. Selina nodded and Angie continued.

"We don't know. Tad did, but he said he couldn't tell us, not yet."

Now it was Mort and I who exchanged a glance.

"Are you saying you didn't really come up here to do a story on the murder rate in Cabot Cove?" Mort asked the two of them before I could.

"Yes and no," Selina responded this time. "Tad was doing the segment on Cabot Cove specifically for *Stalker*. But he was here working on another story, too."

"The one he said was too big for *Stalker*," Angie elaborated. "It's why we got worried when Tad didn't answer his phone or door."

"You thought he was in danger?" I asked them.

"*He* thought he was in danger," Selina answered, looking toward Angie. "At least that's what he told us."

"From who exactly?" Mort asked.

"Tad didn't say."

"Just that it was big, the biggest story he'd ever worked on," Angie added.

"And he didn't say what it was?" Mort pushed.

Both women shook their heads.

"But we did get one shot out by the 'Welcome to Cabot Cove' sign," Selina said, seeming to just remember that. "Tad wanted us to shoot him holding something."

"Holding what exactly?" I asked them.

"I don't know what it was," Selina continued.

"We can show you the footage, though," said Angie. "Maybe you can tell us."

She rose from the bed and moved to the camera case, fishing the camera itself out as Selina spoke.

"We probably shouldn't be showing you this, but if it helps you figure out why Tad killed himself or . . ."

Her voice tailed off again, and she shuddered slightly at the thought she'd left uncompleted.

Angie had the camera cued up to the footage shot at the town line she wanted Mort and me to see, visible through a cell-phone-sized screen that opened to the side.

"Stop it there!" I said, spotting something in the shot. "Can you zoom in on that a bit, so I can see what it is Tad was holding?"

Angie nodded and worked some magic with some tiny buttons, enlarging a section of the screen to better reveal the object in Hollenbeck's hand as he stood in the shadow of the **WELCOME TO CABOT COVE** sign. It was grainy and indistinct, but just sharp enough for me to identify.

A colonial document carrier, virtually identical to the one Mort and I had found in the chest buried in my backyard.

Chapter Nine

It was the same size and composition as the one that contained the slave manifest attesting that the much-celebrated founders of Cabot Cove were slave traders. Almost as if they were a matched set of early American portfolios, right down to the leather twine wrapped vertically to keep the flap sealed and contents in place.

"Did he tell you what it was, or what it contained?" I asked both women, getting the jump on Mort this time.

They shook their heads.

"We never even saw it before," one of them said.

Mort chimed in. "What about these places you spent the day shooting . . . what'd you call it?"

"B-roll," they said in unison.

"B-roll," Mort repeated.

"The locations will be in our shooting log," said Angie the producer. "Time we were there, anything of note to add to the narration, so we can keep all the shots straight when we edit the story together."

"But it wasn't the story you thought you'd come here to shoot, was it?" I asked producer Angie, figuring she outranked cameraperson Selina.

She shook her head.

"Was there any narration accompanying the shot I just saw?"

Angie hedged, suddenly uncomfortable. "I'm not sure we should . . ."

"Sure," said Mort, "I get it. First Amendment and all that. But need I remind you your boss is lying dead a few doors down, likely the victim of murder?"

"He's not our boss," Angie said defensively. "Wait, did you say—"

"Murder?" Mort finished for her. "You bet I did. And I haven't determined yet whether you're potential witnesses or suspects. What you do and say next will go a long way toward determining that."

Angie nodded toward Selina, who proceeded to rewind the footage and turn up the sound so we could hear the narration accompanying the shot of Tad Hollenbeck holding the document carrier for display. It was twilight, the scene having a spooky feel to it. I wondered if Hollenbeck had purposely avoided the use of portable lighting to set the mood with the **WELCOME TO CABOT COVE** sign in the background of the shot.

"This is where our story begins, at least part of it," he began. *"Right here in Cabot Cove, Maine, around two hundred and thirty years ago. It's a story about greed, murder, and a history never told. It's a story about a crime per-*

petrated on the American people that persists until this day, because it's remained cloaked in the shadows cast by powerful individuals who have resolved to cover up the truth at all costs. It's a story about American history we'd like to tell ourselves is a myth, a lie. But the real lie was told by the men responsible for what happened here, men whose fortunes were built on the backs of broken spirits. Part of that fortune, a secret treasure, went missing in the 1790s and has never been seen since. Until now."

The shot ended there, new footage picking up somewhere else entirely with Hollenbeck not even in the picture.

"Did you have any idea what he was talking about, either of you?" I asked both women.

"I wasn't even listening, to tell you the truth," said Selina.

Angie shrugged. "I listened, but Tad was prone to exaggeration and hyperbole. I assumed that's what was happening here."

"You mean like last night's *Stalker* promo that got him taken off the air?" Mort said, not bothering to disguise the edge in his voice.

"That was just a teaser to get people to tune in."

"Sure." Mort nodded. "Like opening up Al Capone's vault to uncover that, wait for it, it was empty. Were you as shocked as I was by that, Mrs. Fletcher?"

"I must not have been watching," I said.

Mort looked disappointed I hadn't backed him up and turned back to Angie and Selina. "Did either of you hear or see anything that stood out while Mr. Hollenbeck was holed up in his room?"

"We were supposed to all go to dinner, but Tad said

he was too tired and begged off," Angie offered. "So we—Selina and I—went to that coffee shop across the street."

"We both had hamburgers," Selina added. "They weren't bad."

"You have a receipt?"

"We paid by credit card. I've got it somewhere. I can get it for you, if you like."

"Later," Mort said, not wanting to break the flow of his questioning. "Do you remember when you got back to your room?"

"Just before nine thirty, when our meeting about tomorrow's schedule was about to start. We called Tad's cell, but he didn't answer."

"We figured he'd turned off the ringer because he was tired, like he told us," Selina added. "We kept calling and then knocked on the door when he didn't answer. He didn't respond to that either."

"We could hear the television playing, so we figured he had to be inside." Angie picked up this time. "That's when we called nine-one-one."

"We were worried."

"Why didn't you just pack up and go home when word came down that Tad Hollenbeck had been fired?" I asked, drawing a glare from Mort.

The women looked at each other but didn't respond.

"Answer her question," Mort told them, no longer glaring.

"He said he'd pay us personally for our time," Selina said, when producer Angie still failed to respond.

"We're both freelance, not exclusive to *Stalker*, so we didn't see anything wrong with that."

"Tad said he was sure he could place the story elsewhere," Angie elaborated. "He didn't even seem to care about being fired by *Stalker*. He said this would be a story everybody wanted, even the networks."

"That story involving the spot Hollenbeck recorded in the woods earlier today," I concluded, looking to both of them for confirmation.

They looked at each other, neither providing it.

"We're going to need the footage you shot today," Mort told them.

Producer Angie hedged. "I'm not sure I'm authorized to hand that over."

"Who owns the camera?"

"Er," started Selina, "I do."

"Since we're actually freelance," Angie clarified.

"That means you're authorized to hand it over. And, just to confirm, Mr. Hollenbeck never elaborated to you on the contents, if any, of that old document carrier he was holding?"

Both women shook their heads.

"Mort," I started, wondering if the document carrier might still be somewhere in Hollenbeck's room.

"I know, Mrs. F.," he said, reading my mind. "But there's one more thing I need from these ladies first."

In addition to the memory card containing the footage they'd shot, Angie and Selina produced the logbook that contained the times and places of all the shooting completed that day. Having donned a fresh pair of latex gloves, Mort handled it gingerly in sliding it into a plastic evidence pouch that resembled an oversized Ziploc bag. I searched my memory for a time when his predecessor, my good friend Amos Tupper, had followed similar steps at a crime scene. But I couldn't remember Amos ever even slipping on a pair of latex gloves.

"Sheriff?" Angie started tentatively, as if there was something she had to tell us but really didn't want to.

Mort looked at her, waiting.

"There's one thing you should know," she continued. "Mr. Hollenbeck was very agitated today, wasn't he, Selina?"

The cameraperson nodded.

"I think something had upset, at least disturbed, him," Angie elaborated.

"Could you be more specific?" Mort requested.

"That's just it. There isn't anything specific, at least nothing he shared. Getting more details about those bodies seemed to set him off for some reason."

"You mean the remains found in my backyard yesterday?" I interjected.

"That's right. A set of old bones and another, more recent set, maybe no more than a year according to either the news reports or Mr. Hollenbeck's sources; I'm not sure which."

"And he gave no indication as to why that upset or disturbed him."

Angie shook her head. "I'm sorry."

Mort made some additional notes on the memo pad he had plucked from his pocket again. "I'm going to need you ladies to stay put for a couple days."

They both sighed and shook their heads to show their displeasure.

"I promise to have you out of here by Christmas Eve," Mort said.

After he had locked the evidence pouches containing both the shooting log and the memory card in a compartment in the rear hold of his SUV, we rejoined Seth in the room where Hollenbeck had died and we donned latex gloves.

"What are we looking for?" Seth asked as I began with the desk drawers while Mort started on the dresser.

"An early American document carrier," I told him.

"Like the one from that old chest?"

"Almost identical."

"What was Tad Hollenbeck doing with it?"

"I believe it was a prop, a reproduction, something he picked up online or in a specialty shop to use to tease his story about Cabot Cove. But whoever murdered him wouldn't have known that."

Seth joined us in a thorough search of every potential hiding place the beat-up room offered, including under the mattress and in the crawl space accessible via the single small closet. Mort quickly reverted to his days as a New York City homicide detective in his methodical approach and frequent instructions cast to Seth and me. I must say I was impressed, as I always am when Mort swings into true investigative mode. You can take the cop out of Manhattan, but you can't take Manhattan out of the cop.

We finally gave up after we'd been at it for a half hour with no results.

"I think we may have found our motive for Tad Hollenbeck's murder, Sheriff," I ventured.

"Assuming it was murder and assuming he didn't stash the document carrier somewhere else."

"Assume it was and that he didn't, for a moment," I suggested. "This is Cabot Cove, after all."

"Man comes to do a story on the spate of murders in Cabot Cove and ends up murdered himself," Seth mused. "You can't make that stuff up."

"Right," Mort added. "Might end up a segment on *Stalker* itself."

"If they can find a reporter brave enough to cover it," I interjected.

"I've got an idea," said Seth. "Maybe Hollenbeck figured there was a connection between the murder rate and something that happened back in the 1790s."

"You mean like there really might be something in the water, Doc?"

"I was thinking more along the lines of a curse over something our local forefathers did."

"A curse?"

Seth threw up his arms, showcasing hands still encased in latex gloves. "Hey, I didn't say I believed it. But *Stalker* is tabloid television at its best. Or worst, depending on your perspective."

"Guess what my perspective is," Mort told him.

Seth didn't bother, stopping midstep when he spotted something on the worn, faded carpet, which looked as if it had never been replaced.

"Think I found something here," he said, crouching.

Mort crouched alongside him just to the right of the head of the bed, even with the late Tad Hollenbeck's chest, while I leaned over to follow Seth's gaze toward a pair of black strands too thick to be hair. More like shavings of something, though I had no idea what.

Mort lifted a tweezers from a utility pack clipped to his gun belt and used it to ease both black shavings, or whatever they were, into a fresh evidence bag.

His phone beeped with an incoming text message, just as he slipped the bag into his pocket, soon to join the others in the locked compartment of his SUV. "State police are here," he said.

The head of the crime scene unit seemed none too pleased by Mort's report that he'd already searched the room, without elaborating further. Call it partial disclosure, barely enough to maintain a modicum of professionalism.

"I noticed you didn't mention anything about the document carrier," I noted, once the three of us had turned Hollenbeck's corpse and motel room over to the state police. "Or the shooting log."

"Because there was nothing to mention. We're not even sure at this point the document carrier Hollenbeck was holding was anything more than a prop he bought at Staples. Don't forget that he recorded us opening the chest at the station last night. He could have seen you remove the real document carrier and concocted this whole thing based on that."

"What about the shooting log?"

"It's our case, Mrs. F. The state police are merely assisting."

"Think they see it that way?"

"I don't really care how they see it. I didn't take this

job to pass off investigations of local crimes. And I want to know what Tad Hollenbeck was really up to in Cabot Cove."

We dropped Seth off at home. He'd had a long day with the rehearsal and all, and his woolen Ghost of Christmas Past costume was really starting to itch. I couldn't help but smile at the look the state police crime scene unit flashed him, maybe thinking he was a ghost haunting the motel; the dilapidated condition of the Surfsider certainly suggested it went back long enough to be haunted.

"Better get you home, too, Mrs. F. Hey, I just thought of something: When was the last time I dropped you off on Candlewood Lane instead of Hill House?"

"Nice to have order restored."

"Yes, ma'am, including a murder."

"You're forgetting something, Mort," I said as he pulled away from Seth's home, his trusty Volvo, which was already old when he bought it, sitting in the driveway.

"What's that?"

"Hollenbeck's shooting log," I told him. "How about we have a look at where else he was around town today?"

"In the hope it might give us a clue as to who killed him?"

"You read my mind."

We headed to the sheriff's station instead of my home to examine the logbook in more detail. After we set up shop in Mort's office, procedure dictated we don latex gloves to preserve the chain of evidence, even in the case of the logbook. I dragged a chair over and placed it next to Mort so we could examine the pages together. The book was just what its name indicated, a third of the pages full of specific dates and times associated with story segment assignments that served as separate headers for each individually categorized story.

The last pages in the logbook were written in neat penmanship I took to belong to either Angie or Selina. Sure enough, Angie's initials followed each of the meticulous entries, which seemed far more sophisticated and detailed than what I would have expected from a tabloid TV show like *Stalker*.

The entries were simple and straightforward enough, not a single address a mystery to anyone living in Cabot Cove. I reduced my normal careful scrutiny to a mere skim to keep up with Mort's near speed-reading through the material, his eye far more practiced at such things than mine. I thought again of Amos Tupper and tried to picture him doing the same thing Mort was. He'd been living with his sister in the Midwest somewhere since retiring as sheriff, and I resolved to call him Christmas Day as I always did.

"Anything stand out to you, Mrs. F.?" Mort asked me, waiting a few moments for me to catch up.

"Well, Angie and Selina were right about none of these locations being even remotely connected to the murder scenes Hollenbeck said they were shooting."

"What was that term for what they were shooting?"

"B-roll."

"That's right. The question being, B-roll for what?"

"The story Hollenbeck really came to Cabot Cove to tell, I suspect."

Mort flipped through the pages of the logbook again. "You see anything here I must be missing? Besides the cemetery and the entrance to town, there are those five residential street addresses, none of which was the site of a past murder."

"No, but—"

I stopped, a light bulb going on in my head.

"Mort, do you have a phone book?"

"Phone book? Do they even print those things anymore?"

"Switch on your computer, then, and bring up the town database."

He settled in behind his keyboard. "Why?"

"Because I just realized something."

Chapter Ten

Well, I'll be," Mort managed, looking up from his computer screen, which was now displaying the five names associated with the addresses in question.

My hunch had turned out to be right. The five homes before which Tad Hollenbeck had shot background footage earlier in the day belonged to the descendants of the original founders of Cabot Cove: Earl Grove Hutchinson, John Van Webb, Franklin McMullen, Wyatt Rackley, and John Henry Cabot. The bloodlines of all five had been sustained to this day in some form, distant or otherwise.

That meant that by all accounts, in stark contrast with Hollenbeck's claims about his intentions, his presence in Cabot Cove seemed indelibly connected with the colonial-era chest that had been found in my backyard. First, we'd watched him flash a document carrier that was a near twin of the one I'd examined the night before. And now the footage Hollenbeck had shot the very day he'd almost certainly been murdered bore an undeniable connection with our town's original five founders. Men who, according to the founding documents contained in that old chest, had settled Cabot Cove in order to maintain their lucrative slave-trading business after such practice had been outlawed. But the only history I was interested in right now was what had really drawn Tad Hollenbeck to Cabot Cove.

"Maybe Hollenbeck was right after all," Mort noted, finally looking up from his computer screen.

"About what?"

"This town. Maybe it really is cursed somehow. Maybe we're still paying the price for the founders' stake in the slave trade that brought them up here."

"That doesn't sound much like fodder for a story on *Stalker*, though, does it?"

"I'm sure Hollenbeck would have added in some restless ghosts or something. And he couldn't have known about what turned up buried in your backyard until he got here, right, Mrs. F.?"

I'd already considered that myself, of course. It suggested that Hollenbeck could have had no idea that the document carrier he'd displayed during that shoot in the woods was a virtual twin of the one whose contents I'd examined the night before.

"Mort, do you have that memory card containing the camera footage handy?"

"Oh, glad you reminded me," he said, and produced the small plastic evidence pouch containing it from a side pocket of his sheriff's jacket. "I need to inventory this, too."

"Can we take a look at it again first?"

"Don't tell me, the footage from the entrance to town with Hollenbeck flashing that document carrier."

"I want to listen to what else he said while the camera was rolling, besides what we listened to back in Selina and Angie's motel room."

Mort shrugged, nodding slightly as he eased himself from his chair. "The tech stuff's not exactly in my bailiwick, but have at it, Mrs. F."

There was a slot on the side of Mort's computer fitted to the memory card's specifications, and I eased it in until it clicked home. Icons with language detailing each of the individual shots the crew had completed that day lit up across the screen, and I clicked on the one labeled *TOWN SIGN*. Sure enough, there was Tad Hollenbeck standing there in the sign's shadow, 230-year-old document carrier held for his audience to see. I turned up the desktop's volume as he nodded toward the camera and began.

"A brutal murder that might well have been the first ever in this blood-soaked seaside village. It wouldn't be the last, not by a long shot, rooted in the greed and treachery on which Cabot Cove was founded by men whose pioneering spirit and Yankee charm were belied by a terrible truth that had to be hidden at all costs."

Here, Hollenbeck turned sideways so the camera could sweep about the area beyond the sign, passing over the stumps of long-dead trees and still-living branches laid bare by autumn and the approaching winter.

"This land bleeds that truth, because it was here the first murder victim ever claimed in Cabot Cove was laid to rest

*absent a proper funeral or blessing. Perhaps the deadly seeds
that sprouted to haunt this town ever since were planted
that day. Perhaps that victim's blood stains not just this
land but the whole of the town that takes its name from John
Henry Cabot, one of the five men who settled this place
having no idea of the murderous rites they had released. The
small, bucolic town of Cabot Cove just might be the murder
capital of the country, and tonight we're going to take you
back to that tradition's lurid origins."*

The footage ended there and brought the screen
back to the shot listing I'd clicked on originally.

"He's talking about the owner of those bones killed
by a hatchet, isn't he, Mrs. F.?" Mort asked me.

"I suspect so. Notice what he didn't mention,
though?"

"The remains of the victim killed more recently, for
starters," Mort said.

"Or the chest."

Mort weighed that for a moment. "And now Hollenbeck is dead and that document carrier he was
showing off is gone, which leaves us where exactly?"

"With a need to have a talk with those five descendants of the original founders of Cabot Cove."

I finally got home just past one a.m. to find a voice-
mail message on my landline. One of the ways I'd
celebrated my return to 698 Candlewood Lane was to
at long last ditch the old-fashioned physical answering
machine I'd used for years in favor of my cable provider's version, which pretty much did the same thing,
only better and more efficiently.

The call was from none other than private detective

Harry McGraw, who was the finest investigator I'd ever worked with. Harry might have been ornery and self-deprecating, but his creativity and contacts knew no bounds. I couldn't think of a single time he'd ever disappointed me when I came to him in search of answers. He was a pit bull when it came to information.

"Jess, I wanted to be the first person to call and welcome you home. And if I'm not the first person, I'd still like to welcome you back home. Here's hoping your house doesn't burn down again, especially with you in it."

According to the voice mail's time stamp, the message had been left an hour or so before, right around midnight. Like me, Harry was a night owl.

With that in mind, I called his number, even though I probably shouldn't have at such an hour.

"What are you calling me for?" he groused, answering after the first ring. "Don't you know what time it is?"

"You called me less than an hour ago."

"It wasn't as late then."

"And you were the first. Thank you."

"First what?"

"First to welcome me back home."

"I did? Must have slipped my mind. So, what's so important you had to call me so late?"

"I wanted to say thank you."

"At one thirty in the morning?"

"You told me you never go to sleep until around two."

"When did I say that?"

"A whole bunch of times."

"Because it's true," Harry told me. "Bill collectors don't call late at night. I like to enjoy the quiet. Maybe I should hire one of them to recover what you owe me."

"You never send me any bills to collect."

"It's going to be my New Year's resolution. I'm going to send twice as many this coming year."

"What's two times zero, Harry?"

"You know I was never good at math. I hear you've been busy."

"Really?"

"No, I just thought I'd say that. Annual Christmas play, is it?"

"I'm narrating again," I said, sighing.

"Hope you do a better job than last year, Jess."

"How would you know? You weren't even there."

"I read the reviews. If the critics were right, you should stick to books."

"The only reviews ran in the *Cabot Cove Gazette* and the local high school paper."

"Yeah, those sophomores can be tough to please." He paused. "So, is it true, little lady?"

"Is what true, Harry?"

"About this reporter who had the misfortune to find himself in Cabot Cove over the holidays, where it's murder under the mistletoe instead of kisses."

I wasn't surprised the news about Tad Hollenbeck had gotten out so quickly. Harry probably had an Internet alert set up for *Cabot Cove*.

"Please tell me you're not involved," Harry resumed.

"I could," I told him, "but that would be a lie."

I heard him sigh. "Okay, I'm listening."

"It's a long story."

"I love bedtime stories, Jess. And the timing's just right."

"Ever heard of the reporter?"

"Tad Hollenbeck? He did a story on me once for *Stalker*."

"Really?"

"No, but I had you going there for a second, didn't I? Did he come to Cabot Cove to do a story on deadbeat mystery writers who never pay their bills?"

"He claimed to have come to Cabot Cove to do a story on our supposed unusually high murder rate."

"Nothing supposed about that."

"Anyway, Harry, it appears he came here to do a different story altogether."

"Tell me more. You know how much I love a mystery."

"This one involves the town founders, who, it turns out, were slave traders."

"Right," Harry huffed. "That was a rare occurrence in the late eighteenth century."

"There's more."

"I'm still listening."

"It's too early to try explaining, too many holes that still need to be filled in."

"Want me to poke around this Hollenbeck character, Jess? You know, see what rocks I can uncover."

"I believe the saying is closer to what you find when you turn those rocks over."

"I know, but that costs more. I figured I could save you a little money."

* * *

Harry said he'd call me back as soon as he had something, but not until after nine in the morning. Needless to say, my call with him had left me too amped up to fall asleep right away in spite of the hour, rekindling all my thoughts about the circumstances surrounding Tad Hollenbeck's murder and its connection with the founding fathers of Cabot Cove. I couldn't get my mind off that document carrier pouch he'd been brandishing for that shot in the woods at the far edge of town, miles from the shoreline.

Cabot Cove offered the perfect mix of geography for both marine commerce and manufacturing, at least perfect by colonial and early American standards. Of course, those two pursuits were far from mutually exclusive, given that yarns and fabrics brought in by Portuguese traders from the West Indies and Asia were turned into textile products in factories just a few miles from the bustling port those five founding fathers had constructed.

I finally drifted off to sleep at what must have been around three in the morning, only to be awakened by my cell phone ringing five hours later.

"Sleeping in this morning, Mrs. F.?" Mort greeted me.

"Going in early, Sheriff?"

"My wake-up call was from the state police crime lab. They confirmed it was a bullet that killed the female murder victim whose remains were found in your backyard, a standard nine-millimeter. They also identified her as between twenty-eight and thirty-five years old, five foot six in height, and weighing in at a hundred and twenty-two pounds. Bone structure indicated she was an athlete, likely a soccer, field hockey, softball, or lacrosse player. Apparently they were able to find evidence of healed breaks to the lower extremities that suggested one of those."

"What about when she was murdered?" I asked him.

"According to the crime lab, she's been dead between ten and sixteen months, pretty much exactly what Seth said. They're working on narrowing that down even further."

"I'm impressed, Sheriff."

"Sometimes old-fashioned police work really does work wonders."

"Then I guess I can go back to sleep."

"Not a chance, Mrs. F. It's time for us to see what these descendants of the original founders have to say. Maybe they noticed Hollenbeck filming on their land yesterday. Maybe he asked their permission. Maybe they talked to him and can provide a clue as to who his murderer might be."

"Are we considering them as potential suspects, Mort?"

"Depends on how the interviews go," he told me.

Chapter Eleven

We started with Sheila Del Perrio that Wednesday morning, a direct descendant of Earl Grove Hutchinson who'd surrendered the name only upon marrying her husband forty-five years ago, right out of college. The Del Perrios had actually moved into the Hutchinson family home, which Earl built in the early eighteen hundreds. It was one of the many historical-plaque houses that adorned the streets of Cabot Cove, its place in history duly acknowledged by the hand-engraved wooden testimonial that hung to the right of the home's front door.

Sheila was an off-again, on-again member of the Cabot Cove Friends of the Library and a major supporter of all our efforts even during her off-again periods. I'd called ahead to alert her that Mort and I would be stopping by, and she promised to bake us up some of the cookies that put her among Cabot Cove's most popular residents. She'd done all the baking at Cabot Cove's most popular restaurant, Del Perrio's, for a generation before passing the torch on to her nephew. Her diabetes prevented her from enjoying her own wares, but that didn't stop her from always having a plate ready for those who stopped by for a visit.

Sure enough, when Mort and I arrived the house smelled of gingerbread and cookie dough, evidence of a fresh batch Sheila was cooking for the holidays. Both gingerbread and Toll House cookies filled an oversized plate set on a coffee table in a sitting area of the great room Sheila used whenever she was entertaining. She was an elegant woman whom I could never recall not being fashionably dressed and coiffed, even during the kind of economic downturns that substantially reduced the family restaurant's revenue and once had even threatened to shutter it. Today was no exception, with Sheila garbed in a dress I thought I recognized from the window of a fashionable women's boutique that had recently opened up shop on Cabot Cove's main drag just across the street from Del Perrio's Restaurant.

"Of course I heard," Sheila said to Mort and me, once we were all seated, leaving me marveling at the elegant collection of striking needlepoint pillows of Sheila's own making that adorned the couch and nearby chairs. "The whole town's talking about it. Famous reporter comes to Cabot Cove to do a story on all the murders here, only to be murdered himself. The height of tragic irony."

Mort let that go as best he could. "I'm not sure I'd call him famous."

"All the same, Sheriff . . ."

"Did you know he shot some footage outside your house yesterday?" I asked Sheila.

"What on earth for?"

"That's what we were hoping you could tell us, Mrs. Del Perrio," Mort interjected.

"The sheriff and I are proceeding on the theory that Tad Hollenbeck's interest in Cabot Cove was connected with the town's founding and the men behind it, Earl Grove Hutchinson being one of them."

"You don't say."

Another reason sleep had eluded me the night before was the very real possibility that among the five people Mort and I hoped to interview today was a murderer. The motive for whoever had killed Tad Hollenbeck and made off with the leather document carrier he'd been holding in that camera shot seemed undeniably connected with Cabot Cove's past, specifically the founders from whom these people were descended. Picturing Sheila Del Perrio killing so much as a fly was a stretch. The children's ward at Cabot Cove Hospital carried the Del Perrio name, and her foundation was the primary source of funding for both the town's senior center and the animal shelter, which had never euthanized a single creature, thanks to Sheila's unending commitment to civic duty.

"But why would the late Mr. Hollenbeck be interested in the Hutchinson family home?" she wondered aloud.

"We don't believe it's the home, so much as something buried deep in Cabot Cove's history," I explained as Mort looked on, perfectly content to yield the floor to me at this point.

"Involving those bones dug up out of your backyard, Jessica?"

"The older set quite possibly, given that the remains date back all the way to colonial times."

"Older set? You mean there were *two*?"

Mort nodded. "The more recent remains date back only a year or so, Mrs. Del Perrio. I'm already checking missing persons databases for possible matches, since no woman's gone missing from Cabot Cove in that time frame. In fact, no one's gone missing at all since I've been sheriff."

Sheila Del Perrio looked from Mort to me. "It certainly sounds like the two of you are facing quite the challenge. You think Mr. Hollenbeck's murder is somehow related to our town's history?"

It was I who nodded this time. "He hinted as much in his narration of the footage shot outside your house and the homes of the four other descendants. He referred to a mystery that's never been solved involving great riches," I said.

"You mean like a treasure?"

"Does that ring any bells with you, Mrs. Del Perrio?" Mort asked her.

"I've heard legends about the source of Earl Grove Hutchinson's fortune my entire life."

"Any of them involve the slave trade?"

Sheila frowned. "There were rumors to that effect, yes. But you should know that his son Abel was heavily involved with the formation of Maine's part in the Underground Railroad, both in terms of resources and money."

"History does have a way of balancing itself out," I noted.

"What other legends stand out in your mind, ma'am?" Mort asked her. "You just said something about treasure."

"I didn't mean the kind buried in a chest of the sort that was dug up from Jessica's backyard two days ago. The five founders of Cabot Cove were already eminently successful businessmen when they settled here. And the vast wealth they later accumulated was always thought to be a product of both their seafaring and manufacturing efforts."

"You don't believe that to be the case?"

"They turned a rocky shoreline into one of the most noted northern ports of the time, yes, Sheriff. But that pretty much claimed the bulk of their existing fortunes, and they were already leveraged to the hilt, so they weren't able to borrow any more from banks. Yet under John Henry Cabot's stewardship they built and maintained the largest collection of textile mills and factories across all of New England, New York, and Pennsylvania, and no one knows exactly where the money came from to do that. Can I confess something to you both?" she asked us.

"If it's murder, Mrs. Del Perrio, I strongly suggest you consult a lawyer," Mort quipped.

This drew a smile from her. "No, nothing like that. Would you hold it against me if I told you I occasionally watched Hollenbeck's television program, *Stalker*?"

I watched Mort stiffen, afraid to turn my way or even meet my glance.

"I wouldn't call myself a fan exactly," Sheila continued. "You know, from time to time when I was flipping through the channels."

"We understand," I offered, "don't we, Sheriff?"

Mort nodded, still reluctant to look at me.

"Well, I always thought there was something familiar about Tad Hollenbeck."

"Familiar how?" Mort asked her.

"I can't say exactly. I suppose it was his business to appear familiar, but this was different. I can't say how exactly or elaborate any further. He just seemed, well, familiar."

"Could you be more specific?"

"I'm afraid not, Sheriff," Sheila Del Perrio said.

I watched Mort squirm a bit in his chair. "Would you mind if I asked you an awkward question, Mrs. Del Perrio?" he asked.

"Of course not."

"Where were you last night between the hours of eight and ten o'clock?"

Sheila grinned at that. "Now, that's a first. I've never been considered a suspect of any crime before."

"And you're not considered one now," Mort told her. "I'm just trying to be thorough here."

"It's a simple answer, Sheriff. I was hostessing at the restaurant last night. So there are well over a hundred people who can account for my whereabouts. Would you like me to make you a list?"

Next on *our* list was Terry McMullen, the great-great-great-great-grandson of Franklin McMullen, who had opened Cabot Cove's first fishery and canning business. Both of those businesses had closed long ago, and the family fortune was just a memory now, as was the case for any number of the moneyed gentry who'd been unable or unwilling to modernize their interests to keep up with the times. I could imagine Franklin McMullen opening his fishery and cannery, never envisioning competitors who operated virtually automated assembly lines laying waste to his more staid business practices ages later.

Today Terry McMullen was one of Cabot Cove's hardscrabble sorts who still managed to carve out a living on the sea as a commercial fisherman. He and his crew would go out for days at a time in search of deepwater cod, flounder, and swordfish. He and my old friend Ethan Cragg were elder statesmen in that regard, the de facto leaders of our docks.

Mort had phoned Terry McMullen but received no response, not a terribly big surprise given that he was almost certainly out at sea, meeting the demand of local stores for Christmas Eve. Sure enough, his boat, the *Resolute*, looked to have just returned to port, and Terry was in the process of both supervising and participating in the unloading process of what looked to be quite a haul.

He was dressed in rubbery pants and a matching top with a floppy fisherman's cap draped over his thinning locks and leathery face. He wore thick gloves over his hands that hid the scars and scraped-raw flesh from encounters with hostile fishing nets, and a pair of sneakers that were blindingly white. One thing Mort and I knew already was that McMullen must have still been at sea when Tad Hollenbeck was being murdered the night before.

He spotted us coming and turned his nose slightly, just as I did over the odor of fish that dominated the docks, definitely unpleasant for one not more accustomed to it. The two deckhands who normally joined him out at sea had disappeared into the bowels of the boat by the time Mort and I got there, on their own or on McMullen's orders I couldn't know for sure.

"What is it this time, Sheriff?" he groused in his gravelly voice.

I seemed to recall he'd had more than his share of run-ins with Mort and his deputies over complaints lodged by the harbormaster, as well as encounters with local suppliers over the quality of his catch and resulting remuneration. Several of these dustups, I recalled, had been heated and had come very close to ending violently. Terry McMullen's temper was well-known around town, which might have made him a fitting suspect for Tad Hollenbeck's murder if he hadn't likely had an airtight alibi. I'd heard Mort also had to respond to an altercation he had with ICE agents after someone had falsely phoned in an anonymous tip that his Latino deckhands were undocumented.

"Just a friendly visit, Terry," Mort told him.

"It's never friendly when you show up," Terry said, removing his gloves and swabbing his hands with a ragged cloth he casually discarded as he approached us. "And what's she doing here?" he added, pointing a finger toward me.

"Happy holidays to you, too, Mr. McMullen," I offered.

"There was a murder in town last night," Mort told him. "Fellow by the name of Tad Hollenbeck."

"Never heard of him."

"He was a tabloid television reporter for a show called *Stalker*."

"Never heard of that either. I don't watch much television. Dulls the mind. I prefer books."

"How nice to hear for a change," I commented.

"I mean *real* books, like history," McMullen said, eyeing me derisively, "not that fluff you write."

He swung back toward Mort, as if I wasn't there at all.

"You mind if we hurry this up, Sheriff? I don't want my catch to spoil."

"Tad Hollenbeck seemed to enjoy a particular interest in the five founders of Cabot Cove. We thought he may have contacted you in that regard."

"I just told you I never heard of the guy, so I already answered your question. But let me put it this way to make sure I'm clear: No, he never contacted me and I got no idea why someone would be taking an interest in Franklin McMullen and the other founding fathers. I ever tell you how those others tried to screw him?"

Both Mort and I shook our heads, since his question seemed to be aimed at both of us in this case.

"No," I said, "but I recall some scuttlebutt about that over the years. Something about dealing him out of the big stuff they were up to, turning Cabot Cove into the Boston of the north as far as trade was concerned."

"Did you ever hear anything about the town's founding fathers being involved in the slave trade?" Mort picked up from there.

McMullen shook his head and flashed a supercilious smile. "Were you born yesterday, Sheriff?"

"Keep talking like that and maybe I'll take a closer look at the validity of your commercial fishing license."

McMullen backed off defensively. "Hey, I didn't mean nothing by it. It's the way business was done back then, that's all. You want to look down on all the northern businessmen who supported slavery, you'd end up with a pretty bad crick in your neck. So, you asked me if I've ever heard about it and the answer is, nothing definitive. But stuff gets passed down through the years, enough to make me figure my ancestor and the others were on the same boat as plenty others."

"Tad Hollenbeck was outside your house yesterday," I told him.

"What are you doing here again?"

"I'm with him, Mr. McMullen," I said, gesturing toward Mort.

"And that's all you need to know," Mort added. "Let's stay on the subject here."

"Why should I care if Hollenbeck was outside my house yesterday?" McMullen challenged. "Maybe he was selling Girl Scout cookies."

"He was recording a segment for *Stalker*," I noted, not bothering to add that Hollenbeck had been relieved of his duties, at least temporarily.

"And I was out at sea, so I wouldn't know anything about whatever Hollenbeck was up to."

"He seemed to believe a fortune was out there

somewhere, squirreled away by Franklin McMullen and the other founders."

"You mean the men who screwed Franklin? I can't be sure of much, but I am sure if his former partners came into a fortune, they would have cheated him out of his fair share. Instead, he watched his businesses go belly-up and died a pauper pretty much. I've heard it told three of Cabot Cove's other founding fathers were the richest men in New England for a time."

"The fourth being Wyatt Rackley," I elaborated. "He left Cabot Cove and staked his claim in the West; at least that's what history says."

"I don't know a thing about that. But if he did split from Cabot Cove, it was with a chunk of money that rightfully belonged to the McMullens. Hey, Sheriff," he said, swinging toward Mort. "What's the statute of limitations on rip-offs like that?"

"Five or six lifetimes ago, Mr. McMullen. Thank you for your time."

"Well, Mrs. F.?" Mort posed, after we'd drifted out of earshot.

"He's lying about his knowledge of Wyatt Rackley leaving Cabot Cove."

"How'd you sniff that out exactly?"

"He referred to the other three founding fathers of Cabot Cove being the richest men in New England, when the number should have been four. But he knew Rackley wasn't one of them because he was already gone."

Before Mort could respond, my cell phone rang and

I fished it from my bag to see *HARRY MCGRAW* lit up on the caller ID.

"I'm with Mort, Harry," I greeted him, putting the phone on speaker and raising it between us.

"Good. Always nice to be able to deliver news to him directly. Hey, Mort."

"Hi, Harry."

"Did Jessica tell you she asked me to look into the dearly departed Tad Hollenbeck?"

Mort scowled, his gaze locked on me. "What do you think?"

"I'll cut to the chase, then. Hollenbeck's his real last name, all right, but his real first name is Lewis."

"Is that what you called to tell me, Harry?" I jumped in.

"I'm just baiting the hook here, little lady. See, Hollenbeck's grandfather's name was J. H. Cabot."

"Don't tell me, *J. H.* for *John Henry.*"

"Right as rain, little lady. And that makes Hollenbeck a descendant of the original founders of Cabot Cove, too."

Chapter Twelve

I almost dropped the phone.

"You still there, Jess? Did she faint or something, Mort?"

"I'm here, Harry," I said. "Just trying to process this."

"You said you suspected *something*."

"Not that," I said, eyeing Mort. "But it does clarify what really brought Hollenbeck to Cabot Cove."

"You mean it wasn't about all the murders?" Mort quipped. "I thought he might be giving me cause to retire."

"You already retired, from the NYPD anyway," Harry reminded him over the phone. "Just like I would if certain clients would ever pay their bills. Good thing I love what I do, since I'll probably be working until I'm ninety."

"It also explains why, according to his producer and cameraperson, Hollenbeck didn't seem overly concerned about being suspended," I said, recalling something that had stood out in our interview with them the night before. "Because he thought he was chasing something bigger and much more personal."

Mort nodded. "I think it's time we paid a visit to a Cabot descendant who still uses the family name."

Asa Cabot, the only descendant of John Henry living in Cabot Cove, professed to have never heard of Tad Hollenbeck, much less the fact that anyone by that name was a descendant of John Henry Cabot as well. He had long been estranged from his sister, Grace, and knew she had a son and a daughter, which he claimed to be the extent of his knowledge.

We found Asa at home, a mansion on the bluffs overlooking the sea that had been the largest home in Cabot Cove for as long as anyone could remember. We had called ahead even though there was no reason to. Asa Cabot was always home, suffering from a severe form of agoraphobia that had left him housebound for almost two years now.

His mansion resembled something out of a Victorian novel, dark and in the grasp of overgrown foliage that seemed to have squeezed the life out of the sprawling three-story structure. There was not a single Christmas decoration anywhere in sight. Today was dreary and overcast, but I had the sense that this weed-riddled place would have somehow held to that atmosphere even if the day were bright and shiny, as if sunlight stopped at the property's edges. The stiff December wind off the ocean sent tree branches rattling against the windows, further adding to the dark aura of the Cabot family home, which at first glance appeared to have been abandoned altogether, like something from a Gothic horror tale.

Cabot was also a germaphobe, necessitating that Mort and I remove our shoes and slip on disposable slippers of the sort airlines used to hand out for free on long flights. We were also required to don surgical gloves and masks to minimize the risk of spreading any contagion we might be carrying. A man I took to be either the butler or Cabot's personal assistant directed us to a neat pile of both, laid out on a mahogany table set beneath a beautiful seascape painted by Winslow Homer himself. He was a big man with broad shoulders his suit coat struggled to contain, his hands like calloused slabs of meat that looked like they could crush walnuts. He wore his hair closely cropped to his skull; *high and tight* I believe was the term in military lexicon. He introduced himself to us as "James." He didn't provide a last name and we didn't ask for one.

Asa Cabot was waiting for us in his book-lined study, old-fashioned thick drapes drawn over the windows to shut out whatever meager light might sneak through the cloud-drenched dreariness beyond. He was standing before one floor-to-ceiling set when the double doors closed behind us, the blinds peeled back just a sliver, as if he were peering out at someone he didn't want to notice him. Even without the light, it was clear that the hardwood floor had been polished to a glimmer, save for some irregular patches where the wood looked mottled in a virtual straight line as if it had been subjected to a leak or spill of some kind.

Cabot stood so still he seemed to have grown out of the floor. He was a rail-thin man, tall and almost skeletal, with sunken cheeks and sagging jowls. The lack of sunlight had turned his complexion sickly, so that it looked pale yellow in the study's ambient light spraying out from lavish lamps. An old-fashioned smoking jacket swam over his shoulders, evidence of a time when Asa Cabot had been the rawboned, hands-on industrialist known for digging trenches with his work crews at various construction sites across New England. Years back, prior to the onset of the agoraphobia, he had been known throughout town for regaling locals with stories of Cabot Cove's founding, passed down for generations from John Henry Cabot himself. Today I felt like I was looking at a shell of that man.

"Thank you for seeing us without an appointment, Mr. Cabot," Mort greeted him.

"Thank you for appeasing an old man's foibles by donning the masks and gloves," he said to both of us, before fixing his stare on me alone. "And how are you keeping, Mrs. Fletcher?"

"Fine, so long as my fingers find the keyboard often enough. By the way, your book collection is positively magnificent."

He turned to join my gaze in that direction, seeming to revel in the sight of books neatly arrayed in the set of floor-to-ceiling bookshelves, as I did. "I have boxes more in storage. Perhaps we could discuss my donating them to the Cabot Cove Library."

"Mr. Cabot, that would be wonderful!" I beamed.

"Then let's make it happen, Mrs. Fletcher, once we dispense with the business at hand." Cabot looked toward Mort. "I must say your call surprised, even startled, me, Sheriff," he said in a scratchy voice that was a far cry from the booming one that had needed no megaphone to address those construction crews he'd been fond of joining himself. "My nephew, you say, murdered right here in Cabot Cove?"

Mort took off his hat and nodded. "I'm sorry for your loss."

"It's hardly a loss when I never met the young man and barely knew he even existed. Haven't thought about him, his sibling, or my sister in years. I couldn't even tell you if she's still alive."

"Well, we can be certain her son isn't, as of last night, anyway."

"Lewis," Asa Cabot recalled, his eyes widening at the memory. "That was his name."

"He went by Tad."

"Why?"

"I imagine he found it more fitting for television."

"Tad?" Asa scoffed, rolling his eyes. "I guess it depends on what kind of television show you're watching." His gaze locked on me, suddenly softer and more reflective. "More people should spend their time in libraries like Cabot Cove's. I so enjoyed the presentations I did there on the town's history."

"We'd love to have you in for another talk whenever you feel up to it, Mr. Cabot," I said through my surgical mask, which made it feel as if I was talking, quite literally, to myself.

An almost whimsical look crossed his face. "Again, I so enjoyed those presentations. The crowd was always so engaged, and it was the only time people looked at me for something I could share with them other than money."

"History makes for a fine currency in its own right," I told him.

The whimsy slipped from his expression, replaced by reflection. "You know, I haven't left this house since right around the time of my last talk. When would that have been?"

"Almost two years ago now," I recalled. "And it would be only fitting to have you back once you're able to venture out again."

"I wake up every morning hoping this will be the day. Sometimes the sun is shining and I can smell the freshness in the air through the windows. I open the door but my feet won't move. The doctors don't know what caused my condition, how to treat it, or whether it will ever go away."

"I had a character in a book once who suffered from agoraphobia."

"And how did things turn out for him, pray tell?"

"He solved the murder. He was the hero," I said.

Cabot smiled, seeming to take some comfort in that. "And you've come here today hoping that I, too, might be able to help solve a murder, in this case my nephew's."

"When was the last time the two of you spoke?" Mort asked him.

"I already told you, never."

"I was talking about your sister."

"Grace? I believe she was pregnant with him or her other kid when we had our troubles."

"Would you be comfortable discussing those?" I interjected.

"Why not? Although I suspect she wouldn't be comfortable at all, given that she was the catalyst behind our estrangement."

I waited for Asa Cabot to continue.

"My sister stole money from me, Mrs. Fletcher, a great deal of it. Families, right?"

"I have a rather large one myself," I said, looking forward even more to Grady's arrival, to give us some time together ahead of Christmas Eve.

All this talk was making me regret not seeing more of the nephew Frank and I had raised these past few years, and I resolved to rectify that starting this holiday season. Of course, when we'd made these arrangements for his family to come for a visit I'd had no idea I'd be ensnared in a murder investigation, although that would be nothing new for Grady. He was a direct party to several of the cases I'd taken a personal interest in over the years, including one in which he was accused of murdering his boss at an accounting firm he was working for in New York City. I looked forward to striking up a closer relationship with Grady's wife, Donna, as well as eight-year-old Frank, who for the past few years had aged before me only in the annual family Christmas card photos that I'd taped to the wall like frozen fragments of time.

"Did your nephew try to make contact with you

when he got to town?" Mort asked, pen poised over his open memo pad.

"I don't believe he'd have known how, short of knocking on the door."

"And he didn't do that, knock on your door?"

Asa Cabot shook his head. "No. I'm quite certain of that. My assistant—you met James—would have informed me of such unpleasantness immediately."

"Then you're not aware of the fact he shot some footage outside your house yesterday, late afternoon, just a few hours before he was murdered."

"If James had spotted someone trespassing or snooping around, he would have called your department, Sheriff. Or handled it himself," Cabot said as an afterthought, with a chilling edge to his voice. "Can you provide any notion as to what the footage concerned?"

"Your nephew believed the founding fathers, John Henry Cabot included, harbored a secret that persists to this day," I chimed in. "Can you shed any light on that, Mr. Cabot?"

Cabot flirted with a laugh, at least a chuckle, the gesture looking uncomfortable on him. "Secret, you say. The question would be, which one?"

I stepped a bit closer to him. "You're aware of this business about all five men being involved in the slave trade and that being their original reason for coming north."

"They were all businessmen, Mrs. Fletcher," Cabot said. "They went where the money took them, as all businessmen are prone to do. As for the slave trade, I suspect they believed if it wasn't them, it would be someone else profiting at their expense. And that pursuit, as reprehensible as it was, set the stage for all they built here that has provided a livelihood for thousands and thousands of families over the years."

He took a few steps closer to me, stopping in the twin sprays of light from matching lamps set atop tables on either side of him. The light made his skin look almost translucent.

"Modernity has bred conscience, Mrs. Fletcher, and as welcome as that conscience might be, it offers a lens the past is better not viewed through. Colonial times and the end of the Revolution brought with them their own sets of challenges men like John Henry Cabot had to overcome in order to succeed. They, like their ancestors today, were forced to resort to compromise, primarily of their moral values, in order to continue building America."

"What about a secret fortune—unclaimed, vanished, or both?"

Asa Cabot smiled thinly at that. "John Henry Cabot would have had no reason to conceal a secret fortune when the fact that he had amassed a vast fortune was known to all, Mrs. Fletcher."

"Then perhaps his partners chose to conceal it from him," I proposed. "Did you hear about the colonial chest and two sets of bones that were found in my backyard a few days ago?"

"I seem to recall reading something about that in the *Cabot Cove Gazette*."

"Let me add something to the story. Whoever belonged to the older set of bones was killed by a hatchet blow to the head. And you may also be interested to hear that contained in that old chest were the long-lost founding documents of Cabot Cove, including a manifest from a slave ship."

Cabot nodded slowly. "Explaining how you learned about John Henry Cabot's and the others' involvement in the slave trade."

"Something from that time was the motive for the murder, and it's linked to that of a second victim a year or so ago, Mr. Cabot. Tad Hollenbeck came to Cabot Cove in search of a fortune he believed was rightfully his."

"Who was this second murder victim?" Cabot asked, either intrigued or anxious or both.

"The victim's identity has yet to be determined," Mort told him, adjusting his surgical mask. "Mr. Cabot, I need to ask you for the record where you were last night between eight and ten o'clock."

"The time this Tad Hollenbeck was murdered, then."

"Your nephew, yes."

"I was here, Sheriff, within ten feet either side of where I'm standing now. The same would be true if you asked me about the night before that and so on, going back a lot of nights now."

"Good enough," Mort said. "Again, I'm sorry for your loss, Mr. Cabot."

"And I'm sorry I don't feel it more. I suppose I should call my sister to express my condolences. I'll see if I can find her number somewhere, or perhaps drop her a note."

The big double doors opened, held by James, who must have been anticipating our departure.

"I hope you feel up for a return engagement at the library soon, Mr. Cabot."

"It'll be the second visit I make once I'm able to venture out again, Mrs. Fletcher."

"What will be the first?"

His expression turned almost whimsical. "Riding in the founders' carriage in the Christmas Day parade. I've so missed that these past few years."

Mort held his gaze upon me as we climbed into his Sheriff's Department SUV. "What's on your mind, Mrs. F.?"

"Asa Cabot's personal assistant, James. Even if he wasn't suffering from agoraphobia, Asa isn't the kind of man who'd take a life with his own hands."

"Right, Mrs. F., why bother when you can pay someone else to do it?"

"I was thinking that maybe we should have interviewed him as well."

"Maybe, but I don't see him as the type to take somebody out the way Tad Hollenbeck was killed. Broken neck or single bullet to the brain maybe, but not ground-up sleeping pills."

"He's got military written all over him, Mort."

"A professional, in other words."

"Well, yes."

"Would a professional be likely to forget to leave a glass of water on the night table?"

"I suppose not."

"Case closed," Mort said.

"I only wish. And it wouldn't hurt to check James out, would it?"

"And just how do you propose I go about that, without even a last name to go on?"

I pointed toward my shoes. "He handed these back to me after we left Asa Cabot in his study. That means we've got his fingerprints."

We'd barely driven off when my phone rang with a call from Seth.

"Where are you? You're late."

"Late for what?"

"Play rehearsal. It was supposed to start twenty minutes ago, remember?"

I checked my watch. "I'm so sorry. Tell everyone I'm on my way. Mort will drop me."

"You're with Mort? Doing what?"

"What do you think, Doc?" Mort said, loudly enough for Seth to hear.

The rehearsal proved to be a welcome respite from the rigors of my ruminations on how one of the descendants of Cabot Cove's founding fathers might have been complicit in the murder of Tad Hollenbeck. I stood at the podium, reading glasses donned to better regard the script in which my narrative portions had been highlighted in yellow. The rehearsal went very well, the cast once again energized by being in full costume. I looked at Seth in his Ghost of Christmas Past regalia, stifling a chuckle over what the state police crime scene unit must have made of him the night before at the scene of Tad Hollenbeck's murder.

We breezed through the rehearsal, which was being recorded so the cast could see how well they were hitting their marks and making their prompts. Before I knew it, the fearsome Ghost of Christmas Yet to

Come arrived and I changed my cadence and tone to reflect his terrifying stature.

"Quiet and dark, beside him stood the Phantom, with its outstretched hand. When he roused himself from his thoughtful quest, he fancied from the turn of the hand, and its situation in reference to himself, that the Unseen Eyes were looking at him keenly. It made him shudder, and feel very cold."

I recalled how much the Ghost of Christmas Yet to Come had scared me as a little girl the first time I saw the movie, the superior Alastair Sim version. That was the thing about *A Christmas Carol*; it was truly timeless, and it meant as much to me today as it ever had.

"They left the busy scene, and went into an obscure part of the town, where Scrooge had never penetrated before, although he recognized its situation, and its bad repute. The ways were foul and narrow; the shops and houses wretched; the people half-naked, drunken, slipshod, ugly. Alleys and archways, like so many cesspools, disgorged their offenses of smell, and dirt, and life, upon the straggling streets; and the whole quarter reeked with crime, with filth, and misery."

Something grabbed me in that moment, something in Dickens's description of the streets, the way all sudden realizations do, with the feeling of a vise in the pit of my stomach. In that moment, I grasped what had been bothering me about the visit Mort and I had paid to Asa Cabot, specifically those mottled stains in the wood that seemed to progress in a straight line from the double doors to his stance by the windows.

"Jessica?" Seth prompted, snapping me alert again

with no concept of how long I'd gone silent in my narration.

"Let's take a break," I said, then cleared my throat and aimed my next words at him alone. "I need to call Mort."

Chapter Thirteen

That sounds like a stretch even for you, Mrs. F.,"
Mort commented when I finished, pouring cold water
on what I'd realized just moments before.

"They were footprints, Mort," I insisted again, referring to those spots on the floor the light had barely
given up.

"And what if they were? Maybe they were what's-
his-name's, the big guy."

"James," I reminded him. "And from what I recall,
his shoe size is likely thirteen or fourteen. The stains
left on the floor were closer to half that."

"You get a look at Asa Cabot's feet, too?" Mort asked
me, still unconvinced.

"He was wearing slippers."

"Did you get a look at his slippers, then?"

"Not enough to tell you their size. But the trail of

what I believe were footprints led straight to that closet in the back corner of the study."

"You believe Cabot ventured outside, despite his agoraphobia."

"Makes you think, doesn't it? At the very least, it calls into question his alibi for Tad Hollenbeck's murder. Those stains must've been fresh, Mort, and being left last night would explain why they didn't vanish when the floor was cleaned."

Mort lapsed into silence, telling me he was at least considering my theory.

"Faking agoraphobia is hardly a crime, Mrs. F. And just because he may have ventured outside doesn't mean he ended up at the Surfsider to murder Hollenbeck."

"No, maybe he had help with that. Did you get anything on James's fingerprints yet?"

"You know it's Christmas week, don't you? World tends to spin a bit slower over the holidays. Everything takes longer and it's only going to get worse the closer we get to Christmas."

"Doesn't give us a lot of time to catch our killer, Mort."

"Tad Hollenbeck will still be dead after New Year's, and the cause will still be murder."

"Speaking of which, we still have two more descendants of Cabot Cove's founding fathers to interview. And we need to make a stop at that diner across from the Surfsider."

"You souring on Mara's all of a sudden, Mrs. F.?"

"We need to check out the alibis of Angie and Selina," I said.

* * *

But Thursday morning started with a visit instead to
Shady Willows, an assisted-living center where a
great-great-great-great-great-grandniece of Wyatt
Rackley now resided. Rackley was the founding father
who'd pulled up stakes and ventured west, unable to
quell his pioneering spirit and thirst for adventure.

At least that's what the town history books said, the
same books that had made no mention of the founders' involvement in the slave trade. Mort and I arrived
just as the chair-yoga class was breaking up amid a
sea of red and green decorations, with an artificial
Christmas tree surrounded by presents piled high set
in the corner. We made our way straight to Clara Wizzenhunt, listening to background Christmas music
that might have been on the same loop as what was
playing in Seth Hazlitt's office.

"Mrs. Fletcher!" she greeted me, her knees cracking
as she lifted herself from her chair. "Are you speaking
at lunch again today?"

"No, Clara, not today."

She regarded the clock on the wall. "And, look at
that, it's hours to lunch anyway. I only just ate breakfast. I'm not as good with time as I used to be."

"I know the feeling."

"And I see you brought along the sheriff. Might he
be speaking at lunch, perhaps to enlighten us about
crimes targeting the elderly?"

Before Mort could respond, her gaze found the wall
clock again.

"Silly me. That's not it at all, is it?"

"Could we speak with you, Mrs. Wizzenhunt? It should only take a few minutes."

Clara flapped a hand in the air before her. "Let it take as long as it needs. There's nowhere else I need to be right now." Her full blue eyes found mine, flashing surprise. "Jessica, when did you get here?"

We kept her deliberate pace from the recreation hall to the dining room, where a midmorning snack was being served. Jell-O, it looked like, served out of those single-serving, peel-open containers. There were also tea and coffee available. I got myself a tea and fixed one for Clara as well, while Mort poured himself a coffee from one of those refillable urns.

"I'm the envy of Shady Willows with all those signed books of yours," she told me.

"How nice of you to say that, Clara."

"I let people borrow them from my room, but I refuse to keep them in the library. Can't have them being checked out and not returned." She looked about the nearby tables and lowered her voice. "Some of the residents here tend to be a bit forgetful, though I don't suppose I'm breaking any news there."

"What do you know of Wyatt Rackley?" I asked her.

"My ancestor? Why, I haven't thought about him in, well, a very long time. What do I know of him? Not much beyond what everyone else does, what all the stories say about his coming here with the others to build this town from scratch." She leaned closer to me, stealing a glance at Mort. "That man has a gun," Clara whispered.

"He's the town sheriff," I told her.

"What town?"

"Cabot Cove, the town built by Wyatt Rackley and those other four men. But he wasn't as wealthy as those others, as I recall," I noted, "was he?"

Clara grinned at that. "My long-dead uncle was something of a charlatan. A con man, you might call him today, blessed with a unique ability to ingratiate himself with those of means. And it wasn't for their company, if you get my drift."

"Money," Mort interjected.

"Isn't it always, Sheriff? What Uncle Wyatt lacked in dollars, he made up for in good old-fashioned ingenuity. The other founding fathers welcomed him into their midst because they needed an engineer to design and build the port that literally put Cabot Cove on the map."

Mort had his memo pad ready, his pen held like a sword in his grasp. "Rackley was an engineer?"

"Rackley?"

"Your ancestor," I prompted Clara.

"Engineer? He dabbled in it, like he dabbled in a lot of things. But the closest he ever came to actually building anything was a tree house as a boy that collapsed, injuring his sister. But he was expert at surrounding himself with people who knew what he needed to know and learning from them almost by osmosis. He'd take their ideas and regurgitate them as his own. You might say he was a thief, intellectually anyway. Even the old family stories make mention of that—proudly, I might add."

"And what do they say about his decision to head west?"

"They mostly celebrate his pioneering spirit, while bemoaning the fact that he never returned to the town he helped found. In fact, he never returned east at all. Wyatt left his family behind with the intention of moving them out once he was settled."

"You mean he never got himself settled?" I asked Clara Wizzenhunt.

"Either that or he never summoned his family once he did. The family history is a bit vague on that fact."

"What about his relationship with the other four founders?" Mort asked her.

A quizzical look claimed Clara's expression. "I don't believe I know who you are."

"Sheriff Mort Metzger, ma'am," Mort said, tipping his cowboy hat before slipping it from his head.

She looked toward me again, voice low and scratchy. "He's lying, Jessica. Amos Tupper is sheriff of Cabot Cove."

"He's one of Amos's deputies," I told her.

"Oh," Clara uttered and looked back at Mort. "I really couldn't say, Deputy."

"What have we here?" a voice boomed from the entrance.

Mort and I turned to find Clara's nephew, Lucas, storming across the dining room.

"Looks like Cabot Cove's finest must have found a crime ring inside Shady Willows."

The derision was clear in his tone, his stridency clear in the stiff gait that brought him to the table we shared with his aunt. Clara Wizzenhunt was a widow who hadn't had any children. Lucas Rackley was the son of her brother and sister-in-law, who'd both perished in a boating accident several years back. Lucas, I now recalled, had moved to Cabot Cove sometime after that to be close to his only living relative and stake out a career as a novelist. I believed he was somewhere around thirty, but he had the look of an ageless man-child in no particular rush to grow up. The fact that his late parents had been of substantial means had enabled his current lifestyle and given license to his whims, a good thing since his literary career had clearly gone nowhere in the year he'd been living here.

"I don't believe we've ever officially met," I said, rising with Mort and extending my hand. "Jessica Fletcher."

Lucas Rackley took my hand in a limp grip and regarded me with a cool detachment somewhere between distaste and envy. "I know who you are. Cabot Cove's resident best-selling author."

"Guilty as charged," I said, forcing a smile.

"I read one of your books once, Mrs. Fletcher. Never bothered with another since I'm sure they're all the same."

"Well," I said as Mort uttered an audible sigh alongside me, "I believe it was Hemingway who said all writers just keep writing the same book over and over again."

Rackley looked as if he found my remark funny. "So you're comparing yourself to Hemingway?"

"Quoting him, anyway."

Only then did he finally hug his aunt, who'd remained seated.

"How's your book coming, dear?" Clara asked him.

"Good progress lately," he said tersely, his eyes fastened on me instead of her. "It's not a mystery, of course."

"Your aunt once told me it's more along the lines of Saul Bellow or Philip Roth," I noted.

"Something like that," the young man said, pleased by the comparison.

"I'd be happy to take a look sometime if you'd like," I offered, drawing a grateful smile from Clara.

"For what? To tell me what I'm doing wrong?"

"I was thinking more like so I could recommend the right publisher."

That softened him up a bit. "Really?"

"My imprint only does mysteries, of course, but I'm familiar with several other houses around town."

"Why don't you sit down and join us?" Clara asked him as Mort and I retook our seats.

Lucas Rackley remained standing. "I just remembered I need to be somewhere else. I'll come back later when you're alone, Aunt Clara."

She looked disappointed, embarrassed by her nephew's tone and behavior. "I suppose that would be okay."

The young man swung back toward us. "I don't even know why my aunt stays in this town, after what they did to Wyatt Rackley."

"And what was that?" Mort asked him.

"Statute of limitations has long passed on the crime, Sheriff."

"Lucas, please," Clara started to implore him, but he shrugged her off.

"I wasn't aware Wyatt Rackley was the victim of a crime," I interjected.

"Is theft a crime? Is assault a crime? Is fraud a crime? Is murder a crime?"

That claimed my attention, but Lucas Rackley was just as quick to back off.

"I'm not saying they killed him, but they might as well have. He came up here an equal partner and the other four founders of this glorious town cheated him out of his rightful share. He realized none of the profits that arose from the docks he designed and built. He got nothing from the fishery, the cannery, or the mills and factories, once they went up. You think it was a pioneering spirit that drew Wyatt Rackley out west? Think again. He left Cabot Cove because he was tired of being used and swindled, and never returned."

"Odd that he left his family behind," I noted.

"The story I always heard was that he sent for them once he reached New Orleans, but for some reason they opted not to join him. There was a lot of sickness in the family at that time, and that's as good an explanation as any."

"Have you ever heard of Tad Hollenbeck?" I asked Lucas, drawing a glare from Mort.

"Who's that?"

"A television reporter for a show called *Stalker*."

"I don't watch television."

"Hollenbeck, it turns out, was a nephew of a descendant of an original founder of Cabot Cove, too, Asa Cabot."

"What does that have to do with me?"

"Nothing necessarily. I just thought I'd mention it, primarily because Hollenbeck was murdered last night."

Lucas Rackley tried not to make any response but couldn't stop his mouth from dropping open slightly.

"He came here on the pretext of doing a story on Cabot Cove's unusually high murder rate," I continued. "It turned out he'd come here to pursue something else entirely."

"And what might that be?" Rackley asked, trying to sound as nonchalant as he could.

"A lost fortune that once belonged to the founders, by all accounts. I'm not saying the fortune ever existed, of course, only that he was building a story around it and some sordid issue in the town's past. You wouldn't know anything about that, would you, Lucas?"

"The town's past?"

"The lost fortune."

"You said it didn't exist."

"I said I couldn't be sure. But if it does, you might be entitled to claim a share of it, just like Tad Hollenbeck."

I couldn't tell from the young man's expression whether this was news to him or not. He looked toward his aunt, as if just remembering she was still there. "If the fortune was real, it would be my aunt Clara who'd be entitled to her share."

"See, Jessica, I told you he was a good boy." Clara beamed, reaching up to take her nephew's hand. "But I have more than enough funds to get by."

"You'd have a lot more if the other four founders

hadn't swindled Wyatt Rackley out of what was coming to him."

"What happened when he went west, Lucas?" I asked him.

"He never returned east—I can tell you that much. There are a lot of stories, one in particular about him opening a gambling hall in New Orleans and making the acquaintance of Jean Lafitte."

"The pirate?"

Lucas Rackley nodded. "The very same. That's what the legend says anyway."

"Mrs. Fletcher is very important at the local library," his aunt Clara interjected. "I was going to ask her to make sure your book is well displayed there."

"I haven't finished it yet, Aunt Clara."

"What?"

"The book."

"What book?" she asked vacantly.

"Well, going into business with the likes of Jean Lafitte would explain why he never came back east," I remarked, looking at Clara. "Wouldn't it, Clara?"

"What?"

"Explain why your ancestor never returned to Cabot Cove after being bitten by the pioneering bug."

"I suppose," Clara said, her mind drifting anew. "Did Lucas tell you he was a novelist?"

I exchanged a glance with Lucas, who could only shrug.

"I was just getting to that, Auntie," he offered.

"Perhaps Mrs. Fletcher can help you. Did I tell you she's a writer, too? Of mysteries."

"I'd be glad to help out in any way I can," I offered again, drawing a smile from Clara.

"I'm surprised you're not out solving the murder of this Tad Hollenbeck," Lucas Rackley said with a smirk.

"We're talking to you, aren't we?" Mort chimed in, no longer able to stomach the young man's attitude. "Hard to be in two places at the same time."

"Oh, so I'm a suspect, am I? Did you hear that, Auntie?"

Clara was scraping the sides of her single-sized Jell-O serving with a plastic spoon. "Hear what?"

"Why don't you tell us where you were last night between eight and ten?" Mort asked him. "Just for fun."

"Just for fun, I was visiting friends in Boston," Lucas Rackley said sharply.

"I assume you could provide their names and phone numbers just to cover all bases."

"Why don't I have my lawyer forward them to your office?" the young man said, the way someone who didn't have a lawyer at all might.

Mort fitted his cowboy-style hat back in place, a sign it was time for us to take our leave.

My phone rang as he rose, and I moved aside to answer it.

"It's Sheila Del Perrio, Mrs. Fletcher. Are you with Sheriff Metzger today?"

"I am."

"Could the two of you stop back over at my house? There's something I neglected to mention yesterday morning I need to tell you regarding your investigation. It may prove quite important."

"We'll be over straightaway," I said, hearing a noise, a loud buzzing, in the background on Sheila's side of the line. "What was that?"

"Just the doorbell. I had a louder one installed because I don't hear as well as I used to. Anyway, I'll have a fresh batch of cookies ready for you. Hurry up if you'd like them warm out of the oven."

Chapter Fourteen

Sheila didn't respond the first time we rang that loud doorbell, or the second time, or the third. Never one great at exercising patience, Mort started pounding on the door with his fist, while I worked my way to a casement window to see if I might be able to peer inside.

"Mort," I managed through the heavy lump that had formed in my throat, my voice barely above a whisper.

It took considerable effort for Mort to break the vertical glass pane next to the front door and chip away enough jagged glass to reach in and unlock the door. Moments later, we had confirmed what the view through the window had suggested: Sheila Del Perrio was dead.

She sat slumped on the couch, the very same spot we'd left her in the day before.

There's something I neglected to mention yesterday morning I need to tell you regarding your investigation. It may prove quite important.

Sheila's last words to me before her doorbell rang, meaning she'd been alive barely twenty minutes earlier.

"Seth's on his way," Mort said, pocketing his phone, which I had no recollection of him using. "No indication this was murder, though, right, Mrs. F.?"

"Nothing obvious, but there wasn't initially with Tad Hollenbeck's death either. In other words, let's not get ahead of ourselves."

"You do have a tendency to do that, Mrs. F."

"Do you blame me in this case?"

"I was hoping you might make an exception," Mort said, "this being Christmas season and all."

"And a season for murder, apparently."

Seth joined us a half hour later, and it was the longest thirty minutes I'd ever experienced. The fact that Sheila was a descendant of Earl Grove Hutchinson had brought us there the day before, but the house felt entirely different, sour and sallow. Death will do that to a place, even when murder isn't involved. But a plate of fresh cookies—gingerbread and Toll House again—was sitting exactly where it'd been then.

That got me to wondering who'd rung the doorbell at the end of my conversation with Sheila. My imagination was already conjuring the worst, and I looked to Seth in the hope that he would present a likely cause of death other than murder.

"I've been treating her for a heart condition for years and she was borderline congestive heart failure," he said, in the midst of his examination of the body. "I recently prescribed Entresto for her and it was working wonders."

Indeed, Sheila looked as if she was taking a nap and nothing more. The day's edition of the *Cabot Cove Gazette* was spread on the coffee table before her, a stack of circulars for last-minute Christmas shoppers off to the side a bit.

"Anything raise any flags, Doc?" Mort asked him.

"Well, her eyes are bloodshot, which could indicate she was smothered or suffocated to death. But the woman's eyes were always bloodshot on account of her diabetes. Not a symptom that affects all diabetics, but it certainly presented in her."

"The pillows are different," I noticed.

Seth and Mort turned my way in unison.

"I'm talking about the arrangement on the couch. It's not the same as yesterday," I noted, pointing to a striking needlepoint design in festive holiday colors. "That was on the easy chair, almost like it was set there specifically for the holiday season."

"So maybe she moved it," Mort suggested.

"But she didn't replace it with another pillow, which means there's one missing."

"She could have spilled something on it," Seth said.

"That's one possibility."

"Care to suggest another, Mrs. F.?"

"Did you check her throat?" I asked Seth.

"You mean for bleeding or mucus buildup? You bet I did, and there was none. Of course, another indicator of suffocation would be petechial hemorrhages in the lungs, but those can only be revealed by an autopsy. And you might be interested to hear that the hyoid bone at the base of the tongue is intact. As you know, Jess," Seth continued, showing off for both Mort and me, "fracturing of that bone is sometimes associated with death by suffocation."

"You're getting good at this, Doc," Mort complimented him.

"I have had more than my share of practice."

"What about her fingernails, Seth?" I wondered aloud.

"What about them?"

"If she was struggling with her killer, there may be some skin residue from scratching present under the nails, or strands of fabric from the missing pillow."

"I was just getting to that," Seth said, fitting his glasses back in place and moving to examine Sheila Del Perrio's nails as if he was about to perform a manicure. "What color was this pillow you remember from this morning?"

"It was a forest needlepoint," I recalled, wondering if one of Sheila's masterpieces of embroidery had helped take her life, "so mostly green and brown."

"I can see some lighter strands, cream or white," Seth noted.

"The couch is white," said Mort, his words aimed at me.

"Still not a lot to go on," Seth said, sounding a bit defensive as he clung to his original diagnosis.

"There's one more thing to check for," I told him, "that being bruising on the chest."

Both he and Mort fixed their gazes upon me.

"Putting weight on the chest prevents the lungs from inflating and prevents the victim from inhaling. The pillow by itself could do the trick, but even a woman with a bad heart like Sheila would struggle mightily. With her killer's weight on her chest, though, her struggles would be much less effective and her ability to suck air from the pillow would be rendered virtually nonexistent."

Seth nodded and moved to examine Sheila Del Perrio's chest. The way he positioned himself blocked a view of his work from Mort and me, until he swung back toward us, stripping his latex gloves from his hands with something between a frown and a snarl gripping his face.

"There's bruising, all right, *ayuh*," he reported. "Minor enough for even a pathologist to miss if he wasn't looking for it."

"You think someone might have placed their knees on the woman's chest while holding the pillow over her face, Mrs. F.?" Mort asked me.

"Elbows and a measure of body weight would have done the trick, too."

Seth seemed to notice something on the carpet and shined his penlight in that direction.

"The two of you may want to take a look at this," he said, holding the penlight steady.

He shined it down on the Oriental rug on which the couch and coffee table were positioned. The beam illuminated something all too familiar.

"Is that what I think it is?" Mort managed, already reaching for an evidence bag in his pocket.

"I believe so," I said, crouching over a thin black shaving, only a bit thicker than a human hair, that looked very much like the two we'd found in Tad Hollenbeck's motel room.

"Will you look at that?" Mort said, scratching at his scalp. "If that matches the ones we found in Tad Hollenbeck's motel room . . ."

He didn't finish his thought because he didn't have to. I watched Mort lift the dark strand of hair, or whatever it was, up from the carpet with a tweezers and drop it into a small plastic evidence bag.

"We need to tell the crime lab to rush the results on that, Mort," I suggested.

"Nobody rushes around Christmas, Mrs. F., unless it involves shopping."

"Murder doesn't take holidays, Mort."

Having interviewed Asa Cabot, Clara Wizzenhunt, the fisherman Terry McMullen, and the late Sheila Del Perrio, we had only a single founder left, John Van Webb. The Van Webb bloodline had pretty much died out, just a lone much-removed cousin still residing within the town borders.

Dan Kinder ran a one-man heating and cooling repair business. He lived in Cabot Cove's oldest apartment complex, instead of a stately home, a testament to how hard it was for ordinary working-class folks to afford to reside in town anymore. Property values continued to soar through a roof that kept getting higher and higher, and small homes nowhere close to the sea routinely fetched offers far into six figures.

I thought of my late husband, Frank, and me buying 698 Candlewood Lane, reflecting on the fact that we'd never have been able to manage that with what Cabot Cove homes were fetching today. I remembered thinking the insurance company's valuation of my home to be wildly inflated; maybe not so much now.

"How well do you know Dan Kinder?" I asked Mort, grateful to be back outside in the cool fresh air, leaving Seth inside to continue his preliminary examination of Sheila Del Perrio's body now that we'd determined murder to be the almost certain cause of death.

"Not very." Mort shrugged. "He's done some work around the house, but that describes pretty much all of Cabot Cove."

I recalled some of the gossip about Kinder that had been going around town for years. "You trusted him alone with Adele?"

That drew a smile from Mort. "Adele's a former Marine, Mrs. F. One step out of line with her and he wouldn't be using that foot for a while."

"He's the last descendant still in town of one of the original founding fathers. We need to have a talk with him."

"Why don't I have one of my deputies track him down and bring him into the station?"

"We'd be better off waiting to surprise him. Go see him tomorrow. And I've got to be at play rehearsal by five. The cast will kill me if I'm late again."

Mort shot me a look at my poor word choice. "Anyway," he picked up, "I'd like to have another talk with that producer and cameraperson before I let them leave town. What were their names again?"

"Angie and Selina, producer and cameraperson, respectively. And I need to have another talk with Fred Hardesty."

"Thinking about adding some golden oldies to your rebuilt home, Mrs. F.?"

"Maybe," I admitted. "But if anybody can help me sort out whatever part Cabot Cove's past plays in all this, it's him. What if we asked him to review some of those historical documents for more clues? It would take twice as long with me doing it on my own, and he's far more expert in such matters than I."

"Well, he is head of the Cabot Cove Historical Society, after all. Rather odd bird, though, don't you think?"

"I'm sure people say the same thing about us behind our backs."

Mort shook his head. "You know what I love about Cabot Cove?"

"What?"

His answer was to turn away and start down the walk toward his SUV.

We stopped at Mara's and loaded the chest we'd placed in one of the walk-ins for safekeeping into the back of Mort's SUV. Then we drove the single block to Fred Hardesty's antiques shop.

"Would I?" he exclaimed, after I explained what I needed him to do. "Reviewing those founding documents? That's the best Christmas present anyone could possibly give me! Speaking of presents, I had the one you picked out for your grandnephew delivered to your house, all wrapped."

"I can't thank you enough, Fred."

He watched Mort carrying in a portion of the documents we'd transferred to a plain cardboard box.

"When you're finished," I resumed to Fred Hardesty, "just remember to—"

"Put them in a fridge or something comparable. I have a closet I converted to a dehumidified chamber for paintings and the like. That should suffice. I'll be here if you need me, Mrs. Fletcher."

"You're not going home, Fred?"

He tenderly patted the box Mort had just laid down on the counter. "Not with these to keep me company."

"Call if you find anything you think I should know," I told him.

I went back to the station with Mort, because I didn't feel like being alone. All murders leave me unsettled, of course. But the connection of these recent ones with the earliest history of Cabot Cove was a wrinkle I wasn't used to, and I couldn't get my mind to shut down. I felt like I do when I lose myself in my writing and end up unable to sleep because I can't get the story out of my head.

Tad Hollenbeck's murder had come in the wake of the discovery of the two sets of remains and the centuries-old documents in my backyard by a work crew. One set of bones had belonged to a man dating back to those early years of Cabot Cove's existence. The other set belonged to a woman who was killed sometime around a year ago. All three of these murders, along with Sheila Del Perrio's now, seemed to have a direct connection with something that hap-

pened in Cabot Cove more than 220 years ago. And
the fact that two descendants of the founders had perished within barely forty-eight hours of each other
suggested that Asa Cabot, Clara Wizzenhunt, Terry
McMullen, and Dan Kinder might all be in danger as
well.

I also couldn't shake our encounter with Lucas
Rackley earlier that afternoon. He was a distinctly unpleasant young man, but the fact that his parents had
left him plenty of money to survive made him less of
a suspect if this was about some mythical lost fortune.
And then I remembered something that sent a chill
up my spine.

Lucas Rackley had long, thick jet-black hair brushed
straight back. Very close to what we'd recovered at
both murder scenes. I was just about to share that re-
alization with Mort, when I felt a vibration in the bag
slung from my shoulder and realized my phone was
ringing. Mort was still jabbering away into his radio's
mic inside his SUV when I finally managed to scoop it
out from inside and saw *HARRY MCGRAW* lit up on the
caller ID.

"Since when do you not answer my calls on the first
ring?" he snapped at me by way of greeting.

"I was distracted."

"Another murder?"

"You guessed it."

"I was kidding, Jess."

"I'm not."

"Don't tell me," Harry resumed, "another heir of
the original founders of Cabot Cove."

"Okay, I won't tell you. But you said *heir* instead of *descendant*."

"Because *heir* implies money. *Descendant* doesn't, and I'm starting to think that's what this is all about."

"You just think of that on the spot, Harry?"

"So, why'd you call me, Jess?"

"You called me."

"I did. It must've been because I knew you were about to call me."

"As a matter of fact, I was."

"Good. Christmas is my slow season, you know. Actually, all months are my slow season, so I have some time on my hands. So what have you got?"

"Wyatt Rackley."

"Who?"

"One of the original founders of Cabot Cove, who fled for parts west around 1795."

"I hope you're not going to ask if I knew him."

"It's one of the things I can't wrap my arms around, Harry, especially since by all accounts he never returned to Cabot Cove and it doesn't appear as if he brought his family with him."

"You did say he fled, Jess. That could explain it."

"Maybe."

"But you're not buying that, are you?"

"Right now, I'm not buying anything, Harry. This mystery seems to have its roots two hundred and thirty or so years in the past."

"So what do you want me to do?"

"Can you look into Wyatt Rackley?"

"The 1790s are a little outside my comfort zone, little lady. Not a lot of people left from back then who can provide firsthand information."

"Rackley settled in Missouri for a time before moving to New Orleans," I told him. "The story is he was acquainted with none other than the pirate Jean Lafitte."

"Well," he noted, "at least he kept good company."

"Bye, Harry. Call me as soon as you come up with something."

Mort looked over at me after I ended the call. "How do you look into someone from two hundred years ago?"

"This is Harry McGraw we're talking about, a man capable of working miracles."

"What was it you were going to tell me before he called?"

I filled him in on what I'd realized about Lucas Rackley.

"Way ahead of you on that one, Mrs. F."

"Why didn't you say something?"

Mort couldn't help but smile. "I wanted to wait until you told me."

I was scolding him with my eyes when a call came over the radio and he lifted the microphone to his lips.

"Go for Mort."

"It's Deputy Muldoon here, Sheriff. I'm over at the diner across the street from the Surfsider Motel, like you told me. Something you're going to want to hear about."

"Can it wait, Muldoon?"

"No, sir," the deputy's voice crackled, "I don't think it can. . . ."

Chapter Fifteen

The alibi Tad Hollenbeck's assistants provided doesn't hold up, Mrs. F.," Mort explained, after he'd clipped the mic back onto its stand.

"They weren't his assistants," I corrected. "One was his producer and the other was the cameraperson."

"Whatever," he said, shrugging me off. "Anyway, according to the server who took care of them at the Bottomless Cup across the street from the Surfsider, one was unaccounted for, for upwards of twenty minutes. Apparently, she left the diner after placing her order and still hadn't returned when her food was served twenty minutes later."

"Which of the two women are we talking about?"

"The producer," Mort said, wetting a fingertip to better flip through his magical memo pad.

"Angie Lawrence," I said, saving him the trouble.

He flipped the pad closed. "I told both women they

could leave this afternoon, but they were still there at
last check."

They were almost completely packed and ready to go
when we got there, Selina Sanchez loading the last of
her camera equipment into the back of their SUV.

"Is Ms. Lawrence still on the premises, Ms. Sanchez?"
Mort greeted her.

Selina closed the SUV's hatch. "We were just getting ready to leave, Sheriff. You told us we could."

"I've got a few more questions. Shouldn't take too
long."

Selina regarded me diffidently, as if to question my
presence without directly challenging it.

"Should we go inside?" Mort asked her, showing a
higher degree of deference than I was used to from him.

Selina nodded and led the way to the room, the
door cracked open in spite of the cold. We entered to
find Angie Lawrence just closing her suitcase.

"Oh," she remarked, spotting Mort and then me.

Mort looked from her to Selina and back again.
"There's a problem with the story you told us about
your whereabouts the night Tad Hollenbeck was murdered."

Selina glanced toward Angie, whose gaze remained
rooted on Mort.

"See, according to your server, Ms. Lawrence, you
left the table after ordering your food and didn't return until after it had been served."

"I didn't lie, Sheriff."

"No? What would you call it, then?"

"You asked where we were around when Tad was

murdered. We said we had dinner at that diner. I never said I was there for the whole two hours."

"So where were you, Angie?" I asked her.

This time, she did glance at Selina, but only briefly. "Tad and I . . ."

"You were having an affair," I completed for her.

"I wouldn't call it that. Relationships between staff members are expressly forbidden at *Stalker*."

"But Tad Hollenbeck had been relieved of his duties that day, hadn't he?" Mort reminded her.

"Yes, but I was still an outside producer for the show. If they found out . . ."

Angie's voice drifted off again.

"How close were the two of you?" I asked, as tactfully as I could manage.

"Not close enough for Tad to tell me anything more than he did when it came to the truth about what really brought him here."

"He never even hinted at what he was really up to?"

Angie thought for a moment. "Not beyond saying he wasn't going to need *Stalker* anymore because he was about to strike gold."

"Those were his exact words?"

"Or very close, yes."

"So by 'gold,' he didn't necessarily mean the real story that had brought him to Cabot Cove?"

That seemed to throw her for a bit of a loop. "No, but I assumed that's what he meant."

"And he never mentioned anything about being a descendant himself of one of the original founding fathers of Cabot Cove?"

"Wait, was he?"

"It appears so, yes."

"He never told me," Angie insisted, a bit of derision edging into her voice, even bitterness. "Apparently, there were a lot of things he didn't tell me, so I guess we weren't as close as I thought we were, after all."

"Your personal life is your own business," Mort told her. "I'm interested in the timeline, as in when exactly you were with Mr. Hollenbeck before he was murdered."

"Then you don't consider me a suspect?"

"It's never a good idea to lie to the police, Ms. Lawrence. . . ."

"I didn't lie."

"Especially when it involves a murder investigation. Do I consider you a suspect? I haven't ruled you out," Mort told her, "but I haven't ruled anyone out at this point."

"It would have been around eight forty-five to nine fifteen," Angie told him, her voice softer and flatter. "The rooms in this place have clock radios with big numbers lit up brightly. Just like that one on the night table over there," she added, directing our attention to bright red numerals you could spot from across the room.

"So between eight forty-five and nine fifteen," Mort repeated, making an entry on his memo pad.

"That's right, Sheriff."

"And how did he seem to you?"

"In what regard?"

"Well, he had just recently learned that he'd been fired," I chimed in.

"He had something else on his mind that was more

important than his gig with *Stalker*. You might even call him excited."

"Did he provide any hint as to what?"

"I assumed it was because of the footage we'd shot earlier in the day, all the things he was hinting at."

"But he was never more specific than that," Mort stated in what I thought had started as a question.

"He said he was going to be rich," Angie told us both.

"So he wasn't upset or disturbed anymore?" I asked her, recalling the observation she'd made about Tad Hollenbeck's mood the last time Mort and I had been here.

"Something was still bothering him, Mrs. Fletcher. He kept talking about the remains found in your backyard, the more recent ones that were only a year old. He'd learned murder was suspected. He couldn't let that go. Now that I think of it, he'd grown more angry than upset."

Mort left me off at the high school just in time for our five o'clock rehearsal of *A Christmas Carol*. He promised to drop off the oak chest at my house later. Even though I'd left a pile of the chest's contents with Fred Hardesty for his examination, I'd kept the bulk of them.

Distracted by that, I read my narration stiffly, in a fog, unable to fully concentrate on the words highlighted before me. My mind kept wandering back to the nuances of an investigation that was getting bigger and more complicated. And, to boot, I began to fixate on the fact that the other descendants of Cabot

Cove's founding fathers might not be safe, and we hadn't even gotten to interview Dan Kinder, a descendant of John Van Webb, yet.

Then I went back to fixating on the oak chest containing the earliest documents from our town's history. Secrets hatched, and kept for more than two centuries, seemed to bear a direct connection with what we were facing now. The only clue linking the murders of Tad Hollenbeck and Sheila Del Perrio was the presence of those thick black hairs or shavings at both crime scenes. Until the state police crime lab weighed in, that clue wouldn't be much of a help to the investigation. And I needed to call Harry McGraw back to see if he'd managed to uncover anything about the fate of Wyatt Rackley, one of the five original founding fathers, who'd ventured west and, by all accounts, never returned.

The rehearsal ended with applause from the cast members and a handful of people who'd watched it from the front of the high school auditorium. It finished with me feeling like I was enveloped by the same fog I'd been in when the rehearsal started, barely remembering the delivery of any of my narration.

Seth had offered to give me a ride back home to 698 Candlewood Lane, and I decided to ring Harry while waiting for him to change out of his Ghost of Christmas Past costume. Turning my phone back on, I saw a slew of missed calls from him that had all come in the course of our two-hour rehearsal.

"I'm returning your call," I greeted him.

"Which one? I called you six times."

"You didn't leave any messages."

"My daughters tell me nobody does that anymore because nobody listens to their voice mails. That's so 'old,' they tell me. When did we get old, Jess?"

"Compared to those the age of your daughters, we were born old."

Harry sighed. "You're depressing me. Maybe I'll go have a stiff drink instead of telling you what I uncovered today."

I felt a quiver of anticipation slip through me. "You told me you gave up drinking years ago."

"Because I couldn't afford the good stuff, I figured why bother? Now I figure maybe it's better than nothing."

"Does this have something to do with Wyatt Rackley?" I prodded him.

"Is that a brand of whiskey?"

"Harry," I said in my most scalding of tones.

"Did you ever try to track down someone from way back in the late eighteenth and nineteenth centuries?"

"Why would I? I've got you."

"Suffice it to say that it comes with its own peculiar sets of challenges, but the Internet and nationwide library systems are not without resources, specifically access to census data and voting rolls for anyone skilled enough to know where to find them."

"Like you, of course."

Harry cleared his throat. "Did I tell you I've got a rental car reserved for the rest of the week?"

"Where are you going?"

"I hear Cabot Cove is a great place to spend Christmas, if you don't mind the bodies dropping. I figure I'd better head up there before any more of them fall."

"So long as you're not about to tell me that Wyatt Rackley is the killer."

"That would be impossible, little lady, because as near as I can find out he ceased to exist around 1795."

"Wait a minute," I said, after my surprise wore off. "You said there were census records and voter lists."

"There are, and tax rolls, too. The problem is Wyatt Rackley's name doesn't appear on any of the three in either Missouri or Louisiana, specifically New Orleans."

"Maybe he didn't vote, pay taxes, or bother registering as a resident where he ended up settling," I advanced. "He was known as something of a con man and a scoundrel."

"Con men and scoundrels leave paper trails, too, Jess, even going back that far in time. And there are also newspapers of the time to consider. Would you believe their content from way back when has been digitized?"

"No, I wouldn't."

"Okay, you're right. But there are searchable databases—not cheap, mind you—that have collated reams of information from those papers. Where should I send the bill?"

"What'd you find in those databases, Harry?"

"Nothing whatsoever pertaining to Wyatt Rackley after 1795, and almost everything I found related to various scrapes he'd gotten into with the law around Boston. There are also a few history books of those times that mention him and even cover his being one of the first of those who uprooted their lives for some quixotic vision of the West, only to find it was pretty much like the East."

"But nothing concrete," I said, trying to make sense of that, "nothing that definitively recounts all these adventures Rackley supposedly had."

"Because by all accounts he never had any. I can't find any evidence he ever left Cabot Cove."

"I'm beginning to think that he never did," I said, realizing something that should have occurred to me before, as Seth emerged from the dressing room area and beckoned me to join him.

"No stop at Mara's?" Seth asked incredulously. "You expect me to eat alone?"

"I'm exhausted," I told him.

"What is it you're not telling me, Jess?" he said, an edge of suspicion clear in his voice.

"Why do you think there's something I'm not telling you?"

"Because you never turn down Mara's, especially when I'm buying."

"Are you buying?"

"No, it was just a figure of speech."

"Breakfast tomorrow?"

He shrugged from behind the wheel of his ancient Volvo. "If I haven't starved to death."

"You finally listened to me," Seth said as he pulled into my driveway.

"What?" I said distantly, my thoughts still jumbled.

He gestured toward my porch. "I'm always telling you to leave the outside lights on this time of year, but you never listen to me. Finally!"

"I guess I must have." I shrugged. "I can't remember what I had for breakfast this morning, so I guess it's no surprise I can't remember doing that either."

"Nine sharp tomorrow morning?"

"Nine sharp tomorrow morning."

I emerged from the blast-furnace heat of Seth's trusty Volvo into the dank, wintry night air, which felt like some snow might still be in the offing. I heard Seth's door clank closed and he shuffled up to me as I neared the porch.

"Just want to make sure you make it inside safe and sound," he explained.

"Quite the gentleman you've become."

He pressed a finger to his lips. "Let's keep that under your hat," he quipped. "Don't want to do anything to detract from the crotchety reputation as an old coot around town."

I trudged up the walk, climbed the porch stairs, and slid my key into the lock. I turned the knob and eased the door inward, glancing back to tell Seth all was well when I felt a pair of arms lock around me.

Chapter Sixteen

Aunt Jess!" my grandnephew Frank screeched, tightening his hold on me.

"Easy there." His father, Grady, beamed, emerging from the kitchen with one of my aprons tied around his waist and his wife, Donna, by his side. "You don't want to break your aunt."

"Grady!" I exclaimed.

Little Frank was still fastened tight to me when I hugged the nephew who was more like a son to me, sandwiching the boy between us.

"Ouch!" he cried out.

But the boy who'd been named after my late husband was grinning when we finally separated; as a matter of fact, I couldn't recall many times he'd ever cried, even as an infant.

"We got in early, Aunt Jess," Grady explained, flapping the set of keys I'd given him years before. "Good thing you didn't change the locks."

He spotted Seth entering behind me, shaking his head at the start I'd given him. "Dr. Hazlitt!"

Grady extended a hand, but Seth swallowed him in a hug instead, his expression one of faux reproach when they separated. "How many times do I have to tell you to call me Seth?"

"I kind of like feeling like a little boy again," Grady told him, "especially this time of year."

"I thought you were coming on the twenty-third," I noted.

"And so we're here."

"Today's the twenty-*second*, Grady."

He tapped the side of his head. "As an accountant, you'd think I'd be better with numbers. House looks great, by the way."

I looked about and saw my new décor had been supplemented by an array of neatly wrapped presents complete with stick-on labels that would make Santa Claus proud. Based on the piles, it was hard to believe there were only four of us, even if one of the four was a young boy. Even with the move back home, I'd managed to finish my Christmas shopping, buying all my gifts in person at Cabot Cove shops, as was my custom. The very last had been that very special present I'd found for little Frank at Fred Hardesty's antiques store.

"Well, I'd best be getting on home," Seth said, smiling as he retraced his steps through the door.

"We can't convince you to stay for dinner?" Grady offered.

Seth shook his head politely. "Got take-out meat loaf from Mara's waiting for me in the fridge I can't let go to waste. But wonderful to see you, young man."

"You, too, Dr. Hazlitt."

Seth flashed him one more look of reproach, shaking his head as he closed the door behind him.

"Where's the Christmas tree?" Grady asked me as Donna looked on, quiet as a church mouse as always.

"I thought we could get one together."

"Really, Aunt Jess?"

"No, but it's better than admitting I've been too distracted to pick one out and have it delivered. I don't want you to think I'm neglecting the spirit of the season."

Grady ran a hand through the hair he'd been wearing the same way since graduating college, although I thought I detected a few sprinkles of gray popping up. "No worries, just leave it to us. We'll find the best Christmas tree still standing in Cabot Cove tomorrow. Since I'm a day early, it'll give me something to do."

Little Frank had the very same hair as his father and his beautiful mother's soulful eyes. Having seen my share of childhood pictures of my late husband, Frank, I remained convinced his namesake bore a striking resemblance to him, especially in the way his smile seemed to angle to the side as if it might be about to slide off his face. That feature had followed my Frank into adulthood, and I could only hope that little Frank would grow up to be the sensitive, caring man he had been.

"Speaking of accounting—" Grady resumed, interrupted when a knock fell on the front door Seth had just closed behind him.

I answered it to find Mort Metzger standing there, a deputy behind him with the old chest that had been inside one of the walk-in refrigerators at Mara's for safekeeping perched on a dolly.

"Where do you want it, Mrs. F.?"

In all the excitement, I'd forgotten I'd asked Mort to have the chest brought over so I could continue my review of its contents while Fred Hardesty was working on his.

"The kitchen would be great, if it's not too much trouble."

"Donna and I are cooking up a great dinner," Grady took the opportunity to interject.

"And I have every intention of returning the favor with a Christmas feast that will be one for the ages. Wait until you see the turkey!"

"The one in the fridge? It looks like it needs a zip code all its own," Grady mused.

Mort looked his way, grinning. "Been a long time," he greeted him, extending his hand.

"You haven't changed a bit, Sheriff Metzger," Grady said, taking it.

"Nothing changes in Cabot Cove, son. You know that. It's truly the land that time forgot."

"I've seen that movie," boasted eight-year-old Frank. "It's got dinosaurs!"

"Which describes the way I feel with all these new furnishings and appliances," I noted. "Mort, can I bother you for another minute?"

"Sure, Mrs. F."

"I'll get back at it in the kitchen," Grady said, fall-

ing into step alongside Mort's deputy, who was wheel-
ing the dolly containing the centuries-old chest.

I stepped out with Mort onto the front porch and
closed the door behind us.

"What about the other descendants of the original
founders?"

"What about them?"

"Have you warned them that their lives might be
in danger?"

"I was thinking of doing one of those robocalls to
the whole town; you know, make sure we cover all the
bases, just in case." When I didn't respond to his sar-
casm, Mort continued. "Yes, I called Asa Cabot and
Shady Willows, too. Couldn't reach Terry McMullen,
so I left a message with the harbormaster to have him
call me as soon as his boat's back in port. And we still
need to pay a visit to Dan Kinder. Anything else?"

"Besides the fact that I'm utterly baffled, no."

"You're never utterly baffled when it comes to murder, Mrs. F."

"An investigation that goes back two hundred and
twenty-five years is a challenge even for me, Mort.
That's why I asked you to bring the chest by. Maybe I
can find some clue as to what happened back then
that people are still being murdered over today."

For dinner, Grady and Donna had prepared beef stew
from the same recipe I'd used when Grady was right
around little Frank's age. I couldn't remember the last
time I'd made it myself and found it exactly as I re-

membered from when I so enjoyed cooking for our little family.

Donna had always been a quiet sort who didn't open up to a lot of people, including me. But we got along very well and I never pushed her to be anything different from what she was. And I could tell from her interactions with her son that she was a wonderful mother. I also caught Grady and her holding hands on numerous occasions both before and during the meal, mostly when she caught us reminiscing about raising Grady in the wake of his parents' tragic deaths.

I'd forgotten how much I'd missed having family around. There was something so special about it, thanks especially to little Frank's presence. It just doesn't seem as much like family unless there are children present, and I was so glad I'd insisted that he and his parents stay here with me for the holiday to celebrate my homecoming.

I had gotten so used to my own company over the years that I'd also forgotten how pleasant it was to have loved ones around and to hear voices other than my own. I'd grown accustomed to the company of strangers in my months residing at Hill House. But it was Robert Frost who said, "Home is the place where, when you have to go there, they have to take you in." I think what he meant by that is the comfort one finds in not needing to be anyone other than oneself. And during dinner I didn't once think of the two recent murders and their connection with the earliest days of Cabot Cove. It was wonderful to give my mind a rest while energizing my heart.

Little Frank tugged me into the TV room after dinner, where the flat-screen I was still learning to operate hung over everything like a sentinel.

"Can you show me how to play my video games on this, Aunt Jess?"

"I would if I understood the controls better myself," I told him.

He scrunched his face up in typical eight-year-old contemplative style, the very same expression I recalled from his father at the same age. "What if I could figure it out? Then I could show you."

"How to play video games?"

"And, you know, find the stuff you're looking for on the TV."

"That would be great," I said, squeezing his shoulder tenderly. "Have at it."

He captured me in about the tightest hug I'd ever felt. "I love you, Aunt Jess!"

"I love you, too, Frank."

A lump formed in my throat after I said that, memories stoked of the many times I'd said those exact words to my late husband. I couldn't speak my nephew's name without thinking of his namesake, a wonderful thing, of course, but one that left me a bit melancholy nonetheless. I don't think I'd ever been prouder of Grady, whom I had to thank for my career as a writer, than I was in that moment. A man can be a success at many things, but all of them pale in comparison with being a good father.

Donna made it a point to insist on cleaning the kitchen herself, a pretext that I realized would allow Grady to spend some time alone with me in the living room out of range of the booming sounds emanating from the TV room, where little Frank had clearly mastered my giant flat-screen's controls.

"I've got some exciting news, Aunt Jess." Grady beamed at me, boyish and wide-eyed as ever.

"Don't make it too exciting," I warned him. "I am getting older, you know."

"I'm going to start my own accounting firm."

That caught me a bit by surprise given the solid salary and job security the company he'd been with for several years provided. Grady was many things, but business-minded wasn't necessarily one of them.

"That's wonderful, Grady," I said, taking his hands in mine.

He frowned, making what I used to call his pouty face when he was a boy. "You don't sound like you think it's so wonderful."

"I'm just tired, that's all," I said, not elaborating on the events of the past few days.

"Really?"

"Well . . ."

The pouty face broadened into a grin. "Have you ever told a lie, Aunt Jess?"

I squeezed his hands. "If you always tell the truth, you never have to remember what you said."

"You think I'm making a mistake?"

"I think you need to think of providing for your family first."

I could see the excitement brimming over in him. "That's why I have to do this. I'm still years away from making partner at my current firm. We've saved up the money I need to get office space, and I'm starting to feel that if I don't do it soon, I might never do it." He paused, that excited sense I'd felt in him ebbing. "You don't think I'm ready, do you?"

I squeezed his hands tighter. "What I think, Grady, is that if you wait until you're sure you're ready to do something, you might never do it. I wrote that first book of mine mostly to take my mind off your uncle's death. If I'd really thought about it, I probably never would have done it when you consider the folly of the whole experience, thinking I could actually find a publisher. And I never would have if you hadn't fished it out of the trash and submitted it to Covington House."

"I had no idea how you'd react when I told you they wanted to buy it, much less saw it as a potential best seller. Who knew, right?"

"You did, Grady. You believed in me enough to go out on that limb with your girlfriend at the time. You knew how much writing meant to me because you watched me pounding away on the keyboard as a boy. And then you made my dream come true." I continued to hold his hands firmly. "Now I'd like to do the same for you."

"What do you mean, Aunt Jess?"

"I'll support your decision to start your own firm on one condition: that you let me back your effort and not touch a penny of your savings."

He threw himself forward and hugged me the same way his son had earlier, and just as tight. For a moment I thought it was the little boy I'd raised I was embracing instead of the grown adult.

"I don't know what to say," he said, easing himself

away and swiping some tears aside with his sleeve. "I wasn't going to ask you for anything other than your blessing."

"I know that. Consider it an investment."

"Done! So long as you let me pay you back with interest."

"Done!" I echoed, even though I had no intention of letting him do anything of the kind.

Grady's eyes fell on the old oak chest that rested on the floor just short of the kitchen. "What exactly is that thing, Aunt Jess?"

Grady insisted on helping with the daunting process of reviewing the chest's contents in search of clues. Donna volunteered, too, after I'd brought them both up to speed with a capsule summary of all that had unfolded in the past three days, sparing them the gory details and lowering my voice when I came to any point I didn't want little Frank to overhear.

I provided both of them with latex gloves with which to handle the pages, which would no doubt be at varying levels of fragility. None of us would handle any documents or other items that appeared severely compromised after weathering so many years. These would be left to professional restorers, while we busied ourselves with only pages that remained intact.

The stacks of yellowed, cracked, and tattered pages made for an imposing sight on my kitchen table, and we ended up relocating the bulk of the stacks to the counter. Many of the documents—most, even—were easy to dismiss because of their dry nature, in the form of manifests, daily business logs, and profit-and-loss statements, along with banking and other financial materials. This would all surely be great fodder for historians like Fred Hardesty, but I was interested in journals, letters, reports, and any other documents that might provide some clue as to what had led someone to take a hatchet to the head of a victim I was all but certain was Wyatt Rackley. Beyond that, I held to the hope that something within these founding documents would form a clear bridge between present and past, helping to explain the motive behind the murders of both Tad Hollenbeck and Sheila Del Perrio.

Grady was hardly intimidated by the process, no stranger to dealing with huge stacks of pages for his clients. Donna, on the other hand, was all out of sorts initially. Her hands shook as she began sifting through the pages, and I could see the magnifying glass I'd provided trembling a bit. But she settled into the process before too long and was flipping through pages at lightning speed, lingering on those pages that fit the criteria I had laid out. She placed those documents off to the side, careful to keep them in their proper order.

"I feel like I was there for the beginning of Cabot Cove, Aunt Jess," Grady commented, seeming to revel in the process he might well have found a welcome respite from dealing with numbers all day. "This stuff is fascinating. I'm lost without my computer, and these men did everything with a quill pen and an abacus."

"I typed my first few books on a Royal typewriter," I reminded him, "if you can imagine that."

"I'd rather not," said Grady, drawing a nod from Donna.

I continued my own deliberate process, finding

plenty of pages of note but none that appeared particularly relevant to the investigation in which I found myself embroiled. That is, until I came to a notebook with a title that grabbed my attention immediately:

THE JOURNAL OF JOHN HENRY CABOT

I felt a surge of excitement that left a buzzing in my head as I cautiously eased the frayed leather cover over to the side. I skimmed the contents initially, paging through material that was utterly fascinating but not at all related, until I came to a section from 1795 I sensed might be just what I was looking for.

"Whatcha doing, Aunt Jess?" little Frank wondered, having appeared by my side.

"Reading."

"Reading what?"

"A journal."

He peered over the tabletop. "It looks old."

"It is, Frank, very old."

"Older than you?"

I watched both Donna and Grady stifle laughs. "Oh, much older."

"That's really old," the boy noted, pushing himself into my lap. "Can you read it to me?"

"I don't know," I told him. "But let's give it a try. . . ."

Chapter Seventeen

From the Journal of John Henry Cabot

Cabot Cove, 1795

He gave us no choice. You may regard these pages as a confession or an explanation if that makes it easier to accept them and think no less of me. When you read them, I ask only that you consider the betrayal that led us down the road we find ourselves on, a road we are now bound to forever. What I write here I have never put pen to before, keeping the secret we all swore to keep until that betrayal forced us to disavow our word. I put all this in writing so that history may judge our actions for what they were and why we undertook them. There is much here that has never been told before. And what has been told before was never told in all its truth. The country knew of our great works in building a town from scratch. Until now, though, the truth of how we built Cabot Cove has never come to light, residing instead in the darkness that welcomed it, and for good reason.

You will judge my deeds and actions, of that I have no doubt, and I ask only that you judge me on what I had to do that was never my stated intention. His actions left us no choice. I had expected my legacy to be many things, murderer never among them. . . .

"Murder," little Frank said, stopping me there. "That's when you kill someone."

I'd altered the language to be more colloquial for a contemporary audience, while not deviating from the substance. To my surprise, little Frank seemed enraptured by the tale of history coming to life, and his parents had paused their labors to listen as well.

"That's right, Frank," I told him. "Very good."

"Someone bad?"

"Sometimes, but not always."

"Good people get murdered, too?"

"Unfortunately, yes," I said, thinking of Sheila Del Perrio.

"Is that who gets murdered in the story, Aunt Jess?"

"I don't know," I said to my grandnephew. "Let's find out."

By 1794, our money was running out. We'd spent everything we had on the port, and now there was precious little left to invest in the expansion we had anticipated. The inability of Wyatt Rackley to contribute his fair share has proven a terrible detriment, leading to a setback we will be hard-pressed to weather.

I trust the others well enough, but not so Rackley. He has proven himself a scoundrel at every turn, and we have only continued to tolerate him because we have already cast our die with him. Nonetheless, the time has come to finally cut our ties through whatever means are necessary. I fear he has swindled us and we were fools to trust him and give him the rope he would hang us with for the one-fifth share he is no longer entitled to and might never exist anyway unless we find a suitable source of fresh income. The Boston banks will hear nothing of us since we left their home shores. They see us as traitors and will not further fund our efforts since we were not truthful about our intentions in coming north. We are at this point quite lost, floundering in the sea with no one to effect our rescue.

It was Rackley who kept us from going under. We trusted him no more but had no choice but to rely on him no less. Rackley was well acquainted with the kind of undesirable sorts with whom we needed to do business on the seas, especially when it came to the import of slaves we would then send overland to points west and south. Scoundrels, I suppose, keep their own company and are loath to betray each other, as if that would break some code held by those of a black heart and always adhered to. But this was too much to turn down, and even if we had the fortitude to reject the overtures that proved a lifeline to our efforts in the north, we would only be opening the door for someone else to take advantage of the riches dropped at our feet.

"Can hearts really be black?" little Frank asked me.

"It's more of a saying to describe bad people."

"Like evil," Grady elaborated, using the term I'd meant to use.

"Like evil," I agreed, "yes."

Little Frank pondered that. "Did you write this story, Aunt Jess?"

"No, Frank, not this one."

"Who did?"

"A man named John Henry Cabot, the man Cabot Cove is named for."

"Wow, he must've been important."

"He was."

"Was he evil?"

"What do you think?" I asked the boy, not sure of the answer myself yet.

"That they wouldn't have named the town Cabot Cove if he was a bad man. He must have done something good, something that helped people, right?"

I nodded. "Good question."

I must now commit to paper something I have never even spoken of outside of the five of us, four now, something that both saved and destroyed us. I bear blame and deserve punishment, for I went into this with eyes wide open and not turning away from the consequences or ramifications of my actions.

With our port open, our primary trading partners were French merchants sailing up through the West Indies and stopping at our docks before making the long eastward journey home with their holds still heavily stocked. Rackley proved his worth in negotiating favored status with such merchants and sea-men for whom coin dangled before them could make them jump like a circus monkey. But our coin had been drained to a frightful level, too much going out without enough coming in, and uncollected receipts becoming a harbinger of our ultimate failure and business death.

It was Rackley who found the opportunity for our work to continue, so we might not need to abandon the cove and return to Boston in disgrace, prepared to accept a much lower station in life, if not prison itself. The depths of the continuing revolution in France had begun to cost us a hefty measure of our trading, which came close to sounding our death knell, until a merchant as unsavory as Rackley came to his brother of black hearts with a deal that matched one desperate party with another.

Rackley informed us of the details of something we had heard only inklings and rumors of, specifically a theft in Paris beyond all reasonable measure. The crown jewels themselves had been absconded with; Rackley was quite specific with the listing of the gems stolen from the Garde Meuble when the revolution was raging.

The Charlemagne crown
Louis XV's coronation crown
The gold scepter of Charles V
The ivory-topped gold scepter known as "le main de justice"
The Ampulla
The coronation sword

There was far more in this pilfered treasure, including orbs, onyx chalices, and assorted historic relics. But what Rackley was most boastful about were the jewels that included the Regent diamond, the French Blue diamond, the Sancy, and the Hortensia. Not all of this inventory was certain to be available from the thieves Rackley knew from the criminal world he often traveled in. But the remainder of the treasure included thousands of diamonds collected through the ages that would be much easier to transfer through the dark channels Rackley was fond of negotiating.

He explained to us that the thieves had climbed up the building's colonnade facing the Place Louis XV and gained access through a window. Once inside, they had broken the seals on eleven cabinets containing the royal crown jewels, as well as the state and coronation regalia. If we could raise the money, the bulk of those diamonds could be ours at a fraction of their true worth and we would be free to use them as tender to expand our interests and realize the dreams that brought us north from Boston. The plans were all laid. All we needed was the capital to bring them to fruition.

"What's 'fruition,' Aunt Jess?" little Frank asked me, still as engrossed by this tale as his parents were.

"It means *brought to an end*," I told him, elaborating further, *"a successful result."*

"Sometimes my dad reads me parts of your books. I'm supposed to stop him whenever he comes to a word I don't know."

I looked toward Grady, who nodded almost shyly.

"I can almost read them myself now, Aunt Jess!"

the boy boasted. "At least some parts," he added as an afterthought. "Can you get back to the story now?"

"Yes, Aunt Jess," his father echoed as his mother nodded up a storm, "can you get back to the story?"

"By all means . . ."

Our mistake was to trust Rackley, but our choices were limited. If we wanted to remain within the world we were building, we had to take unsavory, disheartening measures that would make us lesser men. But we were able to raise the funds required for Rackley's criminal contacts who would broker the deal and required a substantial price up front. Again, with no choice, we did as we must. I never understood until that moment what it meant for a man to sell his soul, and we all sold ours in making this veritable bargain with the devil.

Rackley's criminal contacts extended to New York and Philadelphia, unsavory sorts there who would pay a fetching price for these diamonds they could still sell off at a significant profit. On the surface, money was made at every level from the thieves, their brokers in France, the French traders who traveled across the sea with the bounty, us, and then the criminal element who would make great profits once they found suitable buyers amid the former colonies for our stolen wares.

We were wise in how we conducted our business so as not to draw the kind of attention to our acts that would have branded us criminals, and rightfully so. The diamonds were transferred from our possession over the course of several months stretching to over a year, the process slowing as our needs declined with the building of our businesses in fishing, canning, and manufacturing. The money reaped from the sales of the diamonds financed construction of some of the largest factories and mills in the entire country. Men came north for the work and brought their families to make our settlement feel like a real city. We built schools and churches. Commerce followed and grew and we lost sight of the transgressions that brought us to such heights. We tried to tell ourselves it was all right because no one had been hurt and many, many had benefited from the discomfort of our actions.

Then Rackley informed us he could move no more of the diamonds through his contacts in New York and Philadelphia, that he needed to travel west to the fledging states there. He claimed to know, at least know of, a pirate named Jean Lafitte who bore a special affinity for precious stones and would enjoy nothing more than to purchase a grand portion of our remaining stock. So we blessed Rackley's intention and his mission, still not fully trusting him but having no choice but to acquiesce to his plans. Indeed, he had made us dependent on his efforts, hostage to his dark whims and foibles. Our greatest sin was in looking the other way. Our greatest error was not realizing that such a fool's errand could only end badly.

Which it did.

"I don't like Rackee, Aunt Jess," little Frank noted after a hefty yawn.

I didn't bother correcting his pronunciation of the name. "Me either, Frank."

"You write about people like him in your books, don't you?"

"Sometimes."

"Why do you do that if you don't like them?"

I looked up at that point and saw both Grady and Donna stifling laughs. Ah, to try to explain the intricacies of plotting to an eight-year-old . . .

"Do you remember the first movie we ever watched together?" I asked my grandnephew.

"The one with the dogs, the dogs with the spots."

"One Hundred and One Dalmatians," I reminded him. "The original Disney movie. You remember it?"

"I remember it was really old."

"Do you remember the woman who wanted to turn all those spotted puppies into a coat?"

Little Frank sneered. "She was mean, really mean."

"Her name was Cruella de Vil, and all stories need someone like that because it makes the good people, the heroes, seem better."

"Oh." Little Frank looked down and then up again. "Do true stories have bad people in them like fake stories?"

"All too often, yes."

"I want to see if the bad man in this story loses the way the woman who stole all those puppies lost in the dog movie."

"Only one way to find out," I told him, and went back to John Henry Cabot's journal.

Rackley talked too much. He also drank too much, which made for a bad combination. And shortly before he was to set out on his journey to the West, that tendency proved to be his fateful undoing.

He blabbered to a friend in the local tavern that, yes, he was headed west, but that he had no intention of returning or selling the remaining stores of diamonds to the pirate Jean Lafitte or anyone else. The rest of us shouldn't have been surprised by his treachery, for he had already shown his true nature innumerable times. But we never expected treacherous behavior of this scale. The four of us were men of honor, and even though we knew Rackley to be no such thing, he would not dare cheat us. The fact that he had proven himself by preserving our efforts with the illicit deal he brokered had further ingratiated him with us. After all, the profits we reaped from the sales of the diamonds and other jewels had financed construction of our fishery, cannery, and a textile mill that was envisioned as the cornerstone of bringing industry north.

Our village offered conditions that rendered it ideal for business. Merchants would bring the finest in yarns and fabrics to our shores and leave with their cargo holds packed with the finished products manufactured from their wares. We envisioned a thriving town, a small city comprising laborers as well as fishermen. We viewed such industry in terms of the collective, seeing it as a way to lure the best Boston and elsewhere had to offer to sprinkle our coastline with homes and families. McMullen was a believer in education and insisted on including in our plan the best schools New England had ever seen, so that the youth who migrated here with their parents would know the most prosperous future imaginable.

It was truly a grand vision that Wyatt Rackley was now threatening to besmirch. We could do without the proceeds gained from the sale of the additional diamonds, but we could not abide his treachery. So we agreed to confront him together, challenge him on his intentions, and bid him on his way wherever he desired only after he turned over four-fifths of the remaining diamonds so we might consider ourselves fairer men than he.

Little Frank had fallen asleep on my lap. I was grateful for that, since it spared me the need to massage the fate I knew awaited Wyatt Rackley in the ensuing pages. As much as I'm exposed to violence in investigations like the one in which I was currently embroiled, I utterly abhor it and avoid it in my books at all costs. Even though it was true, I didn't want to subject little Frank to a tale that would end with one of the other four founders of Cabot Cove taking a hatchet to Rackley's head.

"This is an amazing story, Aunt Jess," Grady said softly, so as not to rouse his son.

"Made even more amazing by the fact that it's connected with more murders being committed today," Donna added, growing more comfortable in my presence.

She'd always been shy around me, and I took this particular moment of opening up to be a welcome sign indeed.

"How does it all end?" Donna asked eagerly.

That moved me to return my attention to John Henry Cabot's unearthed journal, lowering my voice to barely above a whisper when I resumed.

I write this entry, committing my acts to paper, so I might someday be forgiven for my sins. We should have known how Rackley would react. We should have known the inevitability of what would come of our accusations and threats lodged against him. We had trafficked in stolen goods, were party in that respect to a crime already made something of legend. We were criminals all.

Rackley did not take well to our charges, sought to deny them all. But he also refused at all costs to turn over the remaining reserves of diamonds to us on the pretext that we no longer had his trust. Our protestations to that effect became more pointed. Charges and accusations became threats. There were four of us and only one of him. Rackley was used to achieving victory with his tongue more than his sword, but we were hearing none of that on this oh so terrible night.

He finally agreed to turn over the remaining diamonds to our care. Then he moved to their purported hiding place and pulled out a pair of muskets instead. The tables had turned, Rackley now threatening us. What do civilized men do when faced with such action? But Rackley had forgotten we'd all fought for our lives in the Revolution and were no strangers to blood.

When he moved to threaten the others, intending, I was sure, to shoot at least one to make his point, I took the hatchet from where it was wedged in my belt and—

I stopped my narration there, no reason to finish the rest of the story out loud. What followed was all there in John Henry Cabot's journal, how he'd taken the hatchet to Wyatt Rackley, lodging a single blow to the head that must have been almost instantly fatal. Then the remaining founding fathers of Cabot Cove conceived a plan where Rackley's remains would be hidden away and the story circulated that he had departed as planned. Since that had been his stated intention, no one close to him, including his family, questioned the move.

I knew that how Cabot, McMullen, Hutchinson, and Van Webb managed to perpetrate the hoax must be contained in the rest of Cabot's journal. Communication and correspondence being what they were in those days, I was sure it made their task considerably easier, just as their status and reputations would have led no one to question them, everyone taking the men at their word with regard to Wyatt Rackley.

"All this," Grady said, voice kept soft as he gestured toward all the material piled on my kitchen table, "was buried in your backyard?"

I nodded. "Along with two sets of bones, one of which almost surely belonged to Wyatt Rackley."

"What about the second set of bones?" Donna asked me.

"A woman, about your age I suspect, who was shot in the area of a year ago."

It was Grady's turn to nod. "So whoever buried the remains and chest in your backyard . . ."

"Very well may have murdered that young woman we've yet to identify."

Donna shuddered. "About my age . . . What an awful story."

"Made even more so by the fact that it's all true."

She looked toward her husband. "Please don't encourage her to write such things."

"In this case," Grady reminded her, "somebody already did write it: John Henry Cabot. I wonder how the people of Cabot Cove will take to the fact that the man the town's named after was a murderer."

I thought of the pretext that had supposedly lured Tad Hollenbeck up here. "I'm sure many will find it perfectly fitting."

"What about the diamonds?" Donna whispered, when little Frank stirred and rubbed at his eyes.

I read ahead in John Henry Cabot's journal a bit. "According to this, they were nowhere to be found in Rackley's home, and it appears Cabot and the others searched it extensively. Cabot believed Rackley must've squirreled them away somewhere, but . . ."

I scanned some more pages, focusing only on sections of note.

"It doesn't appear he and the others ever found them, at least not in the weeks that followed," I resumed.

"So these diamonds—" Grady started in his normal tone.

"Shhh," Donna cautioned.

"So these diamonds," Grady said softer, "must be the treasure this television reporter came to Cabot Cove after. Now, that would have made a great story for *Stalker*."

I tightened my gaze on him. "Please tell me you don't watch that show, Grady."

"Never, Aunt Jess—well, *almost* never." A pause,

then: "Well, only sometimes when I'm flipping through channels."

I rolled my eyes at hearing that yet again. "Either way, I believe you're right. These lost diamonds, hundreds of them potentially, have become the last legacy left to Cabot Cove by the town's founders. They caused one murder in 1795 and, all these years later, two more this week."

"But where are they?" Donna asked. "Does that journal provide any idea at all?"

"No," I told her, "but I know somebody who might be able to."

Chapter Eighteen

Amazing," commented Fred Hardesty the next morning, Friday, the day before Christmas Eve, looking up from his careful inspection of John Henry Cabot's journal, undertaken with the aid of a magnifying monocle held over his right eye, "simply amazing."

He tugged at his mustache with his free hand, a gesture I'd probably witnessed a thousand times. Mort and I had walked over to Fred's antiques shop after having breakfast with Seth at Mara's. The night before had left me utterly exhausted by the time I finished recounting the contents of that section from John Henry Cabot's journal. Grady and Donna, though, stayed up long enough to shift the contents of my refrigerator about enough to make room for the documents long stored in the colonial-era chest, since it was much too large to fit inside itself. There was ample room to maneuver, save for the spot claimed by the

Christmas turkey I couldn't wait to baste and smell cooking throughout the day, since I was planning on stocking up on provisions today. I had since delegated that task to Grady and Donna, though I'd been looking forward to doing some real grocery shopping for the first time in months.

"How close does it come to your understanding of our town's early history?" I asked Fred.

"It's utterly earth-shattering. Feel the floor, Mrs. Fletcher. It's moving beneath our feet." He looked up at me, then back down at the leather-clad document just as fast. "And that business about the founding fathers' involvement in the slave trade to boot . . . This is truly an early Christmas present, on top of all you left with me yesterday. I reviewed them for much of the night but didn't uncover anything nearly as interesting as this."

Fred went back to work under the spray of an old-fashioned adjustable desk lamp beneath that elegant nonworking antique chandelier that hung from the ceiling. He could have modified the chandelier to modern working condition, but a man like him would have found that to be an affront to history. For Fred Hardesty, its true light lay in its history as an ornament that had once hung in some French nobleman's manor. I could only imagine all that had transpired beneath it over the years, and all the history that resided in the chandelier's shadow thanks to the shop's precious wares. To Fred Hardesty it was history at its best, and, like many of his most favored keepsakes that adorned his shop, he'd likely never be able to part with it. Not a great way to make a living, especially given the newly steep rents on Main Street, but I knew Fred would fight to his last penny to operate the shop on his own terms.

"Did you notice the paper, Mrs. Fletcher?" he asked me, barely able to restrain his enthusiasm.

"What about it?"

"Well, as you know, paper wasn't always so bountiful, nor was it cheap, nor was it made from wood pulp like today's paper usually is. Paper, in the post-colonial age, was like most things: precious, and coming as a result of much toil. Important documents were often written on parchment, which is made from lambskin. That would be what the final version of the Declaration of Independence is written on, though not the earlier drafts. No, those were printed on the same thing most books, newspapers, and correspondence would use—what might have been called rag paper, linen paper, or cotton paper. This would be the highest end of that selection," Fred continued, moving the current page down and back up again as if to test its weight. "Not quite as weighty as parchment but heavier than rag, linen, or cotton. That might explain how it weathered the years, and held the ink, so well."

"History may be coming alive for you, Mr. Hardesty," Mort picked up, sounding impatient, "but we've got two murder victims who won't be doing that anytime soon."

Fred nodded. "So terrible about Mrs. Del Perrio. She was a great customer and I used to love watching her meander through the shop, even when she didn't purchase anything. Speaking of which," he said to me more than Mort, "do you plan on telling Clara Wizzenhunt the truth about her ancestor?"

"I hadn't actually given it any thought."

"You ever meet her nephew, Lucas Rackley, Mr. Hardesty?" Mort asked him.

"I believe he's been in the store once or twice, but I can't say we've actually met. To tell you the truth, I found him uniquely unpleasant."

"You and me both." Mort nodded.

Fred looked back toward me. "So, Mrs. Fletcher, you and the sheriff believe these recent murders might well be connected with that of Wyatt Rackley in 1795?"

"Connected more with the missing diamonds," I corrected. "I was hoping you might have some thoughts on that."

"As in . . ."

"As in what may have become of them."

Fred pondered that for a moment. "Assuming Wyatt Rackley did hide the diamonds somewhere they were never found, are we thinking they might still be in the very same place?"

"After two hundred and however many years?" Mort groused skeptically.

"It's possible, Sheriff," Fred informed him, "more than possible if they were hidden away in a wall or a crawl space, maybe buried in a grave or something like that."

Mort and I looked at each other, both of us thinking about that footage Tad Hollenbeck had shot at the entrance to town.

I watched Mort make a note on his magical memo

pad. "So we'd be looking for graves prior to Rackley's killing in 1795. How many of those can there be?"

Fred thought for a moment. "The founders headed up this way in 1791 and at last check of the historical register, I believe there are somewhere around two hundred marked graves in the three years that followed that have weathered the years."

"More than I was figuring," Mort said, looking up from his memo pad.

"And that doesn't account for all the unmarked graves in backyards and land that was wild at the time. I'm sure some families buried their loved ones in the woods."

"I've got something back at the office to help us out, Mrs. F.," Mort said, offering no further explanation.

"So we're operating on the theory—possibility, anyway—that whoever killed that woman at least a year ago also killed Tad Hollenbeck and Sheila Del Perrio. And that he, or she, is the one who buried the evidence in your backyard after digging it up from wherever it was buried before," Mort said after we'd closed the door to Fred Hardesty's antiques shop behind us.

"Never believing it would be found," I acknowledged. "At least not for many years. The only connection between Tad Hollenbeck and Sheila Del Perrio was that they were both descendants of the original founders. That means our killer might well be targeting anyone he believes might come between him and the diamonds."

"People who hold some claim to them, in other

words," Mort agreed, his expression as flat as the Maine Turnpike. "There's something else, too. The state police crime lab called while you were speaking with Fred Hardesty."

He cocked his gaze back toward the door through which we'd just exited, leaving me to wonder when exactly he'd taken that call.

"Turns out," Mort continued, "that those black strands that were found in both Tad Hollenbeck's motel room and Sheila Del Perrio's living room weren't hairs at all. They're plastic, some kind of composite material. The lab's running further tests to identify it. And they came up with something else, too, pertaining to dirt."

"Dirt?"

Mort nodded. "Apparently, the bones found in your backyard had traces of dirt that didn't match your backyard. Lab techs have already gathered samples from other areas around town in the hope of identifying where those remains were originally buried."

His phone beeped with an incoming text.

"Dan Kinder just told us where we can meet him."

Not surprisingly, winter was Dan Kinder's busiest season, what with residents really firing up their furnaces, some of which dated well back into the last century, for the first time. We found him on a job in the middle of a neighborhood fondly known as the Hill because it was perched on one. Considering what Frank and I paid for our home way back when, the contrast with today's real estate values was striking.

With the taxes and all, I didn't know how regular people got by anymore, even though Cabot Cove had initiated several new financial incentives to keep longtime residents from moving, only to be replaced by mostly summer residents who wouldn't hesitate to let their homes go empty for all but three or so months of the year. Longtime residents grudgingly accepted our town's status as a bustling summer locale now, but not at the expense of being forced to relocate.

Kinder had told the owner of the house to expect us, and that owner ushered us down into the basement, where Kinder had been rebuilding an ancient burner for several hours. We found him kneeling amid a clutter of disassembled parts that exposed the guts of a burner that looked like it sprang from the nineteenth century, never mind twentieth.

"Heard you moved back home finally, Mrs. Fletcher," Kinder said, barely looking up from his tools.

"Calling you to make sure my burner is in good working order is one of the things on my list."

"Hope you can wait until after the New Year."

"Based on the last few nights, I should be able to last until then, Dan."

He started fitting the disassembled burner back together again. "So, what's so important you needed to see me on a job?" he said, the question aimed at Mort more than me.

"What can you tell us about John Van Webb, Mr. Kinder?"

"How many times have I been over to service your heating and air-conditioning systems, Sheriff? I think you can call me Dan."

"I'll stick with Mr. Kinder, if you don't mind. More professional."

Kinder lowered the tool he was holding, some kind of wrench. "This is a professional visit?"

"We wouldn't have bothered you if it wasn't."

"Did I do something wrong?"

"Yes," Mort told him, "when you couldn't convince Adele to sleep with the windows closed."

"Once a Marine, always a Marine, right?"

"That's right. You served, too. Gulf War, wasn't it?"

"The real one," Dan Kinder told him. "And I heard you did a stretch in Vietnam."

"Do I really look that old?"

"Your boiler did, as I recall." He lifted the wrench again and resumed working. "So what can I do for you? Since Mrs. Fletcher's here, too, I'm feeling a bit uneasy."

"You heard about the deaths of a man named Tad Hollenbeck and Sheila Del Perrio, I assume."

Kinder nodded from behind the boiler he was putting back together. "*Murder* is the word going around town."

"And rightfully so, both connected to the founding fathers of Cabot Cove. The victims were descendants of two of them," Mort explained.

"Earl Grove Hutchinson for Del Perrio and John Henry Cabot in the case of Hollenbeck," I elaborated.

"Wait a minute," Kinder said, something triggered in his mind. "Is that the Hollenbeck who's a reporter for that show *Stalker*?"

"Not anymore," Mort noted, leaving me wondering if there was anyone in town who *didn't* watch *Stalker*.

Kinder alternated his suddenly incredulous gaze between both of us. "So are you here to tell me I may be in danger?"

"The thought had crossed our minds," I conceded. "But we're really here to see if you knew anything about your ancestor, John Van Webb. If there were any particular stories that have been passed down through the years."

"Like what?"

"The early days in Cabot Cove," Mort picked up, "especially regarding one of the original founders named Wyatt Rackley."

"I know the name," Kinder told us, appearing distracted, "but that's pretty much all. Wait, could we get back to this descendant thing, specifically the murders? Why would somebody be killing descendants of the men who built this town?"

Mort stepped over some tools and stray parts to move closer to him. "That's another reason we wanted to see you, Mr. Kinder. To see if you'd noticed anything or anyone unusual lately, the last week or so."

He shook his head. "No, Sheriff, nothing that stands out."

I started to follow Mort's path to draw nearer to Dan Kinder but spotted something in the process that froze my thinking. There was something I'd been about to say that totally slipped my mind, my attention somewhere else entirely. I stooped and retrieved something from the basement floor as unobtrusively as I could manage.

"Are you aware that Tad Hollenbeck shot some

footage outside your home not long before he died?" Mort asked next.

"First I've heard of it." Kinder's gaze seemed to waver a bit. "Word also was that Hollenbeck was in town to do a story for *Stalker* on the murder rate in these parts."

"We believe that was just a cover," I said. "Did anyone in your family ever mention anything about a lost treasure?"

"Lost treasure? Nothing I can remember, no. You think it has something to do with these murders, Mrs. Fletcher?"

"I think it's what really drew Tad Hollenbeck to Cabot Cove."

"To claim it?"

"More like, to find it."

"You mean the treasure's still here in town?"

"Hollenbeck believed it was," Mort interjected. "That's what brought him here and maybe what got him killed, too."

"We have reason to believe that he and Sheila Del Perrio were murdered by the same person," I added.

"I knew Sheila," Kinder said sadly. "Did some work at the restaurant from time to time. She was a nice lady. So you think this treasure has something to do with her murder?"

I held the floor. "More likely, the killer is after the treasure and figures one of the descendants of the original founders must be hiding it."

"Well, I can't tell whoever it is a darn thing, so I'm safe."

"That's probably how the previous two murder victims felt," Mort told him.

"Know what I think?"

Mort gestured for him to continue.

"That your little visit here is about wondering if I'm the killer, not a potential victim. That's right, isn't it, Mrs. Fletcher?"

"We have no reason to believe anything of the kind, Mr. Kinder," I told him. "Right now we're just following the leads where they go, and there's plenty of reason to believe you may be targeted next."

"Because you're related to John Van Webb," Mort added. "Are you sure you can't tell us anything about him or the other founders?"

"I haven't always been on great terms with my family, Sheriff, so it's not like we sit around the fire talking about such things. In fact, I don't sit around the fire with any of my relatives at all and wouldn't know most of them if I passed them on the street. You want to invite them over for Christmas dinner, I'll give you the numbers I haven't deleted from my phone."

"Well," said Mort, "if you think of anything . . ."

"Sure, Sheriff, I know where to find you. Merry Christmas," Kinder added as an afterthought.

Mort nodded. "We'll see about that, Dan."

"I need to show you something," I said to Mort, fishing about in the top of my bag for what I'd plucked off the basement floor.

I was still fishing about when Mort's phone rang, and he answered it as we continued toward his SUV.

"You don't say. . . . No, put him in a cell. I'm on my

way back now." Mort looked toward me as he ended the call. "You're not going to believe this, Mrs. F., but one of my deputies just arrested Clara Wizzenhunt's nephew, Lucas, for causing a disturbance at Shady Willows—a *violent* disturbance."

"Just like you're not going to believe this," I said, flashing what I'd finally located in my handbag.

Chapter Nineteen

Mort narrowed his gaze on the thin black shavings I was holding in my palm.

"Those look just like . . ."

"Those black strands we thought might be hairs at both murder scenes," I completed for Mort. "They must have come from whatever work Dan Kinder was doing on that boiler."

Mort continued to regard the potential evidence displayed in my palm. "They look like the same shavings we found in Tad Hollenbeck's motel room and Sheila Del Perrio's living room."

"Not too much of a reach to picture some of these getting caught in the treads on Kinder's work boots, is it?" I asked him.

"Not too much, no, Mrs. F. You looking at Dan Kinder as the killer?"

I nodded. "I will be if these come back a match for the shavings we found at the two murder scenes."

Mort slid an evidence bag from his pocket and held it open while I dropped the twin shavings, or whatever they were, inside.

"Why don't we head down to the station and see about that tantrum Lucas Rackley threw down at Shady Willows, Mrs. F.?"

"Did your deputy provide any more details?"

"You bet. He said Rackley wanted to kill his aunt Clara."

The single light in Lucas Rackley's cell in the basement of the sheriff's station made his jet-black hair look like paint slathered over his scalp. He wore the same combination of scowl and smirk on his face I recalled from yesterday at Shady Willows, leaving me wondering if this was the default setting of his face.

Mort unlocked the door and escorted the young man upstairs to the station's single interrogation room, which was also utilized for storage, given the scant use it got in fulfilling its primary function. Mort and I took chairs on the opposite side of the table, his positioned directly in front of Lucas Rackley with mine set off to the side a bit.

"Let's talk about your ancestor Wyatt Rackley, Lucas," Mort said, surprising me by starting out with that.

The scowl became more of a smirk. "Why, am I accused of wanting to see him dead, too?"

"Somebody did, son. In fact, they killed him."

Rackley flashed genuine surprise. He looked at me before refocusing on Mort.

"Am I missing something here, Sheriff?"

"Your marbles for causing a ruckus at Shady Willows, but we'll get to that later. Right now, I thought you might like to know that, by all accounts, your ancestor Wyatt Rackley was a criminal in his own right. And, also by all accounts, he paid the ultimate price for his crimes."

"I've never heard anything about him being arrested."

"Because the other founders took matters into their own hands after they realized he was swindling them. My guess, from what Mrs. Fletcher has told me, is that he'd been doing it for a long time and finally went too far."

"I have absolutely no idea what you're talking about," Rackley insisted.

I looked at him across the table and pictured him as the spitting image of his ancestor, both inside and out. I tried to calculate how old Wyatt Rackley might have been when John Henry Cabot and the other founders killed him, figuring he might well have been about the same age as Lucas was now: mid-thirties, maybe.

"No?" Mort shot back at him, seeming to be enjoying this. "Then can I also assume you know no more about the lost fortune, or treasure, of Cabot Cove's founding fathers than we discussed yesterday at Shady Willows?"

"I don't even recall discussing it, because I know nothing about it, save for the rumors that pretty much everyone has heard over the years."

"Like the one about Wyatt Rackley moving west and never returning?"

"Because that's the truth. Everybody knows that."

"Then everybody's wrong. Isn't that right, Mrs. Fletcher?"

"That would definitely appear to be the case, Sheriff," I agreed, thinking of Harry McGraw's findings.

"I don't believe you," Rackley said belligerently.

Mort looked back at Rackley across the table, the young man's face glowing through a light sheen of sweat. "What I believe is that there's no evidence your ancestor ever lived either in Missouri or Louisiana, New Orleans specifically. You can see my dilemma here, Lucas."

"No, actually, I can't."

"You threatening your aunt with harm if she didn't come clean about the whereabouts of this fortune."

"Or treasure," I added.

Lucas Rackley's face scrunched up into a mask of consternation. "That's not what happened at all. I have no idea what you're even talking about."

"So you didn't cause the kind of ruckus at Shady Willows, including threatening your aunt, that led the facility to call the Sheriff's Department?"

Rackley physically collected himself by rolling his shoulders and craning his neck to the sides. "Do you know what they charge her every month in that place?"

"No, son, I don't."

"A lot, let me tell you. But the place is filthy, the food stinks, her television doesn't get her favorite cable channels, and if you call for an attendant you can die waiting for one of them to show up. Know what sparked my outburst this morning? A cockroach scampering across the floor in her room."

"What about the part of that outburst where you threatened her?" Mort asked Lucas Rackley.

"I didn't threaten her, Sheriff. I was expressing my frustration over her living there."

"And how'd you do that?"

"I told her she was crazy, nuts, for living there. I told her she'd be better off dead."

"Told her?"

"I guess I was speaking pretty loudly."

"Witnesses at Shady Willows said you were shouting."

"I might have been," Rackley conceded.

"The facility's staff noted you brought Wyatt Rackley's name into this," I interjected.

"Maybe," Rackley said, pondering that. "Yeah, I'm sure I did, something to the effect of if she had the money she had coming to her, she'd be able to afford to live in a better place."

"Your aunt has lived in Cabot Cove all her life, Lucas," I reminded him. "I doubt very much she'd want to live anywhere else, even if it was a better place."

"I bet you'd like nothing more than to provide a better living situation for your aunt, isn't that right, son?" Mort asked Rackley, not giving him any time to respond. "Were you aware that reporter Tad Hollenbeck shot footage outside Shady Willows talking about how a descendant of the town's original founders inside might know something about a lost fortune?"

"Haven't we been over this already?"

"Just answer the question."

"No."

"So you didn't pay a visit to Hollenbeck's motel room later that night to press him on the matter?"

"I wouldn't have even known where he was staying."

"Really?" Mort gloated. "So you didn't follow him from Shady Willows back to the Surfsider?"

Lucas Rackley looked visibly out of sorts. At first, I thought Mort was bluffing, but the glint in his eyes told me he wasn't.

"I thought you were asking me about what happened this morning," Rackley managed.

"I am—was, anyway. Now I'm asking you about something else. Did you follow Tad Hollenbeck from Shady Willows back to the Surfsider, where he and his film crew were staying?"

When the young man didn't respond, Mort took in hand an envelope that had been lying on the table separating us from Lucas Rackley and slid a photograph from inside it.

"This was captured on security footage taken at Shady Willows," Mort resumed, sliding the still shot across the table. "Probably the only security cameras in the whole town, much to your misfortune, son. You'll notice your car directly behind Hollenbeck's SUV after security personnel told him to leave the property. They informed me someone had alerted them to the filming from an upstairs room. Your aunt's room faces the front of Shady Willows, doesn't it?"

Rackley swallowed hard. He had the look of a man about to ask for his lawyer.

"I can wait until after Christmas for your answer," Mort said, after he continued his silence. "After all, I'll be home celebrating with Adele, while you're back in that basement cell."

"I know enough about this sort of thing to know you'd have to charge me with something, Sheriff," the young man said finally, trying his best to sound strong and indignant and failing miserably.

"Had some previous brushes with the law, then, have you, son?"

"That's none of your business."

"But it does sound like you know your way around a jail cell, doesn't it?"

"I didn't kill Tad Hollenbeck, Sheriff," Rackley said, sounding more imploring than insistent.

"What about Sheila Del Perrio?"

"I never even spoke to the woman."

"She was someone else who'd stand to profit handsomely if this lost treasure ever showed up. Isn't that right, Mrs. Fletcher?"

"It is indeed, Sheriff," I said, grateful for the chance to get my two cents in. "If she hadn't been murdered."

I could tell that got a rise out of him.

"But not before she called your aunt to warn Clara that Hollenbeck would be paying her a visit," I resumed. "But you already knew that, didn't you? Because you took the call from the front desk when they put the call through to your aunt's room."

"That's according to the facility's call log, son," Mort picked up. "So when Tad Hollenbeck showed up on the grounds, you couldn't have been surprised. I might even venture to say that you were waiting for him."

Lucas Rackley leaned across the table. "Look, I didn't kill Tad Hollenbeck or anyone else, all right?

Yes, I spotted Tad Hollenbeck on the Shady Willows grounds. Yes, I recognized him from *Stalker*. . . ."

Ugggghhh, I thought, *another fan of* Stalker.

"And I followed him back to that motel to ask him what he was doing there because I figured it might have something to do with the treasure. I'm no angel, Sheriff. But I didn't kill Tad Hollenbeck. I waited in the motel parking lot until I was sure he was alone just to talk to him, see what he knew."

"What time would this have been?"

"Right around eight."

Mort and I exchanged a glance. That timing would coincide perfectly with when Angie and Selina went to dinner at the coffee shop across the road. I figured Rackley must have been gone by the time Angie knocked on the door as planned, somewhere around eight forty-five.

"I knocked on the door," Rackley resumed, needing no prompting this time, "and he answered it. I was pretty sure he was expecting someone else."

That drew Mort's and my gazes together again.

"Did the two of you speak?" Mort asked him, not wanting to give the young man too much time to think.

"He wouldn't let me inside, but, yeah, we talked. Not for long, but we talked."

"I'm guessing he didn't take well to your accusations," I advanced.

"I didn't accuse him of anything. I just wanted to see if his being in town had anything to do with the lost treasure."

"And what did he say, son?"

"He pretended not to know what I was talking about."

I chimed in again. "How can you be sure he was pretending?"

" 'Cause he was nervous. Kept looking over my shoulder, like he thought I might have brought somebody else with me."

Or Hollenbeck was looking for Angie to emerge from the diner across the street, I thought.

"So you got nothing out of him, in other words," Mort concluded.

Lucas Rackley shook his head. "Not a thing, Sheriff. And I was never even inside his room. Doesn't that place have security cameras or something?"

"The Surfsider?" Mort said, chuckling.

"I didn't kill him," Lucas insisted to us both. "He ended up slamming the door in my face and I left, because the alternative would've been to kick the door in and get myself arrested, which has now happened anyway."

Mort rose, and I took that as my cue to reclaim my feet as well. "You're free to go, son. On one condition."

Lucas Rackley got up tentatively, as grateful as he was suddenly subservient. It's amazing what even a little time spent in a jail cell can do for a bad attitude.

"Anything," he offered.

"You get back to Shady Willows and apologize to your aunt for that outburst."

Lucas's expression turned sad, even maudlin. "I can only hope she remembers, Sheriff."

"What do you think, Mrs. F.?" Mort asked me as we watched Lucas climb into the back of a squad car to be driven back to Shady Willows, where he'd left his car.

"I don't think he's a killer, if that's what you're asking me. What about that more recent set of bones dug out of my backyard on Monday?"

"Nothing yet," Mort said, the frustration clear in his voice. "Adele might put lead in my stocking, but I'm giving serious thought to staying here as long as it takes to sort through every missing persons report of women matching the general description of our victim."

"Maybe I'll join you, Mort."

"You'll do no such thing, Mrs. F., not with Grady and his family visiting." He checked his watch. "First thing I'm going to do is call in one of my deputies to run those black shavings you lifted from that basement straight to the state police crime lab. Then I'd better run you over to the high school so you don't miss the final rehearsal."

"Is it that late?" I said, feeling my stomach shudder.

"No, but I want to make sure you get there early, so Seth Hazlitt doesn't badger me for the entire next year."

Our final rehearsal before the big performance on Christmas Day went beautifully. I can't say exactly when this particular Cabot Cove tradition got started, because there were varying versions of the story. Since around the end of World War II, though, every Christmas afternoon featured a parade up Main Street, led by descendants of Cabot Cove's original founders riding in a horse-drawn carriage. We'd once had a Founders Day parade as well. When that was dispensed with because of poor attendance, the descendants of the town's founding fathers were placed at the head of the Christmas parade instead.

The high school marching band always participated, although the necessity of gloves some years in especially frigid temperatures made playing instruments difficult. A dedicated Santa Claus float was stored for safekeeping by the town's Public Works Department, sabotaged one year by Charlie Deeks after he was replaced in the starring role. I cringed at the thought of playing Mrs. Claus again this year, hoping against hope I'd be able to find a replacement for Seth as Kris Kringle to get me off the hook.

No matter the weather, residents lined Main Street on both sides for the parade before making their way over to the high school for the grand performance of the year's Christmas play before an always packed house.

"Well, Jess." Seth beamed after we'd received a standing ovation from the handful of people in the high school auditorium. "That went swimmingly, I'd say. It would appear having Grady and company in town has been good for your performance as narrator."

"Speaking of which, Seth, we're still expecting you for Christmas dinner."

He fingered his chin and flapped his floppy woolen garb. "Maybe I should come in costume. Don't want to scare little Frank, though, do we?"

"He'll probably think you're a character from one of his video games, and he'll be attending the play beforehand."

Seth nodded. "I'd best get you back home so you can be with him and his parents."

I realized I hadn't checked my phone since I'd gotten there and had turned it off to avoid any distractions whatsoever. I switched it back on to find seven missed calls from Mort.

"Can you give me a moment?" I asked Seth.

"Sure thing. I need to change out of this thing anyway."

Mort answered halfway through the first ring, after Seth had taken his leave for the dressing room.

"My, aren't you persistent?"

"With good reason, Mrs. F. I couldn't wait to tell you."

"Tell me what?"

"About the set of bones dug out of your backyard that date back only about a year. Does the name Patricia Demps mean anything to you?"

"Not a thing."

"Me either. Her family filed a missing persons report on her just over a year ago, shortly after she disappeared without explanation from a Philadelphia suburb. Age thirty-one. Height and weight match our victim perfectly."

"That's hardly enough to be certain they're the same person, Mort."

"There's more, Mrs. F. Demps was her married name. Her maiden name is Hollenbeck. She's Tad Hollenbeck's younger sister."

Chapter Twenty

Mrs. F.?" Mort prodded, when I lapsed into silence.

"Still here. Just pinching myself. You'd think Hollenbeck might have mentioned something to us about his sister."

"Unless it was something he didn't want us to know, maybe lead to more questions he didn't want to answer."

"Patricia Demps, née Hollenbeck, must have come to Cabot Cove after the same thing he did. Maybe she came on her own, without telling anyone. Maybe her brother finally figured things out and that's what drew him here in her wake."

"No pun intended."

"He suspected as much as soon as he heard about the more recent remains, explaining why he was upset."

"His producer also said he was angry, Mrs. F."

"I know what you're thinking, Mort."

"Sure you do, because you're thinking the same thing."

"That they might well have been killed by the same person, Patricia Hollenbeck being the first of the descendants of Cabot Cove's founders to perish on the trail of those lost diamonds. Oh my," I added, my voice cracking.

"What's wrong, Mrs. F.?"

"I just thought of the Christmas parade, the descendants who lead it every year."

"Uh-oh," Mort said, echoing my thinking.

"Easy targets," I elaborated, "for whoever's trying to eliminate anyone with claim to that fortune."

Mort offered to come by and pick me up, but I told him Seth had already volunteered to drive me home. That allowed him to stay in the office and contact the head of the state police crime lab to turn the results of their forensic analysis around as quickly as possible, since more lives might well be hanging in the balance.

I almost hated to raise that but knew that I had to. Mort would have no choice but to devise a security plan to take into account the fact that the surviving ancestors of Cabot Cove's founding fathers might well be targets on Christmas Day for the same killer who'd already murdered Tad Hollenbeck and Sheila Del Perrio.

Not to mention Hollenbeck's sister, Patricia.

I didn't envy Mort the task of informing whoever had filed the missing persons report that she'd been found. That must be the hardest thing about police work, informing the next of kin of a loved one's death.

It's a scene I hate writing in my books and normally avoid at all costs. But you can't script reality.

Mort would likely wait for the real medical examiner, not Seth Hazlitt in his de facto role, to confirm the deceased's identity by comparing her DNA to that of her more recently murdered brother. I lapsed into silence through the whole of the drive to my home from Cabot Cove High School. The latest mystery in which I found myself embroiled continued to grow more complicated. I thought of the surviving descendants, considering that one of them might be a killer instead of a potential victim. Only Clara Wizzenhunt could hardly be considered a suspect, from the halls of Shady Willows, though we couldn't rule out her nephew, Lucas. Meanwhile, that trail of dried mud I'd spotted in Asa Cabot's study had clearly indicated he wasn't suffering from the agoraphobia he wanted the town to believe that he was. Something had drawn him out of the house no more than a day or so before my visit with Mort and, even if we ruled him out as a suspect, that said nothing of his muscular personal assistant, James. The same was true for Dan Kinder and Terry McMullen, descendants, respectively, of John Van Webb and Franklin McMullen. While I considered them potential victims, too, a case could be made that they were an even better fit as suspects. And what better motive than the lost treasure made up of those diamonds the remaining four founding fathers had never recovered in the wake of murdering Wyatt Rackley in 1795?

I always know when it's time to quit a writing session, and that was the same feeling that struck me as Seth turned the corner onto Candlewood Lane. My mind was on overload and I was having trouble keeping all the facts straight. I realized he'd been talking the whole ride and I couldn't remember a thing he'd said.

"Pleasure talking to you, Jess," he groused as he pulled his trusty old Volvo into my driveway right behind Grady's SUV.

Two surprises greeted me when I stepped through the front door. The first was the most beautifully decorated Christmas tree I'd ever seen, a gorgeous six-foot spruce, and the second was none other than Harry McGraw seated on the couch facing it.

"I thought I'd be waiting until New Year's for you to get back home," he said, flashing that tight smile of his and sipping from what looked like a cup of eggnog.

"Merry early Christmas, Aunt Jess," Grady said, swallowing me in his arms as Donna and a beaming little Frank looked on.

The presents stacked into towering piles the night before had been placed under and around the tree, including mine, which my nephew must have fished out of the closet where he knew I always kept them for safekeeping.

"Looks like Santa came early," Grady said, looking toward his son.

"By the way, Jess, thanks for the invite," said Harry.

"Did I invite you?"

"You sure did. Three years ago. Sorry I'm late."

"Uncle Harry brought presents!" pronounced little Frank.

"Six boxes for you," he told me, "with your past-due bills all crammed inside."

"What's *past due* mean, Aunt Jess?" little Frank asked me.

"In this case, *never sent*," I told him while looking at Harry.

"He let me beat him at video games!" the boy continued.

"Did he, now?"

"He must have. Nobody could be that bad at them."

Harry's familiar scowl stretched across his face. "Call it the Christmas spirit, little lady," he told me.

"Whatever you say, Harry."

"I say we better have a talk."

"You drove all this way to tell me something?" I said to him after we'd adjourned upstairs to my office for some privacy.

"Well, Christmas dinner might have had something to do with it. Remember our last conversation?"

I nodded. "You'd uncovered the fact that there was no real evidence that Wyatt Rackley ever left Cabot Cove."

He matched my nod. "You won't believe what I uncovered next."

"How about the fact that Tad's sister, Patricia, disappeared just over a year ago and might well belong to the more recent of the remains dug out of my backyard on Monday?"

He sighed and shook his head. "Now I know why you don't pay your bills. You must have my office bugged."

"I thought you closed your office."

"Because it was bugged. And that's not the only thing I kind of drove up here to tell you. Nice turkey in the fridge, by the way. I prefer dark meat."

"I'm listening, Harry."

"Did you know Patricia Demps drove a burgundy Altima, leased brand-new? I found traffic-cam shots of it, with matching license plate, on the Maine Turnpike."

"Going back about a year maybe?"

Harry stuck out a hand instead of answering. "Pay up."

"What do I owe you?"

"Let's round it off to a signed set of all your books."

"You don't read, Harry."

"No, but if you don't survive until the New Year, imagine what they'll be worth."

"I'd prefer paying you with a check."

"You'd prefer not paying me at all, little lady. But I can tell you that Patricia Demps must have reached Cabot Cove late afternoon on December fourth of last year. How does that jibe with your timetable?"

"About as close as it gets. What about her car, Harry? Was it ever found?"

He nodded. "In Boston. It was towed off the street during a snowstorm around six weeks later."

"So the car remained in Cabot Cove for a while, several weeks probably," I concluded.

"Hidden away for sure, little lady."

"Until the killer decided to stash it down in Boston."

He nodded again. "I can read your mind."

"What am I thinking?"

"Did Harry find any traffic-camera shots of the Altima heading south on the Maine Turnpike after December fourth? And the answer's no, I didn't."

"Because Patricia Demps's killer knew to avoid them."

"Either a hardened criminal or someone who spends a lot of time reading books like yours to pick up hints on how to get away with murder."

"In my books, the murderer always gets caught."

"That's the point. Patricia Demps's killer must have learned from their mistakes. Anyway, her family has been proceeding on the notion that something happened to her in Boston that accounts for her disappearance. Cabot Cove, by all indications, has never even been on their radar. Any other questions?"

"You wouldn't happen to know what she did and who she saw when she got to Cabot Cove, would you?"

"Not yet, no. But I can tell you her and her husband's finances make mine look good. Suffice it to say that once they declared bankruptcy, there wouldn't be a lot of assets to list."

"They declared bankruptcy?"

"On the verge when Patricia headed up here from Philadelphia." Harry rolled my desk chair forward. "So, you want to tell me about whatever it was she came to Cabot Cove looking for or should I guess?"

"Diamonds?" he posed, after I'd completed an abridged version of the tale from John Henry Cabot's journal. "Why didn't you tell me?"

"I just told you. And I only learned about them myself last night."

He checked his watch dramatically. "Hmm, last night would have been, what, maybe a day ago? A lot of hours without picking up the phone and filling me in."

"I'm sorry."

"For what?"

"Not filling you in about the diamonds."

"What about for not paying your bills?"

"By the way," I said to Harry, "your invite to Christmas dinner comes with a catch."

"What's that?"

"Have you ever played Santa Claus?"

Harry grudgingly agreed to take on the role at the Christmas parade, mostly because he felt like he'd be able to keep an eye on everything while everyone just waited for him to say, "Ho, ho, ho!"

I left Harry upstairs behind my computer and found Grady downstairs alone in the living room, the sound of the monster television on my TV room wall telling me Donna and little Frank were likely watching a movie. The one structural change I'd made to the layout of the house during the renovation was to enclose a screen porch I seldom used and convert it into what people call a media room these days. Having only just moved back here, I couldn't say yet whether I'd get a lot of use out of the repurposed space, but it would certainly encourage little Frank to want to visit more often, and that was good enough for me.

I thought it odd that Grady hadn't joined his son and wife, until I saw his right knee bouncing up and down. That had been a nervous tic of his ever since he was a little boy, which manifested whenever something was bothering him.

I sat down on the couch opposite him in his chair. "What's wrong, Grady?"

He flashed surprise at first, then looked down at his knee and stilled it with a hand. "I wasn't totally honest with you last night, Aunt Jess."

"About what?"

"About why I want to open my own accounting firm. I'm being laid off."

The news hit me like a punch to the stomach. "Oh, Grady, I'm so sorry. You've been with them, my, it seems like forever."

"Since before Frank was born, anyway," he acknowledged. "It wasn't that I did anything wrong, more that the firm is reconstituting itself to focus on financial planning and that sort of thing. I've always been just a regular tax accountant. Always figured that so long as I did my homework and served the tax needs of our clients, I was as secure as it got. The problem is more people are doing their own taxes on the Internet these days, and the ones who aren't are relying increasingly on discount shops like H&R Block."

"Well, you've done a great job with my taxes these past few years," I told him. "Saved me a boatload of money. Doesn't that count for anything anymore?"

"Whatever you're charged is nickels and dimes so far as the firm is concerned. They're still going to offer tax services, but only to the customers who are also looking for financial planning and wealth management. It's a rebranding, and I don't fit into the new brand, or so they tell me."

I could see how much it pained Grady to tell me that, the embarrassment and modicum of shame, not to mention fear over the sudden inability to provide for his family. Donna maintained her own business restoring old books and dabbling in custom binding, but the revenue of that amounted to only a fraction of what it took to raise a family in New York, and I detested the notion of them having to move from the apartment that was the only home little Frank had ever known.

"But I've got a plan, Aunt Jess. I know I can make this work. I'm going to rent space out to accountants looking to downsize, like Herb Katz," Grady said, referring to the accountant who'd done my taxes for twenty-five years until he finally retired for good and I retained Grady in his place. "And I'm going to staff the place with accountants like myself who can bring their own dedicated clients with them."

"Makes perfect sense."

"What if it doesn't work?" he asked me, hands crossed before him, freeing his knee to begin bouncing again.

My response was to rise from the couch and fish from under the tree a present I'd ordered for Grady on rush delivery the night before.

"Here," I said, grinning as I handed it to him.

Grady looked down at the professionally wrapped gift. "Did Christmas come early, Aunt Jess?"

"Open it."

I returned to the couch and watched him peel away the paper instead of stripping it off, somehow making the wrapping look almost reusable. He came to a carton a bit smaller than a shoebox, popped off the top, and eased out the single object it contained.

I watched Grady's eyes beam, his expression virtually identical to the one I recalled from when he was his son's age and Frank's namesake and I were raising him.

"I don't know what to say, Aunt Jess," he pronounced, holding up a desk plate that read, GRADY FLETCHER above PRESIDENT. "It might be the best gift I've ever gotten."

"I look forward to seeing it front and center on your desk wherever you open up that new office. And I don't want you to worry about money. You've got my backing for whatever it takes."

"An investment, remember?" he said, continuing to admire the desk plaque.

"On which I expect an excellent return."

"Count on it."

"I don't need to do any counting, Grady," I said. "That's what I've got you for."

"I'm going to make you proud, Aunt Jess. I promise." Grady beamed, that stubborn knee no longer bouncing.

"I'm already proud," I told him. "Now, come help me get dinner ready so we don't have to disturb Donna and little Frank."

We were well into that process when I heard the sound of someone clearing their throat and turned to see Harry McGraw standing in the kitchen doorway. "Since I'm Santa Claus now, I want you to open one of your presents early."

Chapter Twenty-one

See what I mean?" Harry asked me, angling his chair so I could see the screen on my iMac back upstairs in my office.

"You haven't told me what you mean, Harry, so I've got no idea what I'm looking at."

"Hey, you get what you pay for."

"Where are you eating Christmas dinner again?"

He turned back to the screen. "As I was saying, India pretty much dominated the early diamond trade until their mines dried up and Brazil filled the gap as best it could. Going back even further, descriptions of diamonds date to the fourth century BC, already known back then for their value. Small numbers of diamonds began appearing in European regalia and jewelry in the thirteenth century, in large part due to the fact that King Louis XIII of France passed a law that allowed only those of royal blood to possess them."

"Thus establishing them as rare, and thus valuable."

"Anybody ever tell you that you have a way with words?"

"Not book critics, that's for sure."

"You mentioned how that theft of the French Crown Jewels in 1792 set the stage, in some fashion, for these murders that began a year ago with Tad Hollenbeck's sister. Well, the reason why the French government had so many diamonds, thousands of them, in their possession was because of the edict King Louis issued. That had the effect of dramatically raising prices at the same time Brazil's reserves weren't big enough to meet demand."

"Helping to create the ultimate precious stone," I concluded.

"And on top of that, all that wealth redistribution going on throughout Europe in the late eighteenth century fostered a whole bunch of potential new customers, creating a *perceived* shortage. Near as I can tell, though, there wasn't much of a demand for them in America circa 1795. So this story you read in that journal should have added the fact that those founding fathers who came into those stolen gems almost surely moved them gradually through traders from Europe, where the demand was much higher for diamonds. My guess is those traders used them to curry favor with the kinds of royals of the time who'd reward them with status and power for their trouble. Make them ministers of trade or put them in command of a fleet of trading ships under government control."

"How does that get us any closer to catching a murderer today, Harry?"

He grinned as if he'd been waiting for me to pose that question. "Glad you asked, little lady. Because, near as I can tell, the trend I'd latched onto of ships' captains who visited Cabot Cove suddenly being elevated to positions of grandeur pretty much dried up right around the time of Wyatt Rackley's murder."

"You're confirming that the surviving founding fathers never found Rackley's stash of diamonds. And you're suggesting that fortune remains lost to this day."

"I'm not suggesting it so much as the murders, starting with Patricia Demps's, do."

"You're not just suggesting she learned about the diamonds, Harry; you're suggesting she may have found them, and was murdered as a result," I concluded for myself. "But how can we figure out what it was exactly that brought her up here?"

Harry went back to my iMac. "Care to take a gander at her e-mails from the time to see if we can find out?"

We returned to my office to do just that, as soon as dinner was over. Grady could see I was distracted and insisted on tidying up, freeing Donna and little Frank to go back to their movie, while Harry and I went back to our business.

Thanks to research I'd done for a past book, I had a vague notion of how Harry was able to penetrate the layers of cybersecurity to access Patricia Demps's e-mail account, and I didn't care to know any more than that. He caught me studying him with interest and couldn't resist pausing his toils long enough to comment.

"It's how I've been paid by clients from time to time. Call it taking it out in trade."

"Apparently, I'm not your only deadbeat."

"It goes like this, little lady. Computer hacker or something similar needs some help getting out of a jam, and my fee becomes teaching me the tools of their trade, at least the basic ones. How to hack an e-mail account without a password or even knowing the service provider."

"I'd rather not know the details, Harry."

"That's good, because they're illegal. Don't want to see America's greatest mystery writer busted for cybercrimes."

"Don't want to see the world's greatest detective get busted either."

He went back to work on my keyboard, studying the iMac's huge screen. "Right now, the world's greatest detective is drawing a blank, Mrs. F. Looks like Patricia Demps's Gmail account has been deleted."

"Hardly unusual, given that she's been dead, or at least missing, for over a year."

"Except, according to what I'm seeing here, the account was only deleted one week ago. Ring any bells?"

"Just a few days before her brother, Tad Hollenbeck, showed up in Cabot Cove."

"Interesting," said Harry, "don't you think?"

My cell phone rang early Saturday morning.

"Merry Christmas Eve, Mrs. F."

"Mort?"

"Are you awake?"

"I am now. What time is it?"

"Just after seven o'clock. Make yourself some coffee. I'll be by in an hour. We're going on a field trip to try out a present I bought myself for Christmas."

I recalled him mentioning something about that the other day. "Don't tell me: a red toy Eldorado convertible."

"You make me nostalgic to drive my real one, Mrs. F. Remember I told you I've got something to help us out in those woods?"

"Of course. It was only yesterday."

"See you at eight," he said, and the phone clicked off.

After showering and getting ready, I traipsed down the hall as soundlessly as I could manage so as not to rouse Grady, Donna, or little Frank. It had been so long since I'd had to think that way, and I loved the feeling, the sense of having family close by. I didn't know why I hadn't celebrated more holidays with Grady and his family, and I resolved to start making this our annual tradition.

I reached my office to find the door opened a crack and gave it a push to find Harry slumped in my office chair. If it wasn't for him snoring up a storm, I might have thought he was dead. My iMac was still powered up, but the computer had put itself in sleep mode after Harry had finally passed out in the chair.

Something alerted him to my presence and he jerked awake suddenly, eyes swimming about as if he was trying to remember where he was before they finally locked on me and everything snapped into place.

"What time is it?" he asked, rubbing the sleep from his eyes.

"Little after seven thirty."

His early-morning scowl looked the same as it did the rest of the day. "You always get up this early?"

"Only when you or Mort call."

"Must've been Mort today."

"Indeed. He's picking me up in a half hour, says we're going on a field trip."

"Mind if I tag along?" Harry asked.

"Maybe you should get some real sleep."

"I'd settle for a shower and some fresh clothes. That way I can explain to both of you what I uncovered last night before I zonked out."

Mort arrived at eight o'clock sharp, punctual to a T as always. He greeted Harry, who climbed into the front, leaving the backseat of Mort's Sheriff's Department SUV for me. Before I put on my seat belt, I noticed a long, narrow box resting behind me in the rear hold.

"It's a new shotgun, Mrs. F.," Mort said, noticing my gaze. "So I'll be ready to secure the Christmas parade tomorrow."

"What is it really, Mort?"

"Something we're going to make good use of."

"Where?"

"You'll see when we get there."

"You're a man after my own heart, Mort," Harry said, slapping him on the shoulder.

"Good to see you, too, Harry."

Men.

"Jess didn't tell you I was coming to town?" Harry quipped after we'd set off.

"How could I when I didn't know until you showed up?" I jumped in.

"Good thing I did, too," he told both Mort and me, "or the two of you would still be stumbling around in the dark about John Henry Cabot's two dearly departed descendants."

"What's he talking about, Mrs. F.?" Mort said, eyeing me in the rearview mirror.

"I think it has something to do with Patricia Demps's e-mail account, which was deleted just a few days before her brother, Tad Hollenbeck, showed up in town."

"I dumped both their phone records," Harry elaborated.

"I'm going to make believe I didn't hear that," Mort said before he could continue.

"I didn't dump their landlines, only their cells."

"Did either of them have landlines?"

"No, but that's beside the point. Anyway, I went back two years, about a year before Patricia Demps's disappearance, looking to see how often they spoke with each other. Care to guess the number?"

"It's too early in the morning," I told Harry.

"How about never, not a single call between the two of them?"

I could see Mort's shoulders stiffen behind the wheel. "They were estranged—that's what you're saying."

"I don't know; is that what I'm saying?"

"When a brother doesn't talk to his sister for a year, that's estranged."

"So it's a safe bet Tad Hollenbeck had no idea his

sister preceded him to Cabot Cove by almost a year," I noted.

"Then Patricia Demps's e-mail account gets wiped clean just a few days before Hollenbeck shows up in your nice little town," Harry picked up.

"Meaning maybe he figured out she'd been here before she disappeared."

"Likely on the trail of the same thing he showed up looking for, for my money."

Mort made a right, heading out toward a wooded area on the outskirts of town, not far from that WELCOME TO CABOT COVE sign where Tad Hollenbeck had done his final shot. "Which means maybe something he found in those e-mails is what brought him here."

"The same thing that brought his sister here," I added. "Some clue about the whereabouts of Wyatt Rackley's missing diamonds."

"Too bad for both of them they didn't get along better," Mort noted, as close as he got to waxing philosophical about anything.

"You want to tell me what's in the box?" I asked him, the woods drawing closer.

Mort eased the device from the box, looking like a kid opening up his first present on Christmas morning. The device looked like a more sophisticated version of one of those wands you see people fanning about beach sand in search of hidden coins and jewelry.

"What's that thing do, exactly?" I asked him.

"It's nice once in a while to explain the rigors of real police work to you, Mrs. F.," Mort said, waving it about in the air as he searched for the on switch. "Basically, it finds human remains," Mort continued.

"You mean, like a cadaver-sniffing dog," I said.

"Except Cabot Cove doesn't have a cadaver-sniffing dog, so I ordered up one of these. Supposed to be state-of-the-art, thanks to its ability to detect concentrations of something called NRN in the soil, but don't ask me what that stands for."

"Ninhydrin-reactive nitrogen," Harry explained to both of us. "It's a vapor associated with decomposition that collects in air pockets around grave soil."

Mort and I looked at each other, amazed by Harry's knowledge and fluency.

"What?" he said, noting our response. "It was on the front cover of the last issue of *Detective Monthly*."

"I must have missed that issue," Mort said.

"I think I'm the only subscriber."

"See, the state police crime lab identified this section of the woods as a match for the dirt found on the recovered remains that didn't match the dirt from Mrs. F.'s backyard." Mort finally located the power switch and tested his new toy out. "If they're right, this thing should be able to tell us where in these parts the bodies were originally buried, because that . . ."

"Ninhydrin-reactive nitrogen," Harry completed.

". . . stuff remains in the soil bed after the remains have been removed." Mort patted the top of the wand-like thing as if it were a real live dog. "What do you say we take this baby out for a trial spin?"

Mort's trial spin didn't start out well. The NRN sensor was like a bucking bronco in his grasp, looking more like one of those old-fashioned divining rods that led their wielders about in search of water. We were in search of something else entirely, but Mort had no more control than those old-time diviners.

"Want me to take a crack at it, Sheriff?" Harry asked lightly, not wanting to raise too much of Mort's ire.

"No," he snapped, regardless, "I'm just starting to get the hang of this."

He circled about the clearing near where Tad Hollenbeck had filmed his final shot the day he'd been murdered, expanding outward methodically when the machine failed to register a single thing. Mort had begun to tap its top, as if to coax the thing to life, on the verge, it seemed, of either returning it to its box or breaking it across his knee.

Harry began snapping pictures of the whole process, until Mort caught him.

"One more shot and I'll confiscate that thing as evidence," Mort warned him.

"Nobody would believe this otherwise," Harry said, unable to hold back his grin.

"Keep talking and it'll be your ninhydrin-reactive nitrogen this piece of junk will be homing in on in a few minutes."

Just then, the machine started flashing up a storm across its LED readouts and making a sound like a credit card machine telling you to remove your card.

"Will you look at that?" a beaming Mort said, holding the bottommost portion of the machine over a spot on the ground.

"Right," Harry said, turning away so Mort wouldn't see him grinning even wider, "better late than never."

Using small red flags, Mort staked out the circumference of what we all assumed was the former resting place for a pair of skeletal remains and the oak chest containing Cabot Cove's founding documents.

"Here's the way I see it, Mrs. F.," he said, still holding the NRN sensor as if it were a pet dog. "After our killer murdered Patricia Demps, he buried her body here, along with that old chest and the bones we believe belong to Wyatt Rackley. And here they would have all remained if your backyard didn't present a better alternative."

"Why bother doing that in the first place?" the ever-skeptical Harry McGraw posed.

"Because several developers have staked their claim to a big chunk of this land," I told him.

"At prices that would make Park Avenue residents cringe," Mort added.

"We're all holding on to hope that it never happens," I resumed. "But the killer knew their hiding place might be on borrowed time, so he or she seized the opportunity that my torn-up land provided."

"Good thing you needed a new septic system," Harry noted, a frown worn over his features like an old suit.

"How about I send you the bill?"

"Send a dozen. Then you'll know what it's like not to get paid. I haven't bought a pair of new shoes since your nephew was born."

"Little Frank is my grandnephew."

"I meant Grady," Harry said, flashing his trademark scowl.

Which reminded me of something that had been stuck in the corner of my mind for a couple of days now, since we'd paid Terry McMullen a visit aboard his boat, the *Resolute*.

"Mort, you need to bring in one of Terry McMullen's deckhands for questioning."

"I need to *what*? Why?"

"Because I don't think McMullen was out at sea the night Tad Hollenbeck was murdered."

Chapter Twenty-two

Mort sent Deputy Andy over to the docks, where he picked up Esteban Tuco, one of the two Latinos who worked as deckhands on Terry McMullen's fishing boat, for questioning. He was already seated in the interview room when the three of us arrived, after the dispatcher pointed us in the room's direction. Deputy Andy was standing watch in the doorway, facing him.

Mort ushered Harry and me inside, then closed the door behind him. "You're not in any trouble, Essie," he greeted him. "We've just got a couple questions for you."

Tuco swallowed hard. "Sure, Sheriff."

"You know Mrs. Fletcher here?"

He nodded. "Everybody knows Mrs. Fletcher." Tuco smiled.

The waters off the Cabot Cove coast, like much of the northern Atlantic, had been overfished for years, leading to a depletion of stock ranging from cod to famed Maine lobster. Our local fishermen might not be thriving anymore, but there were enough boats still active and looking for crew to create a small but dedicated community of deckhands. They worked hard and were willing to base their pay on the yield of the catch. For our hearty fishermen, like my old friend Ethan Cragg, fishing was a twelve-month job, backbreaking and brutal, which didn't deter men like Essie Tuco in the least.

His bronzed, leathery skin made me think he'd never used sunscreen in his life. Tuco's hair was thick and mussed, formed into the shape of his fisherman's cap. He looked to be in his mid-forties and was raising three young children with his wife in a two-bedroom apartment a half hour outside of town.

"I remembered something from the other day when the sheriff and I came down to the docks," I told him. "Terry McMullen was wearing sneakers that looked virtually brand-new, not the kind of footwear recommended for working a slippery boat deck at sea. I don't think he was really out at sea the night before. I think you and the other crew member went out alone, and he was there to meet you when you brought the boat back in."

"Is that true, Essie?" Mort asked him.

Tuco looked him square in the eye as he nodded, just once. "I can't go to jail, Sheriff," he stammered, his hands trembling before him atop the steel table. "I didn't do anything, Sheriff, except what I was told."

"And what was that?"

"Not to tell anyone."

"Tell anyone *what*?"

"The truth"—Tuco swallowed hard and then took a deep breath—"about that night you were asking Mr. McMullen about."

Tuesday, the night Tad Hollenbeck had been murdered, I thought to myself.

"What about it?" Mort asked him.

Tuco looked toward me. "You're right, Mrs. Fletcher. Mr. McMullen wasn't on the boat that night."

"He lied to you, *jefe*," Esteban said, resorting to Spanish, as he sometimes did when he was nervous. "And he told me to lie, too. I did what he asked because I need the money for my family. But I haven't slept since because I knew if you learned what I'd done, I'd be a criminal. What is it called?"

"An accessory, potentially," I answered him, "but only if Mr. McMullen committed a crime."

"Do you have reason to believe he committed a crime, Essie?" Mort asked him.

Tuco shook his head vehemently. "No, no, *jefe*. I have no reason to believe that. I don't know what he did or why he told the two of us to handle the load ourselves. He said he was getting sick and needed to rest. But this is a big week for us, one of the biggest of the year with Christmas Eve and all. And the fish, they've been biting."

"You didn't believe Mr. McMullen was getting sick?"

"I've worked for him for four years now. He never gets sick, and even if he was, he wouldn't let that stop him from going out, not this week."

"What else?" Mort prodded.

"Else?"

"That's right."

"Like what, *jefe*?"

"Like, what was he really doing, leaving you and the other crew member to handle the haul yourselves?"

Tuco shook his head, his curls flopping about. "I don't know. I'd tell you if I did. You must believe me."

"Had he been acting strange, Esteban?" I asked him, jumping in.

"Strange?"

"Like nervous, on edge, preoccupied."

Tuco shook his head again. "No, Mrs. Fletcher, none of those things." He fixed his gaze back on Mort. "I don't know any more than what I've told you. I don't know what he was doing that night. I only know he wasn't on the boat like he said he was and I have to think of my family, protect my family. You understand that."

"Of course we do, Essie," Mort told him.

"So you won't tell Mr. McMullen what I told you?"

Mort reached across the table and patted his forearm. "I won't breathe a word of it."

"You promise?"

"I promise."

Tuco looked my way.

"Me, too."

Then Harry.

"Sure. I don't know who you are anyway."

"Where can we find Terry McMullen, Essie?" Mort asked.

* * *

Three of our potential victims had emerged as potential suspects, with Terry McMullen the latest to join the club. He'd been preceded by Asa Cabot, a supposed agoraphobic who'd left a trail of muddy footprints in his study, and Dan Kinder, who might well be connected with both crime scenes by those thin shavings made of a composite material I'd first taken for hairs. That left only Clara Wizzenhunt, whom I felt safe in ruling out, given her confinement to Shady Willows Assisted Living Center. Then again, I still hadn't ruled out her nephew, Lucas Rackley, and I couldn't help but still wonder if he possessed some of his ancestor's criminal tendencies. That gave us four legitimate suspects, all of whom would be leading the Christmas parade tomorrow, with Lucas Rackley standing in for his aunt, who had grown too frail to manage the cold for such an extended period.

Mort and I headed over to the docks with Harry McGraw in tow, after Esteban Tuco said we could find Terry McMullen there. He was in the process of hosing down the deck of his boat after raking in a final, considerable Christmas Eve haul when we arrived. He spotted the three of us coming and turned away, not letting up on his labors. I noticed he was wearing boat shoes today, faded and tattered, with soles that squeaked against the deck surface.

"Merry Christmas, Terry," Mort greeted him.

"Whatever you say, Sheriff."

"Got a minute?"

"No," McMullen said, still having not regarded any

of us directly. "I want to finish this up and get on home, if it's all the same to you."

"Don't force me to place you under arrest," Mort warned him.

McMullen finally regarded him but kept on hosing down the deck. "On what charge?"

"Lying to a police officer—namely me—the other day when you claimed you were out at sea Tuesday, the night Tad Hollenbeck was murdered."

McMullen turned off the hose. "You want to see my sales receipts for that night's catch?"

"You mean the catch your deckhands must have made on their own, since you weren't with them?"

"What gave you that idea?" Terry McMullen snapped indignantly, his tone lowered to a near hiss.

"You ever hear of security cameras, Terry?"

"Yeah, and I heard there weren't any on the docks."

"You heard wrong," Mort said, in what I was sure was a lie, conceived, mostly, to protect and keep his word to Esteban Tuco.

Moments like this brought out the New York homicide cop in him, willing to do whatever it took to catch a killer and close a case. It never ceased to amaze me that Mort had chosen to retire in Cabot Cove, and I wondered if he'd had any idea what awaited him when he and Adele moved to Maine.

"Talk to Ethan Cragg lately?" Mort continued.

"No. Why?"

"Because he asked the Sheriff's Department to have security cameras installed after some thefts off fishing boats like yours. It took some time before we found the funds in our budget, but the cameras have been running since just after Thanksgiving. Not a moment too soon either," he finished, in pointed fashion.

McMullen swept his gaze about the sprawl of our working port, still holding the hose.

"You won't see them, Terry. They're the latest variety, manufactured to blend in with the area so as to be unobtrusive. You know what *unobtrusive* means?"

McMullen stiffened. "You got nothing on me."

"I'd like to know why you lied to me. Pretty stupid thing to do when it involves a murder investigation."

McMullen turned almost hateful as he nodded to himself and then sighed out loud. "I wasn't at sea Tuesday night. There, I admitted it."

"Where were you?"

"Nowhere near where that TV reporter got killed, I can tell you that much."

"You'll have to tell me more than that, Terry."

McMullen gazed about, as if to make sure no one else was close by. His eyes settled on Harry.

"Who's he?"

"Name's Harry McGraw. I thought I'd tag along because you might need a lawyer."

"Are you a lawyer?"

"No, but I can recommend a few criminal lawyers who specialize in keeping killers off death row."

"Last time I checked, Maine doesn't have the death penalty," noted Terry McMullen.

"Then I can recommend some other attorneys."

McMullen swung back toward Mort, as if neither Harry nor I was there at all. "I'm having an affair,

Sheriff, with the wife of another fisherman who works the docks. I think you can see what I'm getting at here and why I lied to you."

"I'll need a name, all the same, Terry. And don't ask me to keep this quiet, because I'm going to need to check your alibi for the time we believe Tad Hollenbeck was killed."

"You never told me how."

"He was poisoned."

McMullen looked as if he almost found that funny. "Do I look like someone who'd use poison to kill someone?"

"You're right. A baling hook would seem more appropriate, and you better hope that woman's husband doesn't have any lying around."

Terry McMullen provided the name and address of the fisherman's wife with whom he was having an affair, and Mort dutifully jotted it down in his magical memo pad.

"What do you make of his story, Mrs. F.?"

"Hey," Harry broke in before I could respond, "what about me?"

"What about you *what*?"

"I'm a trained detective and you didn't ask me that question first?"

"You ever hear of Abby Joyner?"

"The wife? No."

His point made, Mort looked back toward me. "You were saying, Mrs. F."

"McMullen won't have an alibi for the time Tad Hollenbeck was murdered."

"Pretty definitive statement on your part."

"Because I'm pretty sure. The Joyners have school-age children, an eleven- and a twelve-year-old. No way Terry McMullen would have stopped by until they were fast asleep."

"So after around ten, you figure."

I nodded. "Which would have left him plenty of time to kill Hollenbeck and still show up right on time at Abby's house. And I also figure he's on the phone to her right now to revise her memory about the time-line."

"You know," Harry said, flashing his trademark scowl, "I could really learn something from the two of you. No wonder my business is in the toilet."

"Care to weigh in, Harry, give us your two cents?"

"I've only got one, on account of a certain deadbeat client whose initials are J. F. But that guy's a bald-faced liar with more tells than I could count."

"Tells?" Mort repeated.

"You know, signs, like mannerisms or something, that he's lying."

"Oh, I know what they are. I'm curious what you noticed, exactly."

"He tried to appear nonchalant, but there were several times when he answered your questions that he stopped moving, kind of froze. Not all the questions, but a few."

"Any stand out to you?"

"A few, like I said, but mostly when you asked him where he was when Hollenbeck got killed and he said nowhere close. That was a lie."

Mort took off his hat and scratched at his scalp.

"Wish I had a picture of him I could show to that clerk at the Surfsider."

"You do," Harry said, holding up his phone, where a picture he'd just shot of Terry McMullen standing on the deck of his boat was displayed.

"You just got yourself an invite to Christmas dinner," Mort said, handing Harry back his phone after inspecting the picture.

"Jess here already beat you to it. Didn't you, little lady?"

"So long as you count inviting yourself."

"In that case," Mort started, looking toward me, "count Adele and me in, too, Mrs. F."

"I thought you said . . ."

"She changed her mind. I hope you don't mind that I told her not to bother bringing anything resembling food."

"Now that we've got that settled, where to next?" Harry asked through the frown frozen on his face.

"No offense, but I should speak with Mrs. Joyner alone," Mort told both of us.

"In the meantime," I suggested, "how about we go wish Asa Cabot a very merry Christmas?"

Chapter Twenty-three

Asa Cabot was none too happy about making our acquaintance for the second time in such a short period. He was wearing the same old-fashioned smoking jacket he was the first time we were there and an expression bent in derision at our presence, which he had only reluctantly allowed through his personal assistant, James, who looked more like a bodyguard, to my mind.

"This is beginning to resemble one of your mystery stories, Mrs. Fletcher," Cabot said to me, making a show of ignoring Mort and Harry.

All of us had removed our shoes and were wearing surgical masks and gloves provided by James, who'd looked on dutifully while we donned them, not saying a word. His glare was extremely discomfiting, leaving me with the sense I was being targeted instead of simply watched.

I surveyed Cabot's magnificent book collection again, even more awestruck than I'd been the last time. "I haven't had time yet to communicate your very generous offer to donate the remainder of your collection to our little library to Doris Ann, our librarian, but on behalf of the Friends group, I can't thank you enough. It will be a wonderful addition and worthy of a special section for such collections."

Cabot's flat, sallow expression showed some life. "If I didn't know better, I might think you were hitting me up for a donation."

"Then I'm glad you do know better, Mr. Cabot, because fund-raising efforts are already underway, with one significant benefactor having already come forward," I said through the surgical mask.

"Should I bother to hazard a guess as to who that benefactor might be, Mrs. Fletcher?" he asked me coyly.

"She insisted on remaining anonymous."

He nodded, cracking the slightest of smiles. "I'm sure she did, and who can blame her?"

The lighting was a bit brighter in his study today, the angle of the sun enabling its rays to slip through the slats of the drawn blinds. The added illumination cast Cabot's expression as even pastier, to the point where I was struck by the notion that I was conversing with a corpse that had climbed out of its coffin. The way his slippered feet glided across the hardwood floor made it seem as if he were floating in a ghostlike manner. That floor had been polished since our last visit, erasing any trace of the footprints outlined in mud I'd noted the presence of to Mort.

I saw no reason to mince words on that subject.

"May I speak frankly, Mr. Cabot?" I said, taking the lead this time.

"I'd expect nothing less from Cabot Cove's most famous resident."

I smiled my appreciation for his comment. "As we discussed in our last visit, you suffer from an extremely pernicious form of agoraphobia."

He nodded slowly. "Yes, I do, regretfully."

"Then I'm curious, sir, as to how I noticed footprints of dried mud across the floor when we were here the other day that matched the shoes that had been resting near the closet over there."

Cabot looked surprised by my remark, but not unduly defensive. "You caught me, Mrs. Fletcher."

Any thoughts we might have entertained about him confessing to the murders were dashed when he resumed.

"I refuse to take my condition lying down, literally so, and had set a goal for myself to be able to participate in the Christmas parade this year with the other descendants. So I've been following my therapist's instructions to try to venture out a bit farther every day."

"And how's that been going?" Mort asked him.

"Not very well, I'm afraid," Cabot lamented, "not since your last visit, anyway. I haven't ventured outside since, unsettled by all this talk of murder."

"I'm sorry to hear that," I told him, meaning it.

"As am I," he echoed, "given that my goal to retake my place at the head of the Christmas parade in the founders' carriage will have to wait another year."

"So none of these practice runs outside brought you into contact with your nephew, Tad Hollenbeck?" Mort said, taking over the questioning.

"I normally confine myself to the rear of the property. It helps me, soothes me, to be able to look back and focus on my study here. As I recall, you said my nephew shot this video in the front of my property."

"Your property is beautifully landscaped, Mr. Cabot," I complimented him.

"Thank you, Mrs. Fletcher. That comes at no small expense."

"And well worth it, given that our horticultural society has named yours the most elegant collection of flowers and flowering plants in the entire town."

Cabot seemed to come to life within the bulky confines of his smoking jacket. "They asked if they might include my grounds in their annual tour. I said yes, so long as they could provide me sufficient notice."

"I heard it was the hit of the day, sir."

"That means a lot to me, Mrs. Fletcher. Gardening was my late wife's greatest passion, and I see the maintenance of those flowers as a testament to her."

"Then I'm sure you're going to have that rough patch out front tended to before spring, Mr. Cabot."

"Indeed." Cabot nodded. "The season's mums were struck by a blight, a fungus of some kind. We had to rip them all out and retill the ground to avoid the fungus spreading."

"There's no such empty patch anywhere toward the rear of your property, and that retilled patch in the front was a perfect match for the mud trail I spotted here the other day, especially since it had rained the night before."

"I must have misspoken, Mrs. Fletcher, and I might well have indeed made a foray, however brief, to the front of my property."

"Well, did you or didn't you, Mr. Cabot?" Mort asked him.

Cabot looked put off by Mort's tone. "Have you ever suffered from an anxiety or panic disorder, Sheriff?"

"I spent twenty years as a New York City homicide detective, sir."

"I'll take that as a no, in which case you're probably not aware how difficult it is for me to venture out at all. Part of my coping mechanism is to be outdoors physically, even if I don't enjoy a precise recollection of exactly where I was. So I might well have ventured onto the front of my property, even if I have no specific recollection of doing so."

"That mud certainly indicates you did, Mr. Cabot," Mort went on. "And the timing indicates it might well have been while Mr. Hollenbeck was here Tuesday afternoon. Might your recollection be failing you there, too?"

"I take offense at your suggestion, Sheriff."

"Just as I take offense at a pair of murders happening in my town in the past week, not to mention a third one a year ago."

"Am I to be considered a suspect again?"

"Not at present, Mr. Cabot," I said for all three of us, "but I am curious about James."

"James?"

"Your personal assistant."

"I know who he is," Cabot retorted, indignation creeping into his voice, "just not the basis of your interest in him."

"I had a sense he might be ex-military, so I asked Sheriff Metzger to lift his fingerprints off the shoes he asked me to take off, as soon as I got back to the station."

"Turned out Mrs. Fletcher's hunch about the military was correct," Mort picked up, "and that's not all. I asked Detective McGraw to look into things from there."

Detective McGraw? I mouthed to Harry, who could only smirk.

"Detective," Mort prompted, "why don't you take it from here?"

Now I knew what Harry had been doing on his phone for a good portion of the morning, Mort having asked him to do some follow-up while I was out of earshot. Talk about a team effort.

"James Carnevale," Harry said, speaking without aid of notes or a magical memo pad, "has a criminal record. Were you aware of that, Mr. Cabot?"

"And who are you again?"

"Detective McGraw," Harry replied, seeming to enjoy it.

"From Cabot Cove?"

"Boston originally, New York more recently."

"Because I don't recall seeing you in these parts before."

"Well, you haven't really been getting out much, have you? But let's get back to James Carnevale."

"Yes, I was aware of his regrettable brushes with the law over the years," Cabot said, nodding. "I believe in providing second chances, Detective."

Harry looked toward me and mouthed the word *detective* before resuming. "This would be more like third chances, Mr. Cabot. Were you also aware that Mr. Carnevale was dishonorably discharged from the Marine Corps?"

"That was made known to me, yes. He volunteered the information in his interview."

"Did that information include the reason for his dishonorable discharge?" Harry asked, and continued before Asa Cabot had a chance to respond. "It was for excessively violent behavior in a war zone, which seems like an absurdity, doesn't it? Anyway, I'll spare you the specifics. Suffice it to say that Mr. Carnevale was lucky to avoid a court-martial and around twenty years in military prison."

"I assure you, Detective, that I've witnessed no such behavior in the two years he's been with me."

"That's probably because you don't have any prisoner combatants for him to have his way with." With that, Harry leaned in closer to me, whispering, "He called me *Detective*."

"We've got some questions for James Carnevale, Mr. Cabot. I wanted to inform you as a courtesy."

Asa Cabot looked my way, whatever warmth there might have been before having vanished. "So, who do you suspect the killer is, Mrs. Fletcher, me or my personal assistant?"

"I suppose that remains to be seen, Mr. Cabot," I told him.

* * *

James Carnevale was not at his usual post when we emerged from Asa Cabot's study. There was no sign of him anywhere about in plain view, and reluctant attempts by Cabot to rouse him via both walkie-talkie and cell phone failed to even produce a response.

"I'm going to assume this isn't typical behavior on Mr. Carnevale's part, sir," Mort said to him.

"Assume anything you want, Sheriff."

"In that case, let's try this," Mort said, before Cabot had even finished speaking. "If Carnevale turns out to be the killer we're after, it was almost certainly at your behest. I'd like you to keep that in mind, in case the spirit moves you to come clean."

"Come clean," Cabot repeated sardonically. "Your type really does talk that way."

"What type might that be?" Mort asked him.

"Lazy law enforcement types."

Mort cast me a wink. "Well then, I better get back to the office to take a nap."

"Give me one good reason not to cancel tomorrow's Christmas parade, Mrs. F.," Mort said, visibly relaxing as the Cabot estate dwindled behind us in the rearview mirror.

"For starters, you'll have to finish your retirement someplace else—that is, once you get the tar and feathers off."

"The little lady's right," Harry McGraw added. "You should know better."

"Why am I listening to you? You don't even live in Cabot Cove."

"In case you've forgotten, I've had a lot of experience here. And I know the territory well enough to anticipate a public lynching if you mess with one of the town's most cherished traditions."

"Traditions that happen to include murder," an exasperated Mort managed, squeezing the steering wheel. "Or has that fact conveniently slipped both your minds?"

"Precisely why the parade needs to go on," I advised.

"In the hope the killer reveals him- or herself. Is that what you're thinking, Mrs. F.?"

"I am, Mort."

"And so I get to play Santa Claus," Harry added.

Mort looked at him incredulously, about to comment on that when his radio crackled.

"Dispatch to Patrol One," the dispatcher's voice rang out. "Come in, Sheriff Metzger."

Mort slowed the SUV and snatched the mic from its stand. "Go for Metzger."

"We need units at Shady Willows, Sheriff. They just called in a report of a resident who's gone missing."

"They say who it is?"

"Clara Wizzenhunt, Sheriff."

By all accounts, according to reports from the staff, the descendant of Wyatt Rackley had disappeared shortly after breakfast, which meant she'd been missing for between three and four hours by the time we arrived. Her nephew, Lucas, was already on the scene, pacing the halls with the fuse clearly burning down on that temper he was liable to display.

"As I was trying to explain to Mr. Rackley there," the shift supervisor started, eyeing Lucas derisively, "his aunt is prone to these spells where she wanders off for hours at a time. She always comes back on her own, with no idea where she's been or what she was doing."

"It's thirty-five degrees outside," I informed the woman, "so I doubt very much she'll be able to survive for all that long."

Lucas Rackley barged his way into our conversation. "Explain to these people how my aunt simply walked out of this place without anyone noticing a seventy-year-old woman wearing a bathrobe. Explain how it's become a regular occurrence, like you just said."

"Your aunt doesn't just walk out the front door, Mr. Rackley," the shift supervisor said defensively. "She mostly sneaks out through a side door. Once, we found her trying to climb out a window."

"Hopefully on the first floor," Harry McGraw noted.

"I would expect exiting through a side door like that would trigger some kind of emergency alarm."

"It's supposed to, but not when the door's propped open for a delivery or a resident being taken by gurney out to an ambulance."

"And were either of those the case around the time Clara Wizzenhunt disappeared today?"

"We had several deliveries this morning she could have exploited, yes. And, since it's Christmas Eve, we're operating with a skeleton staff."

"Where does she usually go?" I asked.

"Mrs. Fletcher, nobody really knows. She's gone and then she comes back like nothing ever happened."

"So it's possible she might take her leave and return without anyone knowing she was gone in the first place."

I could tell the shift supervisor, whose name tag identified her as Gloria, was thrown by my suggestion.

"I suppose, but it's most unlikely," was all she said in response.

"You better have a better explanation than that when I sue this place for everything it's worth, if anything happens to my aunt," snapped Lucas Rackley.

Up until that moment, Clara Wizzenhunt was the only descendant of the founders of Cabot Cove I didn't consider a suspect. But these "spells" of hers left me thinking along different lines, especially since she had a tendency to return to Shady Willows with no memory of what had transpired in her time away from the facility. And no matter what protocols or precautions the staff managed to put into place, Clara kept managing to find her way outside the building and off the grounds to who knows where.

"Did you notify the Sheriff's Department?" Mort asked the shift supervisor.

While Mort continued to engage the Shady Willows staff, I stepped aside and called Seth Hazlitt.

"Six o'clock," he said, by way of greeting.

"What?"

"You're calling to tell me the time for Christmas dinner tomorrow. It's always six o'clock."

"That's not why I'm calling."

"You haven't changed the time, have you?"

"No, I'm calling about Clara Wizzenhunt."

"A patient of mine forever, until she moved into Shady Willows."

"I'm there now—"

"They prefer their own doctors," Seth resumed, before I could get another word in edgewise.

"But Clara isn't."

"Isn't what?"

"Here. She had what the staff referred to as another of her spells and walked off the grounds again. The staff is out searching as we speak."

I heard Seth utter a deep sigh on the other end of the line. "Her cognitive abilities were starting to betray her when she was still seeing me. She called to cancel our final appointment because she got lost on the way to my office a couple miles from her home."

"How awful."

"I didn't need any elaborate tests to tell me she was suffering from the early stages of dementia. I was going to prescribe one of the newer medications that have the potential to slow the decline when the family got her into Shady Willows' Memory Unit. I've been to visit her a few times, Jess. Sometimes it's like she's her old self, and other days she barely remembers who I am."

"These spells she's been having," I interjected.

"You said she's been wandering off, coming back with no memory of whatever happened while she was gone."

"I'm not sure I said all that."

"You didn't have to. You said enough. What she's experiencing is her mind's attempt to hold on to itself, basically. That manifests itself in these blackout periods where she could do anything a fully conscious person might without retaining any memory of doing it."

"How far could someone in such a state actually wander?" I asked him.

"Jess," Seth started in his cautionary voice.

"What?"

"I know that tone, *ayuh*. What's going on?"

"You know me too well, Seth," I said, looking back toward the main desk, where Mort continued to speak with the shift supervisor and others gathered about, including a pair of uniformed private security personnel.

"How long have we known each other now?"

"Since we were both a lot younger. And my question for you is this: Could someone experiencing a spell like Clara Wizzenhunt commit murder without realizing that they'd done so?"

Before Seth could answer, I heard someone cry out and swung again toward the main reception area, where Clara Wizzenhunt had just stepped through the sliding doors, covered in blood.

Chapter Twenty-four

Seth was talking, but I didn't register a word he was saying.

"I need to call you back," I said, ending the call and dashing back toward the reception desk.

A gaggle of Shady Willows staff members surrounded Clara Wizzenhunt just a few feet inside the door. Mort stood at the periphery, hands on his hips, while Harry McGraw hung back, drawing close to me when I ground to a halt.

"Just business as usual in Cabot Cove, right?" he said, not as lightly as he'd meant to.

"Aunt Clara, Aunt Clara!" I heard Clara's nephew, Lucas Rackley, calling from someplace inside the clutter of bodies around her.

I started to move closer, then stopped, realizing there was nothing I could do to help. Finally, Clara emerged with a Shady Willows scrubs–wearing orderly on either side of her holding on tight. She looked confused, utterly disoriented. Her hair was a tangled mess, and thin trails of blood stained her face from what looked like scratches. But the blood that had splattered her clothes had come from much more than that, and I feared Clara might have injured herself while on her sojourn. She was only a few years older than me, still in the prime of life, as far as I was concerned. What a shame to have her own mind betray her, the despair hitting me especially hard, given, as the old saying goes, there but for the grace of God go I.

Clara's eyes fastened on me as the orderlies dragged her past me, trailed by her nephew and a slew of other Shady Willows personnel, including doctors and nurses.

"Jessica!" she called out, coming to a sudden halt against the determined efforts of the orderlies to keep her moving. "What a nice surprise! What are you doing here?"

"I came to see you," I said, thinking fast.

"Well, come along. I want to hear all the latest goings-on at our little library, which isn't so little anymore."

She beckoned me to follow, and I joined the procession with the grudging approval of those leading the way. They were obviously grateful, as well as surprised, that seeing me had snapped Clara reasonably alert, although she seemed to boast no awareness that her bathrobe and nightclothes were soiled, torn, and streaked with blood. I looked back toward Mort, who was already moving to join me.

"That's a lot of blood, Mrs. F.," he said softly when he reached my side.

We were almost to the elevators.

"Let's not jump to any conclusions, Mort. Shady Willows is a long way from both the Surfsider Motel and the home of Sheila Del Perrio."

"You telling me the thought hasn't crossed your mind?"

"Only long enough for me to dismiss it," I said half-heartedly, taking this a bit personally, since declining the way Clara Wizzenhunt had was my greatest fear.

"Because she's a friend or . . ." Mort let his voice drift off. "You know, people in this kind of fugue state have been known to drive cars, even operate heavy machinery, without any recollection of doing so."

"Seth just told me."

"I caught a couple of homicide cases in Manhattan that followed that pattern, though medication was to blame in those cases."

"And?"

"They were still murderers, Mrs. F. My job is to catch them and let the courts sort everything out."

"I'd better call Seth back," I said, stepping aside with phone in hand.

"What happened?" he asked me, answering before I even heard a ring.

"Clara's back."

"How's she look?"

"Covered in blood, but I don't think it's hers."

"How is she otherwise?"

"Well, she recognized me. That's something, anyway."

I could picture Seth nodding to himself on the

other end of the line. "She'll have her share of lucid periods, but as time goes on the frequency of them will decline as the dementia takes firmer hold. It's the toughest thing I've had to face as a doctor over the years. Worse than cancer, worse than anything. The most important thing you can do is—"

"Jessica!" I heard Clara call from inside her room. "Jessica, are you still there?"

"I've got to go, Seth."

"Again? I wasn't finished."

"Clara's calling my name. I'll ring you back after I've seen her."

"Can't wait," Seth groused, sounding more like Harry.

A pair of nurses were giving Clara a sponge bath as Mort Metzger looked on, supervising the process to gather evidence and making sure none of it was compromised any more than it had already been. He was wearing a pair of the evidence gloves he always carried in his pocket and, for want of an evidence pouch, was securing the woman's bloody, tattered clothes in a Shady Willows laundry bag.

"We're going to need blood samples," he told me as the nurses continued to swab Clara's skin clean of it. "But we can get them off the clothes."

"Jessica!" Clara beamed as if nothing was wrong or out of place at all. "I'm so glad you stopped by. Merry Christmas!"

"Merry Christmas to you, too, Clara."

"Have you met my nephew, Lucas?" she asked me, indicating the young man who was perched to her right.

"Nice to meet you, Lucas," I said, because it was easier.

He grunted a response.

"Do you remember where you were, Clara?" I asked, drawing an approving look from Mort.

"When?"

"While you were out."

"Was I out? Where did I go? Oh yes, I went for a walk. Such a beautiful morning for a walk. Christmas presents!" she added suddenly, her mind veering someplace else entirely. "I must have gone out to buy Christmas presents!" She peered out between the people encircling her bed, her gaze sweeping the room. "But I can't seem to remember where I put them. . . ."

"Did you hurt yourself, Clara?" I asked, drawing a bit closer.

"When?"

"While you were out," I repeated.

She looked down at herself and the sponge bath she was receiving. "Nothing hurts. I really don't remember, Jessica, and I promise I won't miss the next Friends of the Library meeting."

"We missed you at the last one, Clara."

"Books are wonderful things," she said, sounding totally coherent in that moment. "Remember what Victor Hugo said?"

"'To learn to read is to light a fire,'" I started.

"'Every syllable that is spelled out is a spark,'" Clara completed.

"You don't remember where you went on your walk?"

"I remember how fresh the air felt. But it was cold."

"Did you see anyone?"

Her face scrunched up into a tight mask of concentration at that. "I don't remember. I don't think so."

I noticed a clothes hamper in the back corner of the room and gestured toward it for Mort.

"I'm going to need to take the contents of that into evidence, too," he said to the shift supervisor.

She was taking copious notes on her clipboard, careful to document everything. "You'll need some more bags, then, Sheriff."

"Why don't I just take the whole thing? Easier to preserve that way."

His thinking paralleled mine. If Clara Wizzenhunt had murdered both Tad Hollenbeck and Sheila Del Perrio in the midst of her fugue states, there would likely be some evidence attesting to that on her clothing.

"Will you stop by and see me again?" Clara asked me.

"Soon, Clara, soon."

"Promise?"

"I promise," I said, aware I might be returning to Shady Willows much sooner than any of us expected in that moment.

"How's she doing?" Seth asked me when I got him back on the phone a bit later in the hallway.

"To tell you the truth, I'm not sure."

"What about the blood?"

"Other than a few scratches on her face and arms, it's not Clara's."

"That's good, isn't it?"

"I'm not sure about that either, Seth."

"And these scratches?"

"They look like they came from branches, probably

from trees in the woods at the back of the Shady Willows grounds."

"Those grounds spill out onto Route One. She could get anywhere in town from there. Did the people there examine her feet?"

"She was wearing slippers. Badly scuffed up, with the soles pretty much shredded. She's got some blisters, but that's pretty much it. No way I can see of learning exactly how far she went. Unless . . ."

I could tell I'd gotten Mort's attention. "What is it, Mrs. F.?"

"Both times we've seen her this week, she was wearing a watch—a smart watch, if I'm not mistaken."

"You're not . . ." Lucas Rackley interjected from just down the hall outside his aunt's room, having overheard us. "I should have thought of it myself. . . ."

"Thought of what?"

"A few months ago, when she was more lucid and not prone to these spells, I bought her one of those smart watches for her birthday," the young man explained. "She still wears it even though she doesn't use her cell phone anymore, so there's no syncing as far as the data the watch has accumulated. But it still might be there, at least for the last few days."

"How can we find out, Lucas?"

"Her cell phone is now tucked away in a drawer in her room. But I synced the watch to it when I first bought the watch for her, which means the data you're talking about might still be there."

"As in . . ." Mort said, leading Lucas on.

"As in steps taken, distance covered, pulse rate—a whole bunch of things."

"Let's stick with distance, son," Mort said. "You're telling me you may be able to tell us how far she ventured off the Shady Willows grounds?"

"Not where she went but, yes, how far she went. I'm almost sure that data will still be available from today. I'm not so sure about the other recent spells, whenever they were."

"Which the watch might be able to tell us as well," I noted, looking toward Mort. "Starting with the murders of Tad Hollenbeck and Sheila Del Perrio. If both of those deaths corresponded with spells Clara was in the midst of . . ."

I let my voice tail off there, still having trouble picturing Clara Wizzenhunt swatting a fly, much less taking the life of another human being.

"How long will it take you to see what her watch has to tell us?" Mort asked him.

"Shouldn't be long, but first I'll have to find her phone."

"You said it was in a drawer, here at Shady Willows."

"Figure of speech, Mrs. Fletcher. The fact is she could have left it someplace, thrown it out by accident, or lost it altogether. I'll search her room. Here's hoping we get lucky."

"Before anyone else gets killed," Mort added.

Chapter Twenty-five

In spite of the obvious distractions, and my apprehension over the Christmas parade the next day, that night was the best Christmas Eve I could ever remember, at least since Frank died. One Christmas Eve before Grady came to live with us, Frank surprised me with my first flying lesson—that was my present—and I'd gone so far as to fly the trainer plane he'd borrowed myself that first time out. Frank couldn't believe I took to the act so quickly, given that driving frightened me too much to ever get my driver's license. I guess I was lucky having lived the bulk of the last twenty-five years in either New York City or Cabot Cove, two of the places in the country where driving isn't a necessity.

I had gotten little Frank that train set at Fred Hardesty's antiques shop but was terrified he wouldn't like it. His father had been quite the fan of model trains as a boy and spent countless hours in the basement with my Frank playing with the train sets he'd assembled or built himself, which dipped and darted about a hefty portion of our basement floor. I recalled how much Grady had enjoyed that and thought little Frank might take a liking to model trains as well. Unfortunately, I'd donated my late husband's expansive collection to a local children's hospital years ago, so I purchased an ambitiously sized fully restored set from Fred Hardesty, who was quite fond of selling antique toys around the Christmas season.

Fred had explained all the workings to me, but I couldn't remember any of them for the life of me and could only hope Grady maintained enough recollection to make it a project he could do with little Frank just as my Frank had done with him. Nonetheless, my heart was in my mouth when my grandnephew chose that box to be the one present he was allowed to open on Christmas Eve.

The boy attacked it like a rabid dog, just like his father had gone after his presents at the same age. If I didn't know better, I would have thought I was looking at Grady from a generation ago, and not his son. With his parents gone, I walked him up the aisle for his wedding and was in the delivery room the night little Frank was born. Such wonderful milestones to remember and celebrate, and I was doing both in that magical, nerve-racking moment when little Frank tore the wrapping off his first model train set, though I feared the boy might not even know what he was looking at.

"I love it, Aunt Jess!" he shrieked as I held my breath.

I let it out just as he leaped into my arms.

"I've always wanted one of these, but I didn't think they made them anymore."

"They don't, really," I told him, feeling ever so relieved, "at least not like this. It's the real thing."

"Like us," Harry chimed in, fishing out a package he'd placed on the pile earlier and handing it to me. "For you, little lady."

I held the neatly wrapped package in my lap. "You don't want me to wait until tomorrow morning?"

"We're old, like Frank's train set there. We might not make it until tomorrow morning."

"Very funny, Harry," I said, starting to peel back the wrapping—gently, because I almost didn't want to disturb the job someone else must have done for him.

"I'm always a bundle of laughs around the holidays," he said. "More than usual even."

"Oh, Harry," I said, his present revealed inside the box. "I don't know what to say. It's . . ."

His perpetually dour expression urged me on.

"Perfect," I finished.

I took the leather-bound notebook, more along the size of a photo album, gingerly from the box and held it up for all to see the title imprinted on the front in bold golden letters:

MURDER, SHE WROTE

"It's absolutely beautiful," I resumed, holding it like I never wanted to let it go. "Truly elegant."

"Lots of pages for pictures and all your press clippings and reviews."

"Only the good ones, of course," I noted, smiling.

"What are you going to do with it, Aunt Jess?" little Frank asked me.

"Fill it," I said, with my eyes fixed on Harry.

My landline rang in that moment and I eased myself up carefully, so as not to drop my new memories book, the title of which had such a nice ring to it.

"What's that?" little Frank said, looking about.

"My phone, Frank."

"But your phone's right there, on the table," he said, pointing toward my cell.

"That's my other phone, my landline."

"Oh," the boy said, as if he'd never heard of one of those before.

I picked up the cordless phone from its cradle and saw it was Fred Hardesty calling. I moved into the kitchen before answering it.

"Glad I caught you, Mrs. Fletcher. Sorry to be calling on Christmas Eve, but your message did say you needed to speak with me right away."

"Thank you, Fred, and it's me who should be apologizing to you for being such a nuisance on Christmas Eve."

"Nothing to apologize for. I'm still at the store after a banner day of last-minute shoppers. I assume you're calling about those documents you left for me to review."

"Exactly. I was wondering if you'd managed to get any further with them."

"The answer's yes, Mrs. Fletcher. I wish I had a better present for you, but I'm drawing a blank when it comes to all this skullduggery the founders were up to. Not a mention I can find anywhere about what became of Wyatt Rackley's diamonds. I still have quite a bit of material to cover, but so far I still have nothing to report."

"If anybody can make sense of whatever's in that chest, it's you, Fred."

I could picture him twirling his mustache on the other end of the line. "And I'm grateful to have the opportunity to experience history up close and personal. To think I'm reading the actual words of the men who created this town . . . I can't think of a better Christmas present, Mrs. Fletcher."

I thought of little Frank's train set and the beautiful keepsake book Harry had given me, smiling.

"By the way, any word yet on that train set I sold you?"

I peered around the corner to find Grady already assembling the tracks near the beautifully refurbished cars he'd laid out on the floor.

"A smashing success," I told Fred.

"You're kidding."

"I'll take some pictures so you can see for yourself next time I stop in."

"Some things stand the test of time, don't they, Mrs. Fletcher?"

"That's what I keep telling myself, Fred."

I continued watching little Frank, remembering his father in virtually the same pose a very long time ago.

"I'll see you at the parade tomorrow, then, Mrs. Fletcher."

"Count on it," I said, unable to lift my gaze from little Frank until I shifted it to Harry McGraw. "Just don't look for me playing Mrs. Claus this year."

Harry adjourned to my office shortly thereafter, refusing to elaborate on a hunch he was pursuing. He'd barely even used the guest room I'd insisted he take instead of staying at Hill House. It had been so long since I'd had a house full of people, with all four bedrooms occupied, and I can't describe how good that felt, especially over Christmas season. I'd gotten so used to the oddities and luxuries of hotel life that I'd forgotten how rewarding the simple features of being at home were. I'd made the best of my time living in a Hill House suite, forging a new routine without significant enough appreciation of how much I valued the one that had been stripped from me by the fire. Everything was better when you were home, and returning there from wherever I'd been was a simple pleasure I'd tended to take for granted until home wasn't there for me for that extended stretch.

Little Frank fell asleep on the living room rug in the midst of constructing the model train. Grady carried him up to his room with Donna in tow. I was going to stop in to check on Harry before retiring for the night myself but decided not to distract him from whatever labors had claimed his attention when I heard the clack of his dutiful pounding away on the keyboard. I had no idea what this hunch he was pursuing might be, but I'd learned long ago to trust in Harry.

The next morning found him passed out in my

desk chair yet again, snoring up a storm. I'd say that the noise had woken me, except I never was able to settle into a comfortable sleep, not with two murders that remained unsolved—three, including Tad Hollenbeck's sister—and too many suspects to make sense of, all culled from descendants of the original founders of Cabot Cove. Fisherman Terry McMullen had lied about being out to sea when Tad Hollenbeck was murdered, and his affair with Abby Joyner would not have precluded a visit to the Surfsider Motel around the fateful time. The shavings I'd spotted in that basement where Dan Kinder was working on a boiler might well turn out to be a match for seemingly identical ones recovered from both murder scenes. Asa Cabot, meanwhile, had now admitted to venturing outside of his home in an attempt to cure his agoraphobia, and his personal assistant, James Carnevale, with that sordid background, was still missing, as far as I knew. Meanwhile, the fugue states that accompanied the spells that sent Clara Wizzenhunt traipsing about the woods surrounding Shady Willows left her a suspect as well, at least until her nephew, Lucas Rackley, managed to download the information from her smart watch to determine how far she'd actually ventured in her sojourns, which had occurred during the day as well as the night. Even if that data absolved her, though, it certainly wouldn't absolve him.

I was convinced that any of these suspects could just as easily become the next victim. This morning's Christmas parade would see them conveniently confined in a horse-drawn carriage parading down Main

Street, and if the killer was someone beyond these descendants of our original town founders, the opportunity would be there for that killer to strike a final, deadly blow. With this in mind, I planned to arrive hours ahead of the parade's starting time, while Mort was enacting whatever protective measures he'd put in place. It was times like this when I valued his law enforcement expertise most, realizing how lucky we were to have a sheriff of his exceptional experience. Nothing against the likes of Amos Tupper, but Cabot Cove had outgrown having anyone but a professional wearing the sheriff's hat. Someone who understood that crime didn't stop at the borders of small towns like ours. That said, I always called Amos on Christmas Day and resolved to continue that tradition, no matter what else occurred today.

What I couldn't quite grasp yet was exactly how Wyatt Rackley's long-missing diamonds fit into all this. Without a firm idea of how many there actually were, it was impossible to calculate their potential value, which I imagined could stretch into eight figures. That was certainly enough to go around among the surviving heirs, even those beyond Cabot Cove, which raised the question, What if the killer was not, in fact, one of them? Was the killer somehow in possession of the diamonds and seeking to eliminate anyone with a legal claim to them?

My unease was exacerbated by the fact that I had a sense we were nearing the endgame. Maybe I was exaggerating the importance of the Christmas parade from a timing standpoint, but nonetheless I clung to the hope that once Harry McGraw stirred, he would produce some revelation gleaned from his toils behind my computer.

"I don't want to comment on an empty stomach," he said when he finally emerged from my office and went straight into the bathroom.

After a wonderful breakfast prepared by Grady and Donna, with some help from little Frank, who couldn't wait to get to his train set, I pressed Harry again.

"I don't want to comment while I'm digesting," he said this time, from his chair at the kitchen table.

"In other words, you haven't found anything."

"Not yet."

"Are you close?"

"Not yet."

"Is that going to be your only answer, Harry?"

"Can I tell you later?" he quipped, stifling a yawn. "How does anybody sleep in this place?"

"Not in a desk chair normally."

"Good point." He lumbered out of his chair. "Well, I'd better go get properly dressed." He lowered his voice in addressing Donna and Grady. "Somebody convinced me to play San—"

Harry stopped himself just in time when he remembered little Frank in the chair next to him.

"Who you going to play, Uncle Harry?" the boy asked him.

"Sanford Jones."

"Who's that?"

"Very important person in these parts."

"Why? What'd he do, Uncle Harry?"

I nodded at Harry, coaxing him on.

"Well, little man, he was the first merchant to ever open up a store on Main Street," he said, figuring that would be it.

"What did his store sell?"

"Pretty much everything. It was one of those mercantile places."

"What's a mercantile place?"

"Somewhere that sells everything."

"Oh," little Frank said, grudgingly accepting Harry's explanation.

"How'd you talk me into this again?" he asked, turning toward me. "Just so you know, I had a bad experience at a parade once."

"What happened?"

"Would you believe I got run over by a float?"

"No."

"It was a *Star Wars* theme," Harry said. "I won't tell you where Darth Vader's lightsaber ended up."

"Want to head over to Main Street together?" I asked him.

"When are you leaving?"

I checked my watch. "Soon."

"In that case, I'll meet you there."

After Harry disappeared up the stairs, the rest of us retook our seats in the living room from last night to finish the process of opening presents. Christmas was certainly made for kids, and I couldn't imagine it being anywhere near this much fun without little Frank being there. His enthusiasm and excitement bubbled over and spread to the rest of us, leaving Grady, Donna, and me beaming genuinely about our gifts as much as the boy did.

I much preferred watching them open the presents I'd gotten for them, as opposed to opening my own, but I also knew I'd given Grady the greatest gift imaginable by volunteering to back him in his new business venture. What good is money if we can't use it to help the people we love? I didn't really look at it as an investment, of course, and would have been willing to support my nephew even if his whims had been less grounded, as they had been at times in the past. This time, though, the notion of opening up his own accounting firm seemed perfectly reasonable and well-thought-out.

I remember one of my editors saying she was partial to maintaining a hands-off relationship with her authors because she didn't believe you could micromanage the creative process. So, too, you couldn't micromanage relationships with the people who meant the most to you. In my mind, you were all in or you weren't. And I was all in on Grady. I'd long passed the point of providing unquestioned support strictly because of the tragedy of losing his parents at such a young age. I'd long since stopped feeling sorry for him and chose instead to appreciate the wonderful man he'd grown into, even if that wonderful man didn't always make the best business or financial decisions.

As soon as we were done opening presents, Grady offered to drop me off at the head of the parade route on Main Street. I'd risen to grab my coat when I spotted something amid the refuse of torn wrapping and stray bows, something I'd never have noticed at all if it hadn't been for the events of the past week. I leaned over to pluck it from the carpet, feeling my heart begin to hammer against my rib cage.

Because I was holding a black strand identical to the ones we'd found in both Tad Hollenbeck's motel room and Sheila Del Perrio's living room.

Chapter Twenty-six

That made no sense, of course, since this strand had hardly been found at a crime scene. I was utterly flummoxed over how it had gotten here. Of course, it was possible that this particular black strand only resembled the others. Being someone who doesn't believe in coincidence, though, I found that hard to believe, which, of course, didn't give me any notion as to how it might have ended up in my house.

I placed the single black strand in a Ziploc bag to hand over to Mort as soon as I caught up with him at the Christmas parade. Grady dropped me off as planned at the head of Main Street, just before it was closed off at eleven a.m. ahead of the parade's one p.m. start. It would take twenty-five minutes at most for the whole of the procession to make its way from the beginning of the route to the end, the street packed on both sides with residents eager to participate in this longtime Cabot Cove tradition. Grady said he'd be back with Donna and Frank by a little after noon to snag a prime viewing spot along the sidewalk, hopefully close to Mara's so he could have a regular supply of hot chocolate.

I found Mort in the company of a dozen of his deputies, the most I'd ever seen gathered at one time. I held my distance as they reviewed placement and their protective strategy, going through all necessary means to secure the parade in the event our killer showed up.

"Very impressive, Sheriff," I told him after the group had dispersed to take their assigned positions. "Looks like you called everyone in."

"That's not the whole of it, Mrs. F. The state police are assisting as well, handling spotter duty."

"Spotter duty?"

Mort gestured above us. "From rooftops and through windows at the highest vantage points. I'm determined to make this the safest Christmas parade ever."

"Under the circumstances, that's an ambitious goal."

"Oh, and speaking of the state police, the lab called earlier—on Christmas morning, no less—to tell me that those black shavings we found at the two murder scenes didn't match the shavings from that boiler Dan Kinder was working on."

"You mean the black shavings like this?" I asked him, easing the Ziploc bag from my pocketbook.

Mort's eyes bulged as he took it in his grasp. "Where'd this come from?"

"My living room, if you can believe that."

"I can't." He gave the strand a closer look. "It sure

looks like the others, Mrs. F., but we'll need the state police crime lab to weigh in on that. Speaking of which," Mort added, flipping open his magical memo pad, "according to their analysis, what we found at the two murder scenes weren't shavings, but fibers, something called Kanekalon. Mean anything to you, Mrs. F.?"

"Not a thing."

"Me either. Oh, and the state police also informed me that the blood found on Clara Wizzenhunt yesterday wasn't human. And it turns out the remains of a raccoon were found just outside the main entrance shortly after she returned."

I looked toward Clara, who was staring vacantly ahead at something maybe only she could see. "You figure she brought it back with her from where she wandered off to?"

"That's my working assumption, yes," Mort affirmed.

"Well, here's another: Clara could never have been the killer anyway—we were with her when Sheila Del Perrio called, just before Sheila's doorbell rang."

Mort nodded. "Yeah, I knew that. I was just testing you."

"Really?"

"No, but I did manage to call Abby Joyner. I figured that was better than a visit that might make her husband suspicious."

"Why, Sheriff Metzger," I couldn't help but say, "I do believe you've finally discovered discretion."

"Something I didn't need to exercise a lot in New York City, Mrs. F. Anyway, Abby Joyner confirmed she was with Terry McMullen the night of Tad Hollenbeck's murder."

"So I guess we can rule him out as a suspect."

"Ah, but there's more. Would you care to guess where they met for this tryst?"

"Don't tell me the Surfsider Motel?"

Mort nodded. "They were there until eleven o'clock and, to anticipate your next question, yes, Terry McMullen did leave to go somewhere, she says, around nine fifteen. I confirmed the timing with the babysitter she hired."

"How long was McMullen gone from the room?"

"That's the thing. She doesn't remember. See, there was some drinking involved and . . ."

Mort left things there.

"So Terry McMullen is still very much a suspect, but Dan Kinder has slipped back considerably."

"Of the remaining suspects, who does that really leave us with, Mrs. F.?"

Before I could answer, I spotted none other than Asa Cabot emerging anxiously from his car.

The car was a Bentley or Rolls-Royce, something like that, encased in a thin sheen of dust, as if it had been tucked away in a garage for quite a while. The black car's heft and formidable lines made Cabot look small as he climbed out of the front seat, careful with every step, as if the next might sink into quicksand.

"Mr. Cabot!" I called out to him, not bothering to hide my surprise.

He welcomed the sight of a familiar face amid all

the hubbub dominating the parade's starting point here at the head of Main Street and walked deliberately my way.

"Have I come to the right place to take my spot in the founders' carriage, Mrs. Fletcher?"

"Let me direct you to one of the organizers," I said, looking about for one. "I know this couldn't be easy for you, Mr. Cabot. You're a brave man for coming."

"You inspired me not to wait until next year."

"Me? How?"

"With that talk about those presentations I used to give at the library. It made me realize too much of life was passing me by."

"Very courageous of you to make the effort, all the same."

"Thanks to a boatload of antianxiety medication." He shrugged his bony shoulders, then frowned. "I hope you'll still think I'm brave after another hour or so. I'm not looking forward to this, Mrs. Fletcher; well, I am, and I'm not, if that makes any sense."

"It makes perfect sense, sir, and if there's anything I can do for you, please don't hesitate to ask."

"I must say I noticed quite a police presence on hand."

"Doing everything they can to keep everyone safe, Mr. Cabot. That includes you and the other founders' descendants."

"A worthy pursuit indeed, but are they truly a match for the killer?"

I peered at Asa Cabot closer, still not having ruled him out as a suspect. "Let's hope we don't get the chance to find out."

The fact that he'd come alone was enough to tell me that another potential suspect, his personal assistant, James Carnevale, was still nowhere to be found. That said, it was also possible that Carnevale had acted on Asa Cabot's orders in eliminating two of the other descendants in the past five days.

After escorting Cabot to one of the parade organizers to be directed to the right place, I cast my gaze down Main Street, past the floats and local dignitaries assembling into position at the start of the route. Players from *A Christmas Carol*, which we'd be putting on at the parade's conclusion, manned one of those floats. The Cabot Cove tradition was for those manning the route to move immediately to the nearby high school to partake of our performance, one show and one show only. You'd think such a thing would have trouble gaining an audience on Christmas Day, but the status of the play as a tradition of our Christmas celebration led annually to a packed house that was often standing room only. There had even been years when a second performance had been added, but that was before more residents started traveling over the holidays and others aged into preferring a warmer climate as soon as winter reared its ugly head.

Because it was cold, and Christmas, the crowds that would soon pack both sides of Main Street had not yet begun to gather in earnest. I was relying on a combination of adrenaline and anxiety over what was to come to keep me warm, besides a heavy parka, woolen socks, and other appropriate gear for the weather, and so far it was working. I decided to busy myself for the time being by surveying the scene on

my own, while Mort continued setting up the considerable security detail, unprecedented by Cabot Cove
standards.

The parade assembling at the head of Main Street
curled onto adjacent Spring Street. The horse-drawn
carriage that would carry the surviving descendants
of Cabot Cove's founding fathers at the front of the
parade had yet to arrive. It would be driven, as always,
by Averell Cooperman, a local farmer who raised
champion draft horses most thought were Clydesdales
but were actually another, almost-as-large and equally
impressive, breed. They were massive animals that
looked big and muscular enough to pull a freight
train.

I spotted Asa Cabot seated back in his fancy car
with the engine running and heat on for sure, his expression making me wonder if he might drive off at
any moment. I imagined that his agoraphobia was
calmed at least a bit by being inside the familiar confines of his car. Then again, based on the blanket of
dust that clung to the big car's paint like paste, it had
been quite a while since he'd been inside it, never
mind behind the wheel. I felt genuinely bad for him,
though I couldn't say precisely why.

I stopped even with the high school marching band,
which was assembling into position at what would
eventually be directly behind the horse-drawn carriage. I also spotted a number of Christmas-themed
characters in full elaborate costume. One grouping I
identified as Santa's elves had all donned oversized
plastic heads that featured an assortment of beards,
mustaches, and sideburns.

The floats lining up along Spring Street, meanwhile, were mostly those of local merchants who'd paid a nominal fee to ride a float promoting their businesses. Mara's had a float, as did the local bookstore. The Friends of the Library always sponsored one as well, this year to be ridden by elementary school kids wearing costumes from Dr. Seuss's *How the Grinch Stole Christmas*. I could hear the distant riffs of the famed theme song from the television adaptation as the chaperones began to usher the kids on board.

I checked my watch to find there was still an hour to go until the Christmas parade's one o'clock start. I heard the *click-clack* of hooves meeting asphalt and spotted Averell Cooperman riding onto the scene in a carriage drawn by his draft horses garbed in full Christmas regalia. If I didn't know better, I might've thought they were supposed to be reindeer and that it would be Santa Claus, instead of descendants of the founding fathers, who'd be riding in the carriage. Santa's, of course, would be the very last, but the costumed elves would tease the crowd about Santa's arrival by a fake sleigh closer to the front. I caught an elf with a mustache that reminded me of Fred Hardesty's holding his massive plastic head up so he could sneak in a final cigarette before taking his place along the parade line.

A used-car dealership that had been in business forever on the outskirts of town was sponsoring a float dominated by none other than Mort's vintage red Eldorado convertible, looking showroom new.

I saw a smattering of the cast from *A Christmas Carol* starting to climb on board their float, which fea-

tured a scene from Dickens's Victorian England. Seth
Hazlitt was among them; freed from his traditional
role as Santa Claus, he'd come in full costume as the
Ghost of Christmas Past, and I made my way over to
say hello.

"Forget your costume, Jess?" he asked playfully
from aboard the float.

"I don't need it. I found someone else to play Santa,
remember?"

He regarded me with faux derision. "Could've
done better than that all the same, *ayuh*."

"I was too busy preparing tonight's dinner to get
changed."

"Don't forget, I'm bringing the pie."

"Mara's?"

"Mara's," he affirmed with a nod. "A nice variety."

"Same as last year?"

"Of course. What else did you expect?" His expression tightened. "Anything new on the investigations,
anything I should know?"

"Well, the state police crime lab identified the black
fibers we found at both murder scenes."

"Fibers?" he prompted, hearing that for the first
time.

"Something called Kanekalon. Mean anything to
you?"

Seth moved his head from side to side instead of
nodding. "I could be wrong, but I think that's the material that goes into synthetic wigs."

"As in . . ." I started, tugging at my hair.

Seth nodded.

"So we're looking for a killer who wears a wig?"

"Or a toupee. How many times have you found yourself chasing a clue like that, Jess?"

"Never."

"First time for everything."

"This week seems to be full of first times."

"You better check me on that definition," he cautioned. "The Kanekalon I'm thinking of might just as easily be an ingredient in baby formula."

"In which case we'd be looking for a killer who crawls and hasn't learned how to talk yet."

"Good luck to Sheriff Metzger trying to take their statement."

I moved on at that, into the unwelcome chill of the shade to better see my phone's screen. I googled *Kanekalon*, and the first hit that came up proved Seth to be correct. I doubted synthetic hair was the only thing the artificial fiber was used for, but a half dozen pages into my search I still hadn't come upon another.

I strolled up the street in search of Mort to inform him, and was impressed by the positioning of the deputies he'd set in place. I was glad to see they weren't outfitted in flak jackets or carrying the long guns kept under lock and key at the sheriff's station, neither of which fit very well into the festivities. Then again, neither did the presence of a dozen deputies and who knew how many Maine state police officers in the first place. But we couldn't lose sight of the fact that if a murderer was targeting the descendants of our founding fathers, then having them all together at one time might be too great a temptation to resist.

I passed a float sponsored by one of those chain jewelry stores that had moved in, the float dominated by a Christmas tree decorated with diamonds I assumed were fake. That sight left me considering the multitude of very real diamonds that had gone missing before Wyatt Rackley had been killed by John Henry Cabot in 1795. I had hoped Fred Hardesty's expert scrutiny of those historical documents would reveal something of note, and if his efforts failed, I had no idea where else to turn.

I couldn't find Mort anywhere along Main Street, so I made my way back down the street to where Averell Cooperman had now positioned his carriage at the very start of the procession. I saw Asa Cabot approaching it stiffly, alongside one of Mort's deputies, who seemed to be guiding him. I recognized Dan Kinder as well and watched Terry McMullen stamp out a cigarette before hoisting himself on board. Lucas Rackley was making his way slowly up the street, a figure edging along by his side who I realized, impossibly, was his aunt, Clara Wizzenhunt.

"Clara!" I greeted her when I reached them.

"Jessica! Lovely day, isn't it? And Merry Christmas!"

"Merry Christmas to you, too," I said, turning my attention to her nephew.

Lucas wrapped an arm around Clara's frail, bony shoulders. "She woke up this morning and insisted on coming."

Clara wore a puffy navy blue coat that dropped to her knees, over a print dress colored a combination of red and green for the season. It swam on her a bit, testifying to how much she'd deteriorated since she'd last worn it, a bit of melancholy added to an otherwise happy moment. But she was here to take her rightful place at the head of the parade. An orderly I thought I recognized from Shady Willows had accompanied them but was keeping his distance. He was likely to keep pace alongside the founders' carriage, without climbing on board.

"I haven't seen you in forever," Clara was saying. "You must come see me. Promise you will."

I looked toward Lucas, who shrugged.

"I promise, Clara."

"Next week?"

"Why wait until next week?" I said, looking at both her and Lucas. "Why don't the two of you come for Christmas dinner at my house today?"

Lucas looked toward his aunt, whose focus remained solely on me, a big smile spreading across her face. "That sounds wonderful! Doesn't it, Lucas?"

I'd expected him to shrug the question off, but he nodded instead. "What time would you like us there, Mrs. Fletcher?"

"Dinner's at six."

"Then six it is!" Clara chortled.

She hugged me and then accepted her nephew's help in mounting the portable steps that led up onto the open carriage. Before joining her on board, Lucas approached me, lowering his voice enough to make sure his aunt couldn't overhear his words.

"I found my aunt's cell phone and was able to download the data from her smart watch. Her most recent spells don't correspond with the two murders, and the latest covered barely a half mile in total, about the average of the others as well."

I nodded absently—no reason to tell him I had clumsily forgotten that Clara couldn't possibly have killed Sheila Del Perrio. A real-life investigation, in that respect, is not unlike the fictional ones I concoct, in that sometimes things are speeding by so fast it's easy to miss the obvious.

Lucas cast his gaze toward Averell Cooperman's draft horses. "It's funny, but Aunt Clara used to be scared of horses, terrified even. It's one of the reasons she always avoided participating in the parade. I guess she's forgotten about that, too."

Those horses snorted and flopped their heads up and down, one after the other, as if imitating each other.

"Take good care of her, Lucas," I said, squeezing his arm tenderly.

I moved on, trying to spot Mort to fill him in on even more now. The sidewalks were beginning to quickly fill in, residents coming in droves seemingly from nowhere. With parking closed on Main and the adjoining streets, they would've had to park their cars several blocks away and make the rest of the trek on foot. I noticed a pair of kiosks, one on each side of the road, arranged by Mara's and distributing free hot chocolate, candy canes, and Christmas cookies. The scene left me wishing there was snow in the offing— not a big storm, just enough coating to give the scene its final indelible image.

Mort wasn't answering my calls, and I still couldn't find him. I wished he'd given me one of those police walkie-talkies so we could stay in communication. I continued scanning the street for him, my eyes sifting amid the crowds on both sides beginning to fill in every available space, already two-deep in some places and soon to be three or four. Nothing brings people out on a frosty Christmas afternoon better than a longtime tradition like this, and Cabot Cove residents had become even more dedicated to appreciating and preserving such things since the influx of summer residents had almost robbed us of our identity. It was almost as if the fifteen hundred, maybe two thousand, people who came to view the parade did so to hold on to the last vestiges of the old Cabot Cove we were all determined not to let go of.

I spotted a host of floats populated by the members of various Cabot Cove High School boys' and girls' sports teams in full uniform, the basketball players with thick letterman jackets and sweatpants worn over their thin shorts and tank tops in the cold, while the girls wore only light warm-up suits over their uniforms.

I continued my search for Mort along the sidewalks on both sides of the street, and spotted Harry McGraw, in full Santa Claus regalia, climbing up into the plywood sleigh, which buckled a bit under his weight. I made my way there and found him working his tablet, not yet in character.

"Anything to report, Harry?"

"Did I call to tell you I had something to report?" he asked me, not even looking up.

I checked my phone to make sure I hadn't missed a call from him. "Er, no."

"Then I've got nothing to report yet." He looked up long enough to study the growing crowd. "I have to smile and look jolly, don't I?"

I nodded. "You are Santa Claus, after all."

"No problem. I'll just picture you finally paying your bills. That should make me smile."

With that, Harry went back to his tablet.

The sidewalks were now packed two- and three-deep, in some places even four-. I spotted a large figure moving at the rear of the congestion. He looked familiar for some reason, and when he passed by a less congested area, I saw why.

It was James Carnevale, Asa Cabot's personal assistant.

Chapter Twenty-seven

He'd been nowhere to be found when we'd left Asa Cabot at his estate yesterday after informing him of Carnevale's criminal record, as well as his dishonorable discharge from the Marines. I found myself frozen in place right in the center of Main Street. I took my eyes off James Carnevale to search for the nearest Cabot Cove deputy, but when I tried to pick him up in my gaze again, he was gone.

Was I sure it had been Carnevale in the first place? I began doubting what I'd seen, wondering if my imagination had conjured his appearance, conceiving an ending for this story the way I might for one of J. B. Fletcher's mysteries. I tried to breathe easier but could feel pressure in my chest with each inhale. Then I heard a whistle blow three times, the signal lifeguards use for impending danger. These whistle blows sounding from a hundred feet back at the head of Main Street had originated for another purpose entirely.

The annual Christmas parade had begun.

I heard cheers; I heard applause; I heard the pounding drumbeat of the high school marching band as it set out on the parade route immediately behind Averell Cooperman's horse-drawn carriage bearing the descendants of the town's founding fathers.

I moved to the side of the street where I thought I'd glimpsed James Carnevale, moving about the rear of the crowd stacked three-deep in the hope of spotting him again. Before I knew it, the head of the parade had drawn even with me, the descendants waving awkwardly at the throngs assembled on both sides of the street.

For some reason, I waved back. The elves with the immense heads followed the marching band, making a show of banging against one another. The head with the mustache banged into a head with a freckled face, which banged into one that looked as if it had sunburn, and all three elves went down, drawing laughs from the crowd. They lumbered back to their feet, looking perplexed, as a rubbery hand belonging to the mustachioed one worked to affix the whole of that mustache back in place after the comic collision dislodged it. The Friendly Auto Sales float, featuring Mort's pristine Cadillac Eldorado, had to slow slightly to avoid drawing too close.

James Carnevale was nowhere to be seen. Then, just like that, he reappeared. Carnevale's stride took him along behind the rows of spectators. He matched the pace of the horse-drawn carriage down Main Street, seeming to mirror it. Was he there to protectively watch over Asa Cabot or for some other reason entirely?

I needed to locate Mort now more than ever, coming finally upon Deputy Andy, who was one of the few holdovers from the days when Amos Tupper was sheriff.

"Where's Sheriff Metzger?" I demanded when he was in the middle of a friendly holiday greeting.

The smile slipped from his face once he saw my expression. "I haven't seen him in—"

"Call him! Now! Tell him James Carnevale is here!"

"James *who*?"

"He'll know! Just do it!"

I lost Carnevale again but needed only to trace the path of the horse-drawn carriage to find him.

"Sheriff wants to talk to you, Mrs. Fletcher," Deputy Andy said, handing me his walkie-talkie.

"Mort?"

"What's going on? What's all this about James Carnevale?"

"He's here!"

"Where?"

"Moving even with the carriage at the head of the parade."

"Where are you?"

I started moving on in Carnevale's wake, taking Deputy Andy's walkie-talkie with me. "I just passed Mara's."

"Okay. I see you. Stay where you are. I'm coming to you."

"But—"

"Stay where you are, Jessica, and that's an order!"

Mort called me *Jessica* these days only in moments like this. I reluctantly held my ground to await him. The Cabot Cove High School sports teams' floats were moving past me, making me think about how much kids had changed since I'd been an English teacher there. I heard footsteps pounding somewhere close and swung to find Mort dashing up to me in a huff, slightly out of breath.

"Merry Christmas, Mort."

"It will be if no one else gets killed, Mrs. F.," he said, getting his breath back.

"Speaking of which," I said, leaving it there as I gestured toward the head of the parade, where James Carnevale was keeping pace with the horse-drawn carriage.

I realized I was still holding Deputy Andy's walkie-talkie and stuffed it in a pocket of my parka as Mort raised his to his mouth.

"All units, this is Sheriff Metzger. Suspect spotted currently passing in front of Cabot Cove Books. White male, approximately six feet two inches and two hundred and twenty pounds. Wearing dark slacks and black leather jacket. Converge and wait for my signal."

When we looked that way again, Carnevale was cutting through the crowd and heading into the street, even with the founders' carriage, a hand reaching into his jacket pocket.

That hand was just emerging when the sheriff's deputies converged on James Carnevale and Mort ordered them to take him down. They rushed him en masse, spilling him to the pavement, where he disappeared beneath a sea of heavy green jackets. An orange prescription bottle was launched airborne, what Carnevale must have been reaching for when the deputies swarmed him: his charge's antianxiety medication. He'd likely been readying Asa Cabot's next dose.

The commotion spooked the horses pulling the founders' carriage, and they twisted sideways, forcing the floats in their immediate wake to brake to sudden, squealing halts that nearly toppled riders of several and even rocked Mort's beloved Eldorado convertible.

Some of the marching band was still playing and some wasn't, the resulting melody shrill and jumbled. The big-headed elf characters, meanwhile, banged into one another without meaning to this time, the one that looked like Humpty Dumpty stepping all over the mustache that was now missing altogether from that big head's plastic face.

Oh my . . .

Then I turned to see Santa Claus huffing his way toward me. It took me a moment to recall it was Harry McGraw dressed as jolly St. Nick, hands on his knees to catch his breath.

He stripped off his cottony beard. "I've got another one for you, little lady," he said, the tablet I'd glimpsed him working on in his free hand. "I know who—"

"—the murderer is," I completed for him. "So do I, Harry."

He leaned against Mort's Eldorado, looking deflated that I'd stolen his thunder. "And a happy New Year to you, too."

*   *   *

We found Fred Hardesty at his antiques shop well back on Main Street before the start of the parade route. He was sweeping up after his very busy Christmas Eve the day before, seemingly oblivious to what had just transpired.

"Merry Christmas, Mrs. Fletcher," he greeted me, halting his labors. "You, too, Sheriff. I'm afraid I have no further progress to report in my study of those documents, if that's what this is about."

"It's not," said a scowling Santa Claus.

Hardesty's eyes fell on Harry McGraw, still clothed in his Santa garb, minus the beard.

"Were you naughty or nice this year?" Harry asked him. "I'm guessing that murder qualifies as naughty."

Hardesty's mouth dropped open. He looked at me, then Mort.

"I don't think I understand," he managed.

"Oh, I think you do," Mort told him. "I think you understand very well."

With that, Mort stretched a hand toward Fred Hardesty's face and stripped off the fake mustache that everyone in town had thought was real for as long as I could remember.

"Tell him, Mrs. F.," Mort said, slipping the fake mustache into an evidence pouch.

"That's made of Kanekalon, strands of which we found in both Tad Hollenbeck's room at the Surfsider and Sheila Del Perrio's living room."

"We're betting those strands prove a perfect match

for this," Mort added, displaying Hardesty's fake mustache inside the evidence bag.

"I found one in my living room this morning," I told him. "That seemed impossible at first, until I remembered you'd packed up that antique train set for my grandnephew and had it delivered to my house. The strand must have dropped into that box right here in your shop and then ended up on my carpet when little Frank tore it open."

Hardesty ignored my insinuation. "I barely knew Mrs. Del Perrio and I didn't know this Hollenbeck character at all."

"In which case you need to explain something to me, Fred," I said to him. "Sheila's son-in-law was kind enough to open up Del Perrio's before we came over here. You see, just before you killed her, Sheila had called to tell me something she'd forgotten when Sheriff Metzger and I were there the day before. I think it was the fact that you and Tad Hollenbeck had dinner there separately but around the same time early Monday night. Both your names were in the reservation book, and Sheila's son-in-law remembers her introducing Hollenbeck to you after he expressed an interest in Cabot Cove history. That's what she wanted to tell me, and it explains why you killed her, because she was the only person who could definitively link you to Tad Hollenbeck."

I resumed when Hardesty failed to respond.

"Did Hollenbeck tell you what he was after? Did he accuse you of being involved with his sister's disappearance?"

"Maybe Hollenbeck found something in his sister's e-mails that incriminated you," Harry McGraw chimed in, holding up his tablet, which I saw now had a crack right down its center.

"Patricia Demps came to Cabot Cove because she believed you had the founders' long-lost diamonds in your possession," I added. "In fact, she knew you did. Her brother must have figured out the same thing, and that's why you killed him."

"I'm guessing she already knew about the long-lost diamonds when she got here, and she knew just where to find them, thanks to pictures on your website, particularly a picture of that," Harry followed, having jogged the cracked screen to the store's website as he pointed up at the object featured on its homepage.

Fred Hardesty's cherished crystal chandelier.

"How many diamonds are mixed in with the crystals, Mr. Hardesty?" Mort asked him.

"You always said Poe's 'The Purloined Letter' was your favorite story," I remembered. "So I guess it should come as no surprise you hid the long-lost treasure of Cabot Cove in plain view."

"So, what happened?" Mort jumped in. "Did Patricia Demps show up here unannounced? Did she threaten you? Did she have a weapon? Because if she threatened you, and you had reason to believe she had a weapon, we could be looking at self-defense here."

My turn. "You buried her body out in the woods in the same place you'd already discovered the remains of Wyatt Rackley and that old chest. But how did you manage to find them?"

I continued when Hardesty remained silent. "Let

me hazard a guess. You must have come into possession of the crystal chandelier where Wyatt Rackley
had hidden the legendary diamonds, and you recognized them almost immediately, because you'd read
John Henry Cabot's journal. That means you must
have uncovered Rackley's remains and the chest
first. . . ." Then I realized what I'd been missing. "You
didn't find them out in the woods, did you, Fred? This
complex of buildings was the site of Cabot's original
mercantile shop. The basement was all that remained,
a root cellar back in the 1790s, and that's where Cabot
must have hidden Rackley's body and the town's
founding documents."

"Does that sound about right?" Harry asked him.
Then, when Hardesty didn't respond: "I think I'll take
that as a yes."

"Why not just destroy the chest and what was inside?" Mort wondered, sounding miffed. "Why bother
reburying it in Mrs. Fletcher's backyard?"

I could see Fred Hardesty's spirit, and resistance,
breaking as he sucked in a deep breath and let it out
slowly. "If I'd really done that, I might say because it
was a piece of history, Sheriff. I could no more destroy
it than I could cut off my own arm."

"She saw that picture on your website and recognized immediately what she was looking at," I resumed. "But she couldn't be sure, of course, without
closer inspection of the chandelier."

"That's ridiculous, utterly absurd," Hardesty tried
to insist through a cracking voice. "How could she
possibly have been so sure based on a grainy photograph?"

"Because she was a jeweler," Harry McGraw told him.

A pair of Mort's deputies who'd been waiting outside took Fred Hardesty into custody. We watched their patrol car drive off, flashing lights going but no siren. I realized I was still holding Harry's broken tablet and started to extend it back toward him.

"Don't bother, Jess," he said, backing off. "I borrowed it from you. You'd think these things wouldn't break every time you dropped them."

Chapter Twenty-eight

I called Amos Tupper to keep up our tradition as soon as I got home.

"Why, Miz Fletcher, it's wonderful to hear your voice!"

"Merry Christmas, Amos."

"And Merry Christmas to you, too, ma'am. Enjoying a quiet holiday season, I hope?"

"Well, not exactly."

"Do I want to know the details?"

"I'm sure you can guess most of them."

I heard him chuckle softly. "I do miss those times, in spite of the details. We made a difference in Cabot Cove, didn't we?"

"We sure did."

"And how's Mort Metzger getting on?"

"Well, he's no Amos Tupper."

"Ah, Miz Fletcher, that's about the nicest Christmas present anybody ever gave me."

"How about coming out here next year, celebrate Christmas in your old stomping ground?"

"That would be wonderful. I just might take you up on it. I don't get out much these days and it would be great to see all my old friends."

"They all miss you, too," I told him.

"Do they, now? Please give them my best, Doc Hazlitt especially. Mort, too. My phone doesn't ring often, but when it does, I always figure it might be him."

"To ask you to assist in an investigation?"

"To ask me if I want my old job back. You know, Miz Fletcher, not everyone's cut out for life in Cabot Cove."

"True enough, Amos, true enough."

It was the most crowded Christmas dinner I'd ever served, both extensions for my dining room table required in order to seat everyone. In addition to Seth, Harry, Mort and his wife, Adele, Grady, Donna, and little Frank, Lucas Rackley and his aunt, Clara Wizzenhunt, did indeed show up promptly at six. I'd forgotten I'd even invited them but was so happy to see Clara, and even Lucas now, I welcomed them in with open arms. Little Frank barely touched his food because he was so eager to get back to building the model train set he'd opened the night before. I didn't realize how many pieces were actually contained in the box it was packed into until I saw it sprawling across the center of my living room with still more pieces to add before the train set was fully assembled.

I could only imagine how happy my Frank must be with that, assuming he was watching.

Under the circumstances, our performance of *A Christmas Carol* had been postponed. The good news was that instead of a single performance, there would be four leading up to and on New Year's Day. I looked at that as just extending Christmas in Cabot Cove a bit longer, not a bad thing at all. Call the postponement a blessing in disguise.

"You know," Harry said at one point, after little Frank had gone back to his train set, "I almost feel bad for that guy—Fred Hardesty. To think he had those diamonds all these years and never got a chance to cash in on the treasure."

Mort had given the state policemen, who came to the sheriff's station to take Fred Hardesty into their custody, Hardesty's mustache to compare with the black strands found at both more recent murder scenes. A match would seal his fate, which was pretty much sealed already.

"What do you figure the diamonds are worth, Sheriff?" Grady asked.

Mort shrugged. "I'm no expert, and the state police need to bring one in to separate the diamonds from the cut crystals they're mixed with. Why don't we say a lot, a whole lot? And don't ask me who actually owns them, because I have no idea. I'm sure those descendants of the founding fathers will stake their claim, but who knows how it will all turn out?" he said, careful not to include Lucas Rackley in his gaze.

"That the best you can do?" Harry scowled, going

back to his turkey with a shrug. "I should have clipped one when neither of you was looking," he said to both Mort and me. "Compensate myself for clients who never pay their bills."

"Jess," Seth Hazlitt chimed in, "just give me the word and there'll be no pie for Mr. McGraw."

"You bring my favorite flavor, Doc?" Harry said to him.

"How could I when I don't know what it is?"

"You could have asked me, you know."

I looked down the length of the table, including at little Frank's currently empty chair. I was back home at 698 Candlewood Lane with the people I loved and cared about the most in the world.

"To friends and family . . ." I started, holding my wineglass up in the air for a toast.

For just a moment I thought I saw my Frank occupying our grandnephew's chair, raising his glass in a toast with everyone else. But he was gone just as fast as he'd appeared, a happy figment of my imagination.

". . . the best gifts I've ever been given," I finished, at which point I heard a rumbling sound coming from the living room, and then something else.

Choo, choo! followed by the familiar sound of a model train whistle.

I bounced out of my chair a step ahead of everyone else, felt them cluster behind me as we all watched an eight-car toy train steaming along the track little Frank had assembled all by himself.

"Look, Aunt Jess." He beamed. "It works! Isn't it cool?"

"Very," I told him, "very cool."

"Best Christmas ever!" he said, hugging me tight with the controller still clutched in his hand.

"You know what?" I replied, hugging him back. "It just might be."

Read on for an excerpt from
the next *Murder, She Wrote* mystery, by
Jessica Fletcher and Terrie Farley Moran,

KILLING IN A KOI POND

Available in hardcover from
Berkley Prime Crime

As I carefully made my way down the steps of the Amtrak Silver Star, Dolores Nickens stood on the platform waving both arms, her gold bracelets flashing in the bright South Carolina sun. The instant I stepped onto the platform she grabbed me in a crushing hug. I'm sure she pressed out a few of the wrinkles my tan linen suit had collected on the long ride south from Washington, DC.

"Jessica Fletcher! It's been far too long." She held me at arm's length and eyed me critically from the top of my head to the soles of my beige pumps. "My goodness, you never age!"

When Dolores started to lean in again, I took two quick steps backward to save myself from another colossal squeeze and said, "I can't tell you how sorry I am to have missed your wedding. By the time I received my invitation, my nephew Grady had already asked me to babysit while he and Donna went on an anniversary cruise, although their son, Frank, objects strenuously to the term 'babysitting.' He claims to be quite grown up."

"Ah, the young ones—if only they knew how fast the years go." Dolores tucked her hand into the crook of my arm.

"He's like the proverbial weed—his head is already up to my shoulder. Anyway, no matter what his parents call it, he and I have agreed that my official title is 'the adult in the house' whenever Grady and Donna are away."

Dolores laughed. "That's so like you. Always quick with a diplomatic solution. Do you remember sophomore year when I roomed with Lila Huggins, that redhead who always *just knew* she would be a famous artist one day? When she announced she decided to paint a jungle mural complete with lush green trees and assorted wild animals on every wall in our tiny room, you, my dear Jess, saved the day and probably prevented me from lifelong recurring nightmares of cheetahs and panthers and what all."

"I merely told her that since she was going to be so famous in a few short years, she surely didn't want to waste her time and effort painting murals since they aren't portable. How could she leave her masterpieces behind once we graduated? I suggested that she paint her vision of the jungle on those superlarge canvases that were stored in the basement of the arts building. When fame hit she could have them shipped to galleries anywhere in the world."

"And three months later she changed her major from fine arts to psychology. Today she is a well-known Hollywood shrink, appearing on television talk shows all the time. Who would have known?" Dolores chuckled.

A porter carried my luggage off the train and, without missing a beat in her nonstop reminiscences, Dolores led us to the parking lot.

She stopped in front of a snazzy red convertible and swept her arm above the hood. "Voilà! A Porsche 911 Carrera Cabriolet. What do you think?"

I hadn't seen many like it. "Very fancy."

"A gift from Willis. I can't wait for you to meet my new husband. Do you remember all the bad boys I dated in college, not to mention the other two charming but wicked men I ultimately married?" Dolores raised her eyes skyward and sighed at past memories. "Willis is so different. He may seem a little gruff at first, but once you get to know him he is a sweetie pie. It may have taken me longer than most, but I have found the perfect husband."

She popped the trunk, which, surprisingly, was in the front of the car. It barely held my carry-on, so the porter loaded the rest of my luggage in the backseat. I slipped a few bills into his hand and he tipped his cap jauntily. "Enjoy your visit, ladies."

"Elegant, isn't it?" Dolores said as she unlocked the car doors.

"Oh my, it certainly is." I burrowed into the passenger seat. "And so comfortable. Sometimes these fancy cars look a lot better than they feel."

"Willis constantly says there is nothing too good for his doll. That's me. I'm his doll. Seat belt on?"

I gave my seat belt a reassuring tug. "On and secure."

Dolores glided the car out of the parking space, headed toward the exit. "I always say there is nothing like a decent man and a flashy car to keep a lady smiling. So, what do you think, Jess?"

"I think you seem bubbly, energized. Happier than I have seen you in years. You seem like a totally different woman than you were at our last reunion. When was that—four years ago?"

"Just about. Right after husband number two emptied our bank accounts and ran off with mistress number ninety-eight or ninety-nine, whichever she was. Not a problem I will ever face again. Like any man, Willis has his quirks, but philandering isn't one of them. I can work around the silly quirks he does have. . . . Most of the time he treats me like a queen."

Most of the time? I didn't like the sound of that. I wondered what went on in the spaces in between.

Dolores chattered along. "Instead of taking Main Street to Route 321, I am going to wander off our path just a smidge and drive along Taylor Street. I can't wait to show you all the marvelous things Columbia has to offer. The art museum is exceptionally noteworthy— the children's room is really a treat. Then there's the Robert Mills House and Gardens. And of course we must tour the state house. So much history. It wouldn't hurt us a bit to do some shopping in the lovely boutiques that are popping up all over downtown."

As if I weren't already tired from my long train ride, Dolores's enthusiasm began to drain what little energy I had left.

"We can do all our girl talk and catching up while we wander around the city," she continued, "but all that is for another day. Here is our first and only stop. Look."

Look? Oh my, I couldn't miss it. Looming ahead of us: a gleaming silver fire hydrant standing taller than most of the surrounding buildings.

I gaped. "What on earth?"

"Welcome to Busted Plug Plaza," Dolores crowed. "I bet this is a first even for the well-traveled mystery writer J. B. Fletcher."

"It certainly is. I'm at a loss for words."

Dolores turned off the engine. "Dazzling, isn't it? Local artist and sculptor Blue Sky designed it. Jump out and I will take your picture in front of the world's tallest fire hydrant. A picture will be all the evidence you need to prove to those Mainers in Cabot Cove that we Carolinians have a thing or two they can't match."

The size of the hydrant was hard to take in, and I stopped a few feet in front of it. Dolores waved her hand, signaling me to move backward. "You have plenty of room. Plenty. I promise—even if you stand right underneath the lowest outlet cap, with the thick chains hanging down, it will still be way above your head."

Dolores held her cell phone high. "Oh, too much sun. I'm going to move left. Can you turn to your right? Great. Stay there. Don't move."

Initially I felt awkward, as I always do when asked to pose for a picture, but then I relaxed and smiled gamely. In a moment Dolores pronounced us done and hustled me back to the Porsche.

"Now, no more touring for you, young lady. I'll hit Main Street, which will lead us right on to Route 321 and out into the countryside."

"I must say, the last thing I expected was a gigantic hydrant. Who did you say designed it?" I asked.

"Blue Sky. Oh, he has another name, but around here he is Blue Sky, famous local artist. And the hydrant is forty feet high and weighs over six hundred thousand pounds. Can you imagine the work that went into designing and building it?"

I admitted I couldn't fathom it.

Dolores continued. "But now the treasure I want to show off is my home. Wait until you see Manning Hall. Built in the late 1890s, it is a replica of the old plantation that preceded it but that was burned to the ground during the Civil War. The Ribault family owned it for generations, but they fell on hard times, and luckily, Willis's star was in the ascendant. I never dreamed I would live in such a house. Why, it's almost a castle."

I leaned back on the headrest and smiled. Dolores had been through a lot of ups and downs in her life. More downs than ups, to be honest, so I was doubly delighted to see her so happy.

"And I have a grandchild." Dolores's voice softened. "Oh, Jess, wait until you meet her. Abigail is nine years old. Everyone calls her Abby. Such a sweet girl. And smart! She loves to wear her hair in braids, just as I did at her age. So we have that in common. Of course, she never got to meet her real grandmother. Willis's first wife died nearly twenty years ago, so I think Abby might have been longing for a granny.

That's what she calls me—Granny Dolores. It's such a thrilling experience."

"And what about her parents?" I wondered aloud. "How is your relationship with them?"

Her excitement dropped a few levels. "Oh, that is a very sad situation. Abby's mother was Willis's only child, his daughter, Emily. She died from an aggressive brain tumor a few years ago. Very sudden. Very swift."

A worried note crept into her voice. "Emily's widower, Clancy Travers, has sole custody of Abby, of course, but he doesn't have Willis's resources. . . ." She hesitated and then went on. "I sometimes think Willis's generosity is the only thing that keeps Clancy bringing Abby around to visit. It's . . . it's almost as if Willis is *buying* access to his only granddaughter."

"Well, however the access is granted, don't you think it's important for the child to have a relationship with her grandfather? Not to have one would be a real sadness," I said.

"I guess you are right." Dolores stopped to let a car pass before she made a left turn. "In any event, I can't wait for you to meet my new family. Would you mind opening the glove box and taking out the black and silver clicker?"

As I retrieved the clicker, Dolores made a sharp turn and stopped in front of an iron gate anchored by two decorative stone columns, replicas of ancient Roman pillars.

"Give the red button a push," Dolores said.

I did, and the two doors of the gate slid quietly apart. The driveway curved immediately to the left. After a few yards, we turned to the right, and Dolores idled the engine. "Manning Hall. Isn't it something?"

A quarter of a mile or so in front of us, a broad three-story brick house surrounded by a sandstone veranda rose majestically from a clearing bordered by trees flowering with pink and purple bonnets.

"It is indeed. And the trees! What are they?"

"Crepe myrtle. They are very common in South Carolina. I'm glad they bloomed a little early this year so you could see them. And we have a lovely sitting garden with lots of benches, and each section of plants is set off by those large white river rocks that sunshine seems to brighten over time. I know you enjoy a nice garden."

I smiled. "Yes, I do like to putter in my garden at home. Of course, in Maine we don't have as much gardening time as you do down here."

"That's true, I'm sure." Dolores switched back to talking about Manning Hall. "Willis said that the moment he saw the house, he knew he wanted it to be our home. So he made an offer on the house and asked me to marry him all on the same day. That's the kind of man he is. Some would say brash, but I think he's a hardworking go-getter. That's how he has managed to be so successful in business and in life."

Dolores accelerated slowly before again coming to a full stop. "Let's get out here. I want to show you my one contribution to the landscape."

As I opened the car door I heard small splashes.

Dolores hurried around the front of the car to show me a square pond edged by broad timber beams and surrounded by low-lying bushes. "This is my koi pond. All the gardens on the property are so formal and still. I wanted something happy, lively."

We stood side by side and watched dozens of multi-colored fish swim around, sometimes circling one another, sometimes going off on their own. One chubby orange-striped koi stopped in the middle of the pond and seemed to stare at us for a few seconds before continuing on its way.

"Why, this is lovely, Dolores. What made you think of it?"

"When Willis bought the property, the driveway was way over there." She waved her arm vaguely to the left. "He thought that a driveway coming from this angle would be, I don't know, more attractive, and would enhance the value of the property. I always wanted some sort of fishpond, and since they were digging up this whole area anyway . . . I met with a landscape architect and he advised a koi pond. Willis agreed, and here are my sweet beauties. Just watching them gives me such a peaceful feeling."

The fish were mesmerizing. I had to agree that watching them was extremely relaxing.

After a few moments Dolores said, "We'll have plenty of time for quiet contemplation by the koi pond over the next few days. And, as you can see, the sitting garden is right along here, leading from the pond to Manning Hall. But for now let's get you up to the house and settled in your room."

That sounded perfect to me.

We drove the short distance to Manning Hall, and before Dolores finished parking the car, the wood-and-glass French doors of the house opened and a slim young woman wearing light blue jeans and an oversized pink T-shirt bounced down the front steps to greet us.

Dolores popped the trunk. "Marla Mae, this is my dear friend Jessica Fletcher, who'll be staying with us for a while. Would you please see to her luggage?"

Marla Mae gave me a big toothy grin. "Welcome to Manning Hall, Miss Jessica. So nice to see Miss Dolores entertaining a longtime friend." Then she hoisted my suitcase and travel bag and started up the steps to the house.

I went to reach for the travel bag but Dolores put her hand on my arm. "It's fine. It's her job."

We entered an extremely formal foyer. The marble inlaid floor gleamed and the walls were covered with lush brocade. To our left was a wide staircase.

Marla Mae said, "Mr. Willis is in his office. Do you want me to tell him you're home?"

"That won't be necessary. Please take the luggage up to the bedroom at the far end of the hall. Jessica and I will surprise him." Dolores took my arm and led me to a door on the right side of the foyer, a few feet past the bottom of the staircase. She gave a light tap and opened the door. At the same moment we heard a crash behind us. I turned to see my suitcase bounding down the stairs.

A balding gray-haired man who I assumed was Willis bolted up from the chair behind his oak desk and bellowed, "What is going on out there?"

He strode right past Dolores and me and rushed into the foyer. Marla Mae ran down the stairs, trying to grab the suitcase before it landed at the bottom, which it ultimately did with a loud thud.

"Stupid, stupid girl. You can't even do a simple chore like carrying luggage up the stairs. You're done. Fired. Get out now." Willis was red-faced, and his yelling got louder with each word.

I'd stepped around him and gotten to the bottom of the stairs at the same time Marla Mae did. We both reached for the suitcase. When I saw the pleading in her eyes I stepped back and let her rescue it. I think we both hoped that would calm Willis down. It didn't.

He turned to Dolores. "I want her gone. Now."

"I know you do, dear, but we have guests this evening and I need her to serve dinner." Dolores sounded like a mother placating a small child in desperate need of a nap.

Willis grimaced, then nodded. "I'll give you tonight, but"—he pointed to Marla Mae—"that clumsy girl is gone at the end of the week. Is that clear?"

"Very clear, darling. Now, let me introduce you to one of my oldest friends. Jessica Fletcher, this is my husband, Willis Nickens."

I could understand why he was so successful in business. Willis Nickens had the ability to change his entire personality in a flash. He broke into a wide smile, took my hand between both of his, and said, "Dolores has told me so much about you, her old college friend who is now a famous mystery writer."

"Oh, I don't know if I would say *famous*." When anyone used that word in referring to me, it always made me ill at ease. I tried to change the subject. "You have a lovely home, and from what I have seen the landscaping is magnificent."

"Thank you. We are delighted to have you as our guest here at Manning Hall. And believe me when I tell you that being famous never hurt anyone. Dolores will show you to your room. I'll see you for cocktails before dinner." He dismissed us both, reentered his office, and shut the door firmly behind him.

Dolores sighed. "I am sorry that you saw Willis at his worst, Jess. He demands perfection and really goes off the rails when someone fails to meet his expectations. Marla Mae broke a crystal vase last week, and now this. . . ."

I put my arm around her shoulder. "Dolores, the important thing is that you and I will have a few days to spend time together. Anything going on around us will be only so much background noise."

I had no idea how wrong I was.